T0167085

BIRCH

THE BEGINNING

BIRCH
THE BEGINNING

———•◉•———

A NOVEL

A mystical adventure of good over evil, held in a medieval backdrop of Modania . . . .

Gods and demi gods create three wizards to look after the elements and the land and keep them safe from the evil Lord Zelfen. But the fate of all lies in the hands of a simple forest boy—Birch.

Similar to the style of Steven Donaldson with a hint of Terry Pratchett, this novel creates a world of mystery and intrigue, and is often embellished with a sense of humour too!

GEORGE ALEXANDA

authorHOUSE®

AuthorHouse™
1663 Liberty Drive
Bloomington, IN 47403
www.authorhouse.com
Phone: 1-800-839-8640

© 2012 by George Alexanda. All rights reserved.

A catalogue record for this book is available from the British Library

No part of this book may be reproduced, stored in a retrieval system, or transmitted by any means without the written permission of the author.

This book is a work of fiction and as such all characters and situations are fictitious. Any resemblance to actual people or events is coincidental.

Alexgeorge6694@gmail.com

First published by AuthorHouse   02/08/2012

ISBN: 978-1-4678-8505-8 (sc)
ISBN: 978-1-4678-8504-1 (ebk)

Printed in the United States of America

Any people depicted in stock imagery provided by Thinkstock are models, and such images are being used for illustrative purposes only.
Certain stock imagery © Thinkstock.

This book is printed on acid-free paper.

Because of the dynamic nature of the Internet, any web addresses or links contained in this book may have changed since publication and may no longer be valid. The views expressed in this work are solely those of the author and do not necessarily reflect the views of the publisher, and the publisher hereby disclaims any responsibility for them.

Editorial evaluation

I was delighted to read this enthralling fantasy, Birch—The Beginning. What we have here is a good, solid novel with substance and scope to it, a richly textured piece of writing that very skilfully manages to be at once, incisive, tense, thought provoking and highly entertaining

This is a work of fiction of considerable imaginative depth at that, but at the same time, the text abounds with a wealth of perceptively observed detail, obviously the product of real experience, which lends the book a poignant, sometimes quite gritty reality, a dramatic immediacy, which is one of its key strengths. The characters, situations and dialogue are relayed in vivid and lively detail which makes each literary moment seem entirely authentic. As a result, the reader is effortlessly drawn into the fabric of the story, experiencing it as his or her own reality.

The plot is an accomplished device in itself, patiently built, and sparingly meted out with an eye on the necessities of tension, pace, climax and anti-climax. As a result, this story has a plot with considerable substance and texture: the reader's interest is aroused on the opening pages, and the work remains atmospheric until its conclusion.

The written style of this work is another feature of its success. Without being at all self-conscious, this author has found an individual voice, in which he writes with fluency and expressiveness. His style is extremely versatile: at times it is terse and economical; at others it becomes descriptive and quite elegant.

I have no hesitation in saying that this is a highly readable book.

Ann Austin

Dedications

To Margaret in Spirit

To Terry Andrews, it's been a long time coming

To me: Stop smoking those funny cigarettes

A special thanks to Jili Hamilton for her unwavering friendship over

many years, and her help during the production of this novel.

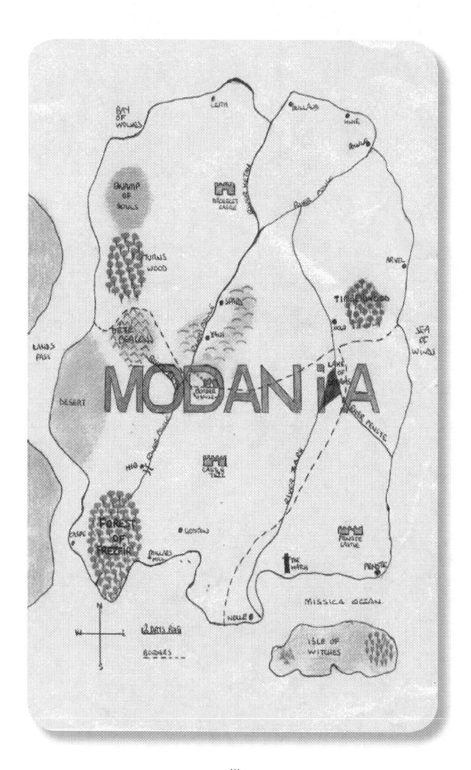

CHAPTER ONE

T HE OLD HOUSE STOOD silently on Millers Hill like a monument to some long past medieval war lord encapsulated in his own thoughts. Its one chimney stack pointed skywards, a menacing finger of defiance that reproached the gods for allowing unsupervised wind and rain to run amok, ravishing, punishing the stonework, crumbling the mortar that had held the stones together and in place for so long.

Ivy trespassed over the stonework as far as the attic windows which surprisingly remained intact. They stared uninvitingly across the rooftops of a village some miles away where, contrary to the beliefs of the younger generation, constant rumours of ghosts, spirits and evil goings on were rife among the elders.

A little way from the house a lone figure stood amongst the bracken and dry twigs. Behind him the forest of Frezfir stood silhouetted against the evening sky. The pines and oaks appeared to be watching his every move, listening to his every thought.

Nervously he began to move toward the house, his eyes searching for any signs of life. The house beckoned him, its hidden secrets wanting to be revealed. Although he could not see any signs of life he could sense that something living dwelt within.

Cautiously crossing the open ground he made his way toward the house. Everywhere was silent. Even the smaller life forms that usually busied themselves on the ground remained silent until he had passed. It was as though imminent danger had been sensed and time had stood still for the brief moment of his passing resuming only when no possible threat was detected.

The veranda was of a wooden construction that announced his arrival, echoing his footsteps as he neared the large front door. He took hold of the brass door knob with both hands, and with a cat-like meow of its hinges; the door opened and welcomed him inside. It was dark inside but small candle fought bravely to allow a little light, a light that outlined the fine interior. The smell of rich leather was pleasing. He closed the door with the heel of his boot; the sound echoed throughout the house as he made to look around.

'Hold' echoed a voice from the darkness above him but before he could react to the situation, an icy grip wrapped around him and held him fast. At the same moment the sky outside darkened, thunder rolled and lightening flashed. He fell weakened to the floor. His eyes widened with the fear of the unknown and his attempts to free himself were futile.

From the shadows with their infinite games of illusion the voice echoed again.

'What brings you to the domain of Lord Torran Wizard of Ice and Fire if it not be that you desire an early grave?

Beads of perspiration dripped into the prisoners eyes; he blinked several times before answering.

'My Lord release me I beseech you. I am but the bearer of a message that I am sure you would want to hear'.

A few moments passed while Torran studied his captive who was unknowingly emanating a crude magical force. He could sense this and he wondered who this visitor could be. He waved his hand once more in the darkness.

'Release' He called

The grip of ice disappeared immediately and as the young man got to his feet, a tall erect figure lit a candle with a flame that appeared to be an extension of his pointed finger. It could be seen now that Torran was dressed in a red and white robe that glistened in the candle light; it seemed to be almost alive. His golden hair fell in curls across his immense shoulders. A youthful face looked sternly at the stranger and piercingly blue eyes had already asked the question.

'Who are you that dare interrupt my meditation?' 'What is this message that you bear?'

'Are you really the Lord Torran?' Enquired the young man. 'I must be sure as my message is for his ears alone'.

'Of course I am Lord Torran. What's more I do not suffer fools gladly. You have tried ice. Would you like to sample fire?'

A red nimbus surrounded the wizard as he raised his hand and pointed a finger.

'No!' Cried the young man. 'It's just that my father the Lord Brin of Castle Tezz . . . .'

'Ah! Interrupted Torran. He lowered his hand and the red nimbus faded and was gone in an instant. For a time Torran looked deeply into the young man's eyes, eyes that reflected a memory of almost half a century past.

It was then that, after an absence of many years Torran was returning home to Millers Hill. It was a lazy day, flies played games in the slanted rays of the mid-day sun. Cattle chewed noiselessly on the sweet meadow grasses and the aroma of herbs filled the air. Two birds argued over a ripe berry as others watched with mild indifference. He breathed a deep breath, savoured the clean air. He was happy to be nearing journeys end.

As he was passing close to Castle Tezz, he heard a cry of distress and immediately his survival instincts took charge. He was no longer the carefree wanderer, but through an age of constant conditioning, had become an animated machine of death and destruction in the blink of an eye to those who might be considered an enemy. Cautiously, almost cat-like he moved towards the sounds, the screams of pain. His eyes darted this way and that, visibly searching, always alert. His ears trained for the slightest hostile sound and reflexes ready for lightening reaction.

He found something quite unexpected. Before him on the ground lay a woman in the latter stages of child birth. He relaxed, immediately regretting that his sudden appearance might have startled her.

'My Lady!' He exclaimed.

He noticed the finery of an important person and the realisation that this woman was of high breeding followed.

'Forgive me for not standing my Lord', returned the young woman. 'You quite startled me and as you bear witness I am indisposed at the moment'.

'I understand my Lady, but how come that you are away from your chambers?'

I am a foolish woman my Lord. I was compelled by some inner feeling to seek a stream and open air, I know not why'.

'It is but one of the many unknown wonders of child birth my Lady'
Many women have, shall we say, strange desires when their time is near.
We must get you to your attendants'.

'No my Lord, I will not move before my child is born. However, if it is
not an imposition upon your good intent, my husband is the Lord of Castle
Tezz. Please have him send my hand maidens and the healer to tend me. If
I were to walk, or ride back at this time . . . .'

'I understand my Lady'.

Lord Torran ran towards the castle, an easy feat for his athletic build.
A large white stallion that had been following him looked up, and then
continued to munch the sweet grass. He knew that when his master ran
towards something, it was normally to make sure that that something
didn't remain in an upright position. The horse preferred the grass.

'Who approached Castle Tezz?' a guard shouted the question from
the battlements when he saw Torran running towards the lowered
drawbridge.

'Stay your weapons', called Torran as he halted near the nervous
looking soldiers. 'I am Lord Torran with an urgent message for the Lord of
Castle Tezz'.

'My Lord' continued the guard'. 'What say your message that I might
deliver it?'

'That his Lady lay in child birth but a short distance away' replied
Torran.

Before he had finished delivering his message, a runner was making
haste towards an inner building. A few moments later a crowd of fussing
women hurried towards him, a plump, balding man of indeterminate age
followed them. With all speed the group was directed to where the young
woman lay. Both men, Lord Torran and the healer, were ushered to a
discrete distance whilst the hand maidens busied themselves in preparation
for the forthcoming event. The still air carried their discounted feelings
over the area where the birth was to take place.

'But out here my Lady?'

'It is where it must happen'

'You will catch your death'.

'I am strong, I will survive'

'If your father were here he would spank you!'

'I have grown from childhood, now stop fussing and continue with
your duties'.

The healer was slowly pacing back and forth. He was whistling a lively tune when Torran posed a question.

'Why call a healer when he is not allowed to go near where he was supposed to be'.

'Well' said the healer, 'I'm not actually here for the birth. I'm here in case anything goes wrong with it'.

'Then they will blame you?'

'Of course'

One of the hand maidens came hurrying towards the two men. The healer, who immediately expected the worst, adopted a serious expression as the hand maiden, almost out of breath, began to speak.

'She . . . . My Lady will not go back to the castle. She insists that the child be born out here, in the open'.

'Let it be so,' said the healer who had had experiences in arguing with women, 'to move her now might prove to be fatal'.

'On your head be it healer', said the hand maiden as she hurried back to her work.

'See what I mean?' he said, looking at Torran.

A strong litter of wood and canvas was delivered in order to convey both mother and child to the castle after the birth. A very large, heavy-set man paced the draw bridge awaiting news of the birth and of his Lady. His broad, bearded face showed signs of concern and his dark eyes were hiding numerous questions. Bare footed, he winced occasionally as he stood on small pebbles. He made a mental note to detail someone for the task of cleaning the court yard of the wretched things. He then noticed that the hem of his light blue robe had begun to collect dust and change colour. He made a mental note of that too!

Shortly after the sun had rested its arc on the distant hills and the air had begun to cool, the party led by Torran was sighted nearing the castle. A Lady without a guard was deemed unthinkable and so Torran, instead of continuing his journey, assumed that position to the fair Lady of Tezz.

Leading the small party he halted at the entrance to the castle and drew his large black bladed sword, a custom to ward off anyone with ill intent. The action was of one movement and the blade almost leapt from its sheath as though alive. He saluted the Lord of Castle Tezz.

'I am the Lord Torran'. It sounded more like a threat than a greeting. 'By choice and the charter of chivalry, guard and protector to the Lady of

Castle Tezz'. He stood in the posture of Knights Guard as the Lord of Castle Tezz approached.

'Well met Lord Torran. I answer as the Lord Tezz of Castle Tezz'.

'Then accept my charge Lord of Tezz for my knightly duties are thus completed'.

Lord Torran sheathed his sword with the same fluid movement.

'I accept your charge gratefully Lord Torran and offer you the hospitality of my humble dwelling'.

'It is with gratitude that I accept your offer my Lord'. Concealing his abundance of joy, the Lord Tezz walked swiftly to his wife's side.

'Well, woman of mine?'

Lord Tezz tried to adopt a look of authority as he asked how his wife had come to wander unescorted from the castle.

'Oh stop that', she said. 'You couldn't be angry if you tried. Here, hold your son and don't smother him with that bristly beard. He's really a dear', she said while looking at Torran and smiling'.

'A son!' exclaimed the Lord of Tezz.

He picked up the tiny bundle and wandered, followed by the others, back inside the castle. Torran gave a shrill whistle and a large white stallion joined the group. The Lord of Tezz was mumbling to the child something along the lines of, 'diddum's doo dare den' or words to that effect. The healer, much to Torran's amusement, was whistling away to himself while taking the blame for all the things that might have gone wrong.

News of the birth had travelled fast and had spread throughout the castle, as a result the kitchens had become a hive of activity. A large chef wobbled around giving orders, tasting recipes for a feast that he knew would be called for. Large chunks of meat roasted slowly over an immense open-grate fire. As it turned it hissed and spat grease which burned away on the white hot coals. The floor was strewn with bird feathers, and in one corner a group of kitchen helpers chopped and peeled, cleaned and washed.

The simplest dish was the fruit; peeled and diced it lay on large platters. The meat and poultry dishes had to be designed, glazed and decorated before being set on long silver trays. The evening drew on and the efforts of the kitchen staff did not go unrewarded.

Mid-evening Lord Tezz called for a feast to be prepared. Local dignitaries had been arriving early for a free feast at Castle Tezz was not to be missed; such was the reputation of the kitchen, and the wine cellar.

The celebration in honour of the first son of Tezz, and also in honour of a visiting knight, was held in the spacious meeting hall. Tables were set in an enormous half circle at the open end of which stood a raised and elongated platform, seats for the lords and ladies and honoured guests. Ancient battle honours adorned every archway and in contrast, warm coloured lengths of woven silks decorated the walls. Several log fires burned along the length of the outer walls and huge candles in hanging baskets provided light. When the guests had assembled, and after a line of servants in uniform had laid out the succulent food, Lord Tezz stood and called for silence.

'My friends, let all formalities this evening be put aside or kept to a minimum as this is a day for joy and celebration. My only duty is to announce the birth of my son. He shall be called Brin. Let everyone hear throughout the land of Modania and beyond that from this day forth Brin of Tezz is my one and rightful heir. I might also say, and in conclusion for I am not a lengthy speaker, that fate and the gods seemed to have chosen his champion and protector. Lord Torran, will you accept this charge'.

To be more or less unknown at that time, yet asked to be the child's protector and Champion, was indeed an honour? To refuse such an honour would not be an outright insult, but it would be most certainly taken as a rebut, especially after the recent event in which Torran had played a major role. After a short pause he stood to much cheering.

'My Lord of Castle Tezz', he began. He bowed slightly to pay homage to his host.

My Lady, members and visitors to this most noble of gatherings. Although youthful in looks I am considerably advanced in years. Even this learned assembly could not even begin to comprehend why this is so and I could not, at this time, offer a reasonable or an understandable explanation. However, having said this I will add that that during my years, never have I received a welcome such as this. I accept this charge gladly, with humility and with all of my heart shall I serve. Let all hear throughout the land of Modania and even in lands beyond, that no man shall harm Brin of Castle Tezz lest it be by slaying me first'.

As Torran resumed his seat the hall erupted with shouts of acceptance, cheers, handshakes and people diving for the succulent food. The feast had begun.

A summer mist clothed the ground which made Castle Tezz look mysterious in the morning light. Tops of small bushes watched an early bird as it chirped its greeting from atop the ramparts. A sound; the little bird opened its wings and was gone as it soared into a sky streaked with yellow and blue. Lord Torran had slept well, had risen early and was now standing in the meeting hall admiring the architecture. Servants had almost but completed cleaning after the feast of the previous evening when the sound of bare footsteps heralded the arrival of the Lord of Tezz.

'Greetings and a fine morning to you Lord Torran. I trust that your comfort was satisfactory'.

'More than satisfactory, thank you my Lord, but what is the question you wish to ask?'

'Alas, I could never conceal my thoughts. I intend no disrespect Lord Torran, but a few points may be clarified I feel. Firstly, during your speech last evening, you mentioned that you were considerably advanced in years, this puzzled me'.

Lord Tezz walked over to the open fire and began to warm his hands. Turning again to face Torran, he continued.

'Secondly, when we first met and you drew your sword in salute, I noticed that the blade was not only black, a rarity today even in these parts, but the blade appeared to have a will all of its own. Lord Torran, forgive me but the history of the ancients is a subject close to my heart. Add the age to a black bladed sword and couple that with a white stallion and I am sure that I have knowledge of you'.

Torran looked into the eyes of Lord Tezz and smiled. 'Not many people remember the legends my Lord of Tezz'.

'Then it is true, I'm not mistaken?'

There was a moment when all was still, a moment when realisation dawned then, as a supplicant would kneel to his master, the Lord of Tezz knelt before Lord Torran.

'My Lord of Tezz, please lest you be seen, it would be unbecoming of the Lord of this castle. I am but a man who is grateful to be with others. I have separated myself from the land and from society for far too long and I am eager for company and yearn for companionship'.

Lord Tezz stood and saw Torran in a different light. He embraced the living history that stood before him. He understood at that point that Brin was safe and that no harm would befall him while Lord Torran was his protector and guardian.

However, Torran had a warning.

'We are now as brothers Lord of Tezz and therefore it is right that I should caution you. Should I at any time have to use my powers for any purpose, I fell that I would have to leave this place. It would be unsafe for others if I were to stay.

'As I understand your motives Lord Torran, I accept your caution. The gods have indeed smiled upon us this day'.

The gods did indeed smile that day and for the many years that Torran stayed at Castle Tezz. During the childhood years of Brin of Tezz, Torran instructed him in in the use of the sword, riding and tracking. He instructed him in the knowledge of knighthood and how to conduct himself; he was a keen learner and, at the request of the Lord of Tezz, he received tuition in history and architecture.

During his lessons in concealment Brin often tried to hide but could never understand how easily his tutor managed to find him. During his teenage years Brin was further coached in the art of jousting and how to upset his opponent by name calling. It was a curious way to do battle but it often worked and with surprising advantages.

'An angry fighter makes mistakes', he used to say.

Name calling became quite a popular game between the two; oft times vocabulary was tested to the point of frustration. These were times of great happiness, but happiness doesn't always last forever. It was during a particularly cold day in autumn when the day was coming to a close, as was a chapter in the life of Brin of Castle Tezz. The trees had lost their brilliant green of summer and birds without number were migrating across a red streaked sky. In the distance a rider wearing battle armour, solid, arrogant in posture and bearing a northern standard. The Black Eagle banner on a background of crimson, waved defiantly in the wind. At the gallop rider and mount neared the southern stronghold of Castle Tezz. On arrival at the gates of the castle the northern knight began throwing insult after insult at Brin.

'Where is this nobleman who prefers to lie with cattle? Show yourself or go back to the field where you were born'.

The news of the intruder flashed throughout the castle and people began to gather. It was common knowledge that the northern peoples were antagonistic warmongers who leapt at every opportunity to belittle and goad the south into combat. This champion had no idea of the danger he faced.

"I will sink my sword into his foul neck", stormed Brin.

'Oh we are angry. Have we forgotten our lessons?' Mocked Torran.

The two looked at each other. Brin was trying to keep a straight face but he had no control. Both fell about laughing at the jibe. The arrival of the straight faced Lord Tezz seemed to escalate the hilarity.

'What are you two laughing about? Do you not both realise that our house is being insulted'

'I will go and dispatch him', said Brin amid a fit of laughter.

Lord Tezz intervened. 'It would be unseemly, Brin, and it would also indicate a lack of confidence in you champion'.

Brin, although frustrated that he would not be able to redeem the family honour personally, accepted the wisdom of his father.

'By your leave, my Lords', said Torran. 'I have something to do that needs my immediate attention. I shall not be long'.

As Torran left to prepare himself, Brin wondered how he could be so sure of Victory. Lord Tezz answered the unspoken question saying that Lord Torran's skills were exceptional. He was not a man to be taken for granted. As they debated what might follow, the battlements began to fill with curious onlookers. Brin and Lord Tezz joined them.

Torran walked at a leisurely pace towards the main gate, and as he did so people were suddenly staring for it wasn't the Lord Torran that they had come to know. This Lord Torran was wearing a red and white robe with the insignia of wizard; it appeared to be alive with strange moving symbols. The was a murmur amongst the crowds as a stern faced Torran ordered the draw bridge to be lowered. The sounds of the chains rattling filled the courtyard as the bridge, with a low groan, fell slowly to the ground.

It appeared to the onlookers that Torran was at ease as he crossed the drawbridge and walked towards an evil grinning knight. This was far from the case. He was battle ready; any movement could be counteracted and each step was part of a pre-programmed attack strategy. Crowds were now filling the lowered drawbridge, faces appeared at every window, watching, wondering what their champion had in mind for he wore no sword, at least none that could be seen. He stood facing the knight for several minutes before he spoke.

'I am the Lord Torran, wizard of Ice and Fire, champion and protector of Brin of Tezz and of his household. Who dares to insult him also insults my person. Go now in peace. If you come and are prepared to do battle I must have knowledge of your name and title so that it may appear on your grave marker'.

'So they now send someone in fancy dress to fight their battles. They don't even supply a horse' called the knight. 'You do own one I suppose'.

'I will repeat myself just once Sir Knight', returned Torran. I am the champion and protector of Brin of Tezz. I would strongly advise you to take back your insults and apologise'.

'Well, well, a champion and protector in fancy dress without a horse and do I perceive, without a sword? Make way for a man lest I carve you like a chicken. It would indeed be easier than roasting one'.

The knight dismounted, drew his sword, and ran screaming a battle cry towards Torran who, still looking at ease, stood his ground. Around him light could hardly be seen at first but it was there, small soft beams of light that appeared to be penetrating his body. A red nimbus suddenly appeared around him; people on the battlements and on the drawbridge stood open-mouthed; some were pointing.

Brin looked questioningly at Lord Tezz but realised that he already knew what the outcome would be. Torran raised his hand and shouted a command.

'Fire'.

A dark, blood-red flame shot forth from his pointed finger. The expression on the face of the northern knight was one of surprise at first, then fear, then immeasurable horror as the flame engulfed him. So intense was the heat from Torran's flame that nothing was left but molten armour and bones where the knight had stood.

'No, it was about the same', remarked Torran.

Brin was the first on the scene as he came running across the drawbridge to where Torran stood. 'That was quick', he said as he peered at the glowing mass that was once a man.

'Heated arguments don't last long', replied Torran.

Torran was still looking at the young man as the mists of time faded and the image of Brin disappeared.

'Ah! Brin the young pup has sired a son at last. What message do you bring for me. Has the old goat-herd learned to write as well?'

Forgetting completely the unquestionable danger, the young man drew his sword and levelled a threat at Torran.

'I am Karl of Brin, Sir Knight. I would strongly advise you to keep a civil tongue in your otherwise empty head and speak no ill of my father lest you have no tongue at all'.

Torran looked upon Karl and once more the reflected image of his father with a certain amusement.

'You are indeed the hot-head that once was your father. I meant no offence young Karl of Brin. Your father and I have a bond between us that will never break, we are very close. I am also your fathers champion and have been for many years. During his tuition we used to call each other names in mock battle, a game that exercised the mind and tended to annoy the opponent. It probably stopped us from getting senile in our old age'.

'My father's champion for many years? Getting senile in your old age? You can't be that much older than me. I find your story very hard to believe, Lord Torran. I suppose you will also claim to have known my grandparents?'

'Yes, I met your grandparents shortly after the birth of your father. I am led to believe that they have retired from public life and now occupy the east wing of Castle Tezz. A move I presume that takes them away from governmental pressures so that they can spend their remaining days in peace and reflection. Now what is this message that makes it so important, and put away that sword?'

Karl shuffled about trying to fathom out this strange lord who called himself Torran. Surely he must be older than the person before him! He re-sheathed his sword whilst trying to remember the exact words that his father had told him to say.

'During my childhood,' he began, 'my father had noticed strange occurrences especially when I was truly angered. For this reason he has asked my favour to seek out the Lord Torran. He has instructed me to say unto Lord Torran alone that I have but seven years left, being eighteen. Secondly, that my father has sired wind and water. It is my hope that you can understand the message for I have no idea what it means'.

'I thought I sensed something in you, mmm, wind and water'.

'But what are these words, Lord Torran?'

'You will understand shortly Karl because to me the meaning is clear. It was no accident when I stumbled across your Grandmother, and it now appears not to have been the desire of a pregnant woman to give birth in the open air next to a stream, but the will of the gods'.

'My father was born outside?'

'In a field'.

'Oh'.

'I must admit that in a way it saddens me that you should be the chosen one. Many of your hopes will be dashed. Many heartaches will be written in the book of your life, and although there will be some good times, sorrow will be your constant companion and despair, your bed mate. You are, however, fortunate that your father recognised the second wizard's reincarnation for you could have been in mortal danger. You are also fortunate that I will be here to guide and to teach you'.

'Second wizard? Reincarnation? By the laws Torran, what is happening?'

'My apologies my lord, my manners are unforgiveable', he said, kneeling and awaiting forgiveness.

'Rise Karl, or should I say Lord Karl of Brin. Lord and Wizard of Wind and Water. There is no need for equals to use titles in private'.

'Lord Karl? Said a confused young man. 'Wizard of Wind and Water? Equals?'

Torran smiled. 'Let us eat and sup wine then I will relate to you, firstly why your father sent you to me and secondly, I will tell you about Wind and Water. In time I will explain to you the development of your powers but for the present you must stay with me. You will become the master and not the mastered'.

'I am afraid the I am more confused than ever, Lord Torran'

'All will be revealed to you that you will understand. All that you do not understand will be explained. Now let us eat, I'm starving'.

Torran led the way ascending the broad oak staircase. The spacious hallway at the top was sparsely decorated but several doors emphasized the immensity of the house. Opening one of the doors he led Karl into a luxuriously furnished room. Soft furnishings were abundant; a low table was inlaid with silver and gold filigree; walls were covered with draped fabrics and silken thread. In the huge fireplace logs burned spreading warmth throughout the room. While Karl made himself comfortable on a soft cushion, Torran left the room returning almost immediately with a tray of cold meats and fruit. A bottle of wine sat comfortably in one of his Pockets.

'Can you prepare food?' Enquired Torran.

'I have had instruction', replied Karl.

'Good because it's your turn to make dinner tomorrow'.

Karl smiled. He felt quite at ease for the first time since his meeting with Torran and he seemed relieved. After the meal and several goblets of wine, Torran told Karl of the history of the wizards.

'In the beginning of time,' he began', the land as we know it was but a waste ground. The soil would yield no plant life; the seas would permit no life forms. No being could possibly survive the terrible onslaught of the elements that ruled the world. The elder gods, Zelfen, Mord and Rosil, Mord's mate, had no interest in the land. They were content to amuse themselves with occasionally observing the frenzied elements do battle with each other.

Mountains crumbled and rivers of molten lava argued rites of passage; fire spewed out to burn and dust settled to smother. Seas greedy for land joined forces with hurricane winds in momentous battles with the ground forces. Ice claimed large areas of land causing surfaces to crack, stemming the flow of water and absorbing it by creating a vast white desert.

To the elder gods this was only of a diversionary interest, something to observe now and then. However, and for many generations, the younger gods sought to acquire the land for their playground. They wanted to bring life and beauty to what was then, desolation.

The god, Zelfen, disagreed with all the arguments and proposals for the land but was finally overruled, much to his anger. A meeting was called for and was held on a large white dais, the place where decrees were made. The younger gods were asked in turn to give an account of their ideas after which, a decision was reached. The result overjoyed them because they were given complete responsibility for naming and controlling the elements, and the design and layout of the land.

Eqwin decreed that his two elements would be called Wind and Water. It is to him that you should look in times of despair'.

'Will he help me?' Asked Karl.

'It was he who made you and did ever a father not love his son? Frezfir named his elements Ice and Fire'.

'Then he looks after you, Torran?'

'Yes and he has done for thousands of years Karl'.

Karl looked open mouthed at Torran, but realised that he was not jesting.

'Calia named her elements Earth and Stone'.

'I would have thought that wind and water would be more a woman's thing', said Karl in jest.

'You don't know Calia, Karl. She is a hard woman and does not take kindly to mockery. Anyway, the three younger gods descended upon the land and for many more centuries learned about its secrets. Control of the elements came second and design of the land third. Each sector of land was given a share of water to sustain life, the life that would follow.

Heat was supplied by the sun, ice so that seeds would know when to begin their life cycle. The gods then divided the time into years, the years into seasons as we recognise them today. Seasons were divided into months, months into weeks, days, hours and minutes. Afterward they revelled in their creation. The land was then peopled and the population began to expand.

Having achieved all that they could, the gods decided to leave the land so that the inhabitants could learn to fend for themselves. So that initially the elements would not revert back to their aggressive natures, the gods created three wizards as caretakers. Each was given command over two elements and the power to control them in small matters. Mind you, if the universe disappeared it would be small matter to the gods but they certainly would like to know if anything appears to be going wrong.

An isolated house, this house was built as a meeting place; only here can the gods appear in person. From the outside the house doesn't look much, even a wanderer would think twice about seeking shelter here. Add a few unsavoury rumours and no-one bothers to call at all, it's so peaceful'

'Who were the three original wizards?'

'I was one'

'You?'

'Yes. The god's first mistake was to appoint two elderly men along with me to act as caretakers. I was quite young and could survive a challenge. They were not so young. After a couple of hundred years we were all challenged by our individual elements, me for the second time. The other two wizards were beaten, they did not survive'.

'Did not the elements run riot?'

'No, and that was the reason why no other person was given the position of wizard. The only other person with powers that lived in the land at that time was a master magician; called himself Master Elio. No-one seemed to know where he came from but his powers are awesome. Some say that he was yet another link with the gods. Others referred to him as a god in disguise. The truth of the matter is that no-one really knew. He just appeared and disappeared from time to time.

Some have even said that he perished long age during a fight with the god Zelfen, the reason that he hasn't been seen for the past few centuries but I'm not sure. Anyway, let's get back to you. I have calculated that you should reach maturity no later than your twenty-fifth birthdate. It was when I matured and stopped aging. I was the only wizard left from three until now and because of this fact there must also be a reason that, at the moment, we are unaware of. I have a strange feeling that something is about to change and we must prepare for whatever it is.

Karl I know not of any forthcoming event but I do know that Wind and Water has arrived and there must be a reason. Earth and Stone must also be here somewhere so we must search for him before whatever is about to happen, happens.

'How will we know if anything's amiss?'

'Have no fear Karl, if indeed there is something wrong in this land it will find us'

'What of this house?'

'The house can look after itself. In fact and the truth be known between us, it has a mind of its own. It would certainly cause a few problems if anyone unknown ventured inside its walls' he said with a grin.

He didn't invite any further questions but explained that time was of the essence; that the next day Karl would begin his instruction. He would learn how to master his elements and to use them to his advantage. He would learn how to fight with the weapons he received but during the conversation Torran noticed how tired Karl was'

'Come Karl, you have had a long day. I will show you to your rooms'. He led Karl along a wide corridor and then, opening a door to his left, he bowed slightly from the waist. 'These will be your rooms for the time that you stay here. May it be long and peaceful?'

'Thank you, Torran; it has been a long day'.

After a reassuring smile Torran left Karl to get accustomed to his new surroundings. Karl entered what he could only describe as a dream, the room was immense. A massive chandelier of crystal and gold chain hung centrally from the ceiling. Gentle heat flowed from a granite fireplace; coloured silks adorned the walls. Near to the fireplace stood a bureau on which were pens, ink and parchment and next to that was a bookcase several shelves high, each shelf with a selection of reading material. A small inlaid table sat centrally and was surrounded with soft cushions.

At the far end of the room an oversized, satin covered bed with drapes and feather mattress looked inviting, so inviting that it was soon occupied. Karl drifted off into a deep and untroubled sleep.

Morning came and the sun showed the land its diamond of fire. Darkness gave way to yellow beams of light that searched the morning mist. Karl opened one eye and viewed a small object as it cocked its head to one side and whistled. Opening the other eye and focussing on the small bird, he realised that morning had arrived. The bird, as though completing a task set many years ago, flapped its wings and flew away into the thinning mist. Karl rolled off the bed and slipped on a loose robe of pale green, one of many laid out for his inspection.

'Karl!' Shouted Torran.

'I'm awake', he replied.

'Will you join me in the living room?'

'Why, are you coming apart?'

This son of Brin might be fun, thought Torran. 'Just follow the aroma' he called.

Karl left his room and followed the tantalising smell of cooking food that lingered in the corridor. When he entered what was possibly the dining room, he saw before him much to his delight, a large platter of eggs, bowls of roasted nuts, berries and bread on a long wooden table.

'I hope you have an appetite this morning Karl'.

Karl didn't reply, he just sat down and began devouring the food.

'Oh I see that you have' said Torran in answer to his own question.

'Mm' was the only comment that Karl could make with a mouth full of food.

It wasn't long after breaking their fast that Torran took Karl on a quick tour of the house and stables. A white stallion nuzzled up to Torran in greeting.

'He's a fine looking horse', said Karl

'He is more than that, Karl, he is a friend'

At that moment a shuffling sound came from the vicinity of the furthest stable and realising that the gods may have been working overtime, Torran asked Karl to investigate. Karl crept quietly so as not to make a noise that would alert any intruder. When he reached the far stable, a black stallion of equal magnificence to Torran's white stallion seemed to appear from nowhere. It pawed the air in defiance of anything living.

'Be calm', ordered Karl

To his astonishment the stallion settled down; walked over to him and nuzzled its head into his shoulder.

'Looks like you have a friend too', said Torran.

'Yes it looks that way I must admit'.

And so it was that Torran began to instruct Karl in the ways of the wizards.

Long periods of time were devoted to meditation, the centralising, isolation and control of all his physical and mental being. Shorter periods included the realisation of the powers of others, defence and attack manoeuvers and finally, how to use the knowledge to control his elements.

Karl became a dedicated student, eager for knowledge and he was a quick learner. Slowly as time passed, the patterns and jigsaw pieces of knowledge began to fit together and he felt not unlike an autoclave as he released, teased small amounts of power from his mind. He gathered his will and let it form instructions; a slight draught, a tiny pool of water. He began to develop more power as he practiced his art.

'Be careful, Karl', said Torran. 'I know that you would like to let go and feel the power that is within you, but not yet. We have to use stealth. If your two elements realise what we are about, that is to say that you are learning to control them, they might decide to try and stop you by testing you before you are ready'.

'They may try to destroy me anyway on my twenty-fifth birthday, am I correct?'

'Yes you are. That's when I had my test and I want you to be ready. You're very perceptive aren't you?'

'I'm beginning to wish that I wasn't'.

Four years drifted by. Karl was deep into learning hidden secrets. He spent most of his free time in Torran's library. Volume upon volume of instruction entered his mind and was locked into every corner of his consciousness. So engrossed was he that he failed to notice just how quickly time was passing. There were no moments of boredom, there was so much to do but as a diversionary tactic, Torran and Karl devised learning games.

'Take that', Torran called as he hurled a small ball of orange light towards Karl.

'Not so my lord', returned Karl as he blocked the attack with a solid wall of wind.

Immediately he counter attacked with a quantity of water which soaked Torran.

'I'm wet', he cried.

'Then dry yourself with your orange light instead of throwing it at me'.

'Ah!' said Torran. 'If I were but a thousand years younger I would tan thy hide'.

'But you would have to catch me first old man. Can you swim?'

'Can you cook?' Returned Torran.

'Yes', said Karl, slightly puzzled.

'Well it's your turn to prepare the evening meal'.

'I fell for that, didn't I?'

On returning to the house, Torran went directly to his study room and was lost in manuscripts. Karl went to the kitchen and busied himself with preparing the evening meal. When prepared, the meal of cured pork and vegetables followed and, between draughts of ale, the two talked at length about what was to come. Torran spoke about the time that he was tested by his elements.

Although it was a lifetime ago, he remembered it as though it was yesterday.

'I'll not say that my test was easy; I was petrified to tell you the truth but I was also determined to be the victor. Basically it is the strength of one's own will, the inner strength of the survival instinct. I remember that I was called to the Dete Beacons. Ice attacked first; I used fire against it and when fire attacked, I used ice against it. I played one against the other and it worked. Maybe this should be your plan. Use one against the other; divide and conquer. It wasn't that simple of course but it's more or less what happened. Anyway, enough of work for the time being. I think it's about time that we went calling'.

'Who do you propose we call on?'

'How about we call on Lord Brin of Castle Tezz'.

'Could we Torran, it will be good to see my father again?'

'I don't see why not, but know this. When we call on Lord Brin, you are his senior; you are the wizard. It may be the only benefit you have because the heartaches are numerous. When you reach the age of maturity you will age no more, you will remain at that age. You will not age in appearance but your mind will know the centuries.

Your parents are different, they will age as time goes by and they will pass from this life as will your friends. Marriage is not recommended for obvious reasons. To watch your wife grow old before you; to watch your sons die of old age is a pain that even I could not bear. I have seen the pain in other wizards, they despaired and ultimately, that was their downfall. Are you prepared?'

'I believe that I am prepared and I understand that it will not be easy. I would not expect it to be so, but I have beforehand knowledge of what is to try me and I will be ready for that trial'.

'Well then my young friend, let us try to find suitable raiment; robes that are becoming for the Wizard of Wind and Water. Why don't you pour out some wine while I have a search about?'

Whilst Torran went, almost secretively to the far end of the room, Karl practiced by having the wine pour itself. He watched with interest as Torran opened a chest, and from it took a smaller one. He also removed something that was wrapped in an oil soaked canvas.

'These are for you, Karl. Others lie here for Earth and Stone'.

He brought forth the chest and laid it on the table; the item wrapped in oiled canvas he placed beside it. Karl took a sip of wine and then proceeded to unfold the canvassed item. He felt a tingling in his fingers as he did so, but continued until a large black bladed sword came into view.

'It's alive!' exclaimed Karl.

'Not exactly, it is your power that fills it. It will become like an extension of your arm, superior to any and all other swords with the exception of one of its kind.

Each of the original wizards was presented with a black bladed sword by the gods.

Two are now claimed, there is one left for Earth and Stone'.

Karl laid the sword on the table and lifted the lid of the chest. He removed a hooded robe. This was not an ordinary robe, but one of light blue and green that sparkled as though it were also alive.

'Let us see what our new wizard looks like in all his finery', said Torran.

Karl clothed himself in the robe then, carefully, he strapped on the sword. The robe did not only look alive, it gave him the sensation of being alive. It started with a slight tingling, almost like pins and needles which increased until he felt a solid charge of energy flow through his body, he felt the power of the wizards.

He didn't hear the strange melody at first, but he did notice a mist that began to appear around them.

As the mist began to grow in size, Karl looked on in wonder as little blue and green lights came from the mist to dance around the room. Torran motioned Karl to keep perfectly still as thunder rumbled and lightening flashed within the mist; little stars appeared to follow its advance.

Suddenly it was gone, the mist, the lights, the stars all gone. Where it had been stood an aging figure wearing similar raiment to that of Karl. Long white hair fell about his shoulders, flawless features and crystal blue eyes showed only love. Both knew that this was none other than Eqwin, young God of Wind and Water' Torran and Karl knelt to pay homage where others would have prostrated themselves before the magnificence that was Eqwin.

'Rise and be at peace, my friends'. Eqwins voice was almost a song. 'You have done well, Karl of Brin, I am pleased with my earthborn child. Now, and before your trial starts, your journey. I cannot tell you where it will lead or what ordeals you will face, for this I have been forbidden to say. Nor can I assist in any direct way, but I know that I have chosen wisely in you. I have seen it during your education. I see it now, and your heart tells me that you will not fail me. You have already received by way of a gift from me, a black stallion. Treat him well, for he will serve you and follow you even to the gates of hell if you so command it. Fear not to call for my guidance for I will be ever with you'.

With that parting salutation, Eqwin, God of Wind and Water disappeared. It was at that moment that Karl felt such a surge of power enter his body that he had to sit down, it was almost painful. Torran who had been closely watching Karl, moved over to reassure him that everything would be alright. He explained that he too had felt the presence of his god enter him when he first put on his wizards raiment in acceptance of service. Karl was not yet in his twenty-fifth year but Eqwin had accepted him and filled him with his presence. He would age no more.

'I think I need a tankard of ale', said Karl

Torran filled two goblets with wine. Handing one to Karl he raised his goblet high.

'Lord Karl, Wizard of Wind and Water, I salute you'.

'And I you, Lord Torran of Ice and Fire'.

A moment, a captured moment when two people looked upon one another with respect and admiration before preparing for their journey. Torran, wearing his wizards robes, packed a few things which included the last wizards chest and sword. Lord Karl for his part packed enough supplies to last two or three days, then, headed for the stables. As he approached, Lord Torran was already patting his white stallion on the neck; he prepared to mount. The black stallion walked towards Karl who fussed with him. They had become alike to Torran and his white stallion; friends.

'Well wizard' said Torran. 'Our journey begins'.

'And may we be as one when it ends', replied Karl.

CHAPTER TWO

T HE EVENING WAS WARM; the last of the daytime birds had ceased their merry tunes giving way to the sounds of night. The mating, challenge and greeting calls of a thousand insects filled the otherwise soundless void. The large full moon shone its dulled brilliance onto the faces of Torran and Karl as they sat astride their mounts; began a slow ride down Millers Hill towards open country. Torran glanced back as visions of the house filled his mind. He saw the living room with its wall coverings of silk, the low filigree table reflecting the blaze from the log fire. He saw Karl as a novice and remembered what fun it was teaching him. He saw the stables where his equine companion of many years, the white stallion, had frolicked in the hay. He wondered whether or not he would return. He smiled to himself, of course I will, he thought. Then he spurred his mount to catch up with Karl who had moved slightly ahead. It was a cloudless night, the small lights of heaven watched with complete indifference as the two riders jostled for position in a race across a field. Cattle stirred nervously and then returned to their slumber amid the tall grasses. Torran and Karl halted at daybreak to rest the horses and eat a breakfast of goats' cheese and fruit.

'We should reach Goston village by late afternoon' said Torran as he opened a bottle of wine.

'How long will we be staying there?' asked Karl.

'Only overnight, but we must be on our guard, a lot of thieves and cut-throats travel this road and we could do without upsetting the local community by removing their men folk'.

Their journey continued about one hour later and by then the day was in full swing. Birds filled the blue sky waiting for the plough to unearth their breakfast.

Occasionally a field worker would look up and gaze at what he would consider to be a strange pair of horsemen riding towards the village. Eventually they reached the main village road. A jumble of derelict buildings laid waste for centuries lined the street, a home for vermin and outcasts. There wasn't all that much of a difference in the appearance of the occupied part of the village, the architecture stood out like a sore thumb.

It was a village that had grown through a long period of time; many different styles had been adopted without regard to period clashes.

Torran was a bottomless pit of information and related to Karl the different styles, structural changes and materials used; good information in case of hostile action. Karl listened intently; he had been interested in the subject as a boy and had learned quite a lot from his father.

Eventually they came to the village inn and after bedding down their mounts, went inside. A silence fell on the crowd of locals using the inn as Torran and Karl entered the public room.

'A room for the night innkeeper', called Torran.

'What are you lot looking at, haven't you seen gentry before?' shouted the innkeeper to the open mouthed crowd.

They immediately returned to their chatter of harvests and weather but kept a mistrustful eye on the visitors. It was as though they too sensed that something was not quite as it should be in the land.

'You will be excusing them my lords. It's not often we have distinguished gentlefolk pay us a call'.

'There has been no offence innkeeper', said Torran. 'Now what about the room?'

'Ah, this way sirs, this way'.

The innkeeper led them up a narrow stairway onto an equally narrow landing. Opening a door he showed them a room.

'It's my best and biggest' said the innkeeper, smiling.

The innkeeper then left the pair and when he was out of earshot, Torran and Karl looked at each other and burst out laughing. The room was minute, the walls were bare and only a small dresser kept company with two small cots.

'I would hate to have seen his smallest room' said Karl.

'Or his worst one', said Torran. 'How about some ale?'

'As long as it's his best ale'

'There's a thought. By the way, if we do by chance meet any undesirable people intent upon robbing or cheating us, try to refrain from using your powers'.

'May I ask why?'

'Well we don't want any stories about wizards being spread around. It unnerves people and is unproductive. If there are any dangers, and we might as well expect there to be some, we wouldn't want to give the perpetrators advance warning of our actions'

'I take your point'.

They left the room and descended the narrow staircase. Torran made a mental note of loose floorboards as if by habit; they entered the public room. Explaining that they were librarians and scribes in search of strange phenomena seemed to satisfy the general curiosity, although many wondered what librarians and scribes were, and no-one knew what phenomena meant.

'It's when things happen that cannot be explained', said Torran by way of a description.

Suddenly the room was filled with countless happenings to livestock, crops and individual homes that couldn't be explained. The more fantastic the story, the larger the listening audience. Karl was slightly bemused by all the stories.

'It's like the story of the one that got away', said Karl.

'Well that one was over two feet long' said Torran as he remembered one day when the two had gone fishing. He had played the fish for over two hours; saw the huge head on more than one occasion and battled with it as it darted this way and that in its attempt to free itself which, rewarded by its efforts, it did. It swam slowly away and splashed the water with its fan-like tail as though to rebuke a would-be captor.

The evening drew on and slowly the room emptied. Karl and Torran retired to their room and tried to sleep along with may six and eight legged creatures. This inn was definitely not one to put on their list of stop overs.

The village watchman walked through the muddy streets, his eyes red from lack of sleep. 'Sunrise', he shouted. 'Sunrise'.

Torran and Karl were already awake and watched as the lonely figure slowly disappeared from view. Daily sounds began to echo through the cool morning air. The sounds of cooking and cleaning, doors opening and closing. The smoke from the cooking fires began to climb its feathery staircase into the cloudless sky.

'Breakfast?' Asked Karl.

'I'll risk being poisoned once', said Torran.

They made their way down to the public room where tables were being scrubbed by an overweight woman; several small children were raking the sawdust covered floor with their fingers.

'What are they doing?' Asked Karl.

'Watch', said Torran.

He strolled over to where the children were searching and undetected he dropped a coin into the sawdust. After several minutes small fingers located the coin and a tiny face beamed. He held up the coin so that others might see his good fortune.

'Is it not worth ten times that coin to make a child happy?' Said Torran.

'And ten times that again', said Karl.

They sat down at a surprisingly clean table and the over large woman who could have been the innkeepers wife served them with bowls of hot oat porridge. A jug of milk was placed beside each bowl and a pot of honey was offered as a sweetener. Although Torran and Karl did not enjoy the sleeping arrangements, the breakfast was certainly making up for it. After the porridge, a selection of fried meats was served and to wash it down a tankard of hot, spiced wine.

Torran and Karl were reluctant to move after such a breakfast, but Karl hinted that he was eager to see his father again. After paying for their keep they made their way to the stables. Torran stopped to purchase two stout poles.

'They are a little on the long side if we are spoiling for a fight', said Karl

'No we are not looking for a fight, but if we are to ride to Castle Tezz, we will arrive in proper style. I have packed our individual colours'.

Karl smiled and nodded his head in approval as Torran tied the poles to his horse. They rode at a leisurely pace towards the edge of the village. As they departed the occupied area, Karl threw a handful of coins to a group of children who were waving. 'At least ten times', he said.

The village slowly faded into the distance and thoughts were of a happy reunion.

The hedgerows flickered past as the horses cantered a rhythmic beat on the soft earth. No one spoke for the most part of the day, both knew their destination, and Karl was perhaps a little over excited at the prospect of greeting his father after so long. The two stopped in the late afternoon for a meal and to let the horses rest, but this was a short stop and they were soon riding again. Not feeling too tired, they rode as the evening began to cool and the sun sank into its earthly tomb, its final rays melting into darkness. Suddenly Karl indicated to Torran that four riders bridged the road some distance ahead.

'Trouble?' he asked

'Could be. Remember, stay your powers'.

They rode up towards the four ill-dressed and mean looking men on horseback; stopped a little distance from them.

'Well now, what 'ave we got 'ere then matey?' Called the obvious leader of the group.

'They are clad in fine robes, must 'ave a rich purse if you ask me', said another to the leader.

Torran moved a little closer. Karl did likewise and both were tense and in battle readiness.

'Why do you bother to block our path?' Called Torran.

The four riders thought that that remark was rather funny and chuckled to themselves. The leader leaned forward.

'Well now'. He spread his hands in a wide arc and smiled to his friends. 'This 'ere is a toll road. Me and my companions 'ave the job of collecting the money'.

'How much is the charge?' Asked Karl.

For a while it seemed that the four riders were having a conference, slight giggling floated into the otherwise silent night.

'Now let me see'. Said the leader. 'I think that what you've got in your purses, your valuables, your fine clothes and may be a couple of good strong 'orses. Yes, that would be fair payment'.

For a moment the four riders burst into hysterical laughter. Then their moods changed, their faces became snarls of hatred as they began to move towards Torran and Brin; they drew their swords.

They didn't appear to see what happened next. They didn't see the two black bladed swords come alive and deal death blows to two of the riders. The leaders head dropped as he stared open mouthed in disbelief at his entrails; then he fell sideways from his horse. The other was trying to hold his head in place; his eyes were full of surprise as his head rolled away from his body. The two other riders, realising that to fight would mean certain death, fled, both in different directions.

'Shall we give chase?' Asked Karl as he wiped the blood from his sword and sheathed it.

'I think not', replied Torran.

He went on to explain that even thieves know when not to tempt fate. Revenge might have been in their minds if they were able to summon enough courage, but Karl and Torran would be long gone riding through the night.

Dawn was picturesque with a red streaked sky welcoming the early morning sun; there was a freshness about it that was so inviting. A mist played around the fields chased by light breezes and leaves raced in groups here and there. Karl suddenly caught a glimpse of something that made his eyes widen and his mouth water.

'Look'! He shouted.

Torran's sword was out, his muscles flexed. 'What is it?' He asked.

'Mushrooms', answered Karl. 'I love mushrooms and isn't it time for breakfast?'

'I wish you wouldn't do that' said Torran as he replaced his sword and relaxed.'

'Do what?' Asked Karl as he dismounted and began searching around.

'Oh nothing. By the way it's your turn for kitchen duties'.

Karl stood up. 'Just a minute, Monday, Tuesday, Wednesday. Oh, so it is'.

Torran smiled a sort of sated Cheshire cat smile then began to pick the small mushrooms. Karl gathered some dry wood and soon had a fire burning while Torran carried over two good handfuls of the fungi.

'Will these be enough'

Karl confirmed the amount and set to cooking a meal of cured bacon and mushrooms, the delicious aroma drifting away into the atmosphere.

'Oh, this is the life', said Torran, mockingly.

'Well it's your turn tomorrow', laughed Karl.

The day began to darken as Karl and Torran prepared to continue their journey. Already a slightly stronger breeze had begun to whisper around the hedges and grasslands, tiny droplets of rain followed intermittently.

'Shall I try to calm it down a little? Well at least until we get to my father's castle'.

'No, try not to expose yourself Karl. As yet it is known that you have the power but it is not known how strong that power is. Don't you see that this just might be a test? Hold on, we should reach Castle Tezz in two or three days'

'As you say Torran. It will be good to see my father again after all this time'.

'Indeed my friend, indeed it will. I'll have to start practicing my name calling'.

'Have you always insulted each other?'

'Of course. If we were to be polite to each other, respectable and gentlemanly, why, we would undoubtedly come to blows'.

Torran burst out laughing at the thought. No, he could not raise an arm to his friend. Furthermore, even the gods could not protect the person who did. Lord Torran was Lord Brin's champion and his oath was binding for all time.

Although Karl had not seen his father for over four years, Torran had not seen his friend for ten times that amount. His mind drifted back to that time once again.

'*My Lord Tezz, it grieves me that this day I must depart. If I was to stay the castle would be besieged by would be champions wishing an early grave. I leave in body but not in spirit, call me and I will respond to that call. Wherever I am, whatever I am doing I shall come*'.

'*Lord Torran*' *said Lord Tezz, clasping Torran's shoulders. 'Should you ever come this way, this is your home. With the knowledge of his fine teacher, Brin will become a fair and just lord; I thank you for that*'.

*His arms sagged at his sides as he turned and walked away. Torran gave a shrill whistle and the white stallion joined him. There were no parting ceremonies, no guards of honour, just a feeling of loss on both sides. Lord Tezz returned to his study and sat down. In his sadness he called out, '*return my friend, one day return*'.*

He hoped that Torran would hear his plea, and he did because two words echoed in Lord Tezz's mind, unspoken words but nevertheless audible. 'I will'.

The distant drums of thunder echoed; huge black clouds hung in the air like ink stained cotton wool pads.

'Any time now', said Karl.

There was an eerie sort of silence when nothing moved and no birds sang. Even the scattered trees seemed poised in anticipation of some major event. Large spots of rain began to fall, slowly at first then, with a flash of lightening and a roll of thunder, the heavens opened.

'You and your big mouth', said Torran.

Karl laughed as rain began to streak down his face to form droplets on his chin. They sheltered under a nearby tree that was not much of a shelter at all, they got wet. Karl sensed something different with this weather as winds began to grow stronger. They were teasing him, buffeting him like a cruel jibe and yet he held his power in check.

Small stones then began to be picked up by the wind and Karl began to suffer bruising and small cuts. He could not protect himself because of the torrential rain, he could see little and still he withheld his power. Water slowly built up turning the earth into lethal mud bogs that could hide a body for eternity.

Karl began to find it difficult to remain upright; such was the strength, the force of his invisible enemy. He could be picked up and thrown at any time and for any distance.

Suddenly, Karl's body resigned itself to the commands of his mind as his power demanded release. He stood erect, his matted hair plastered to his face and the force of the wind having no effect upon him. His eyes became fixed, dark, like ancient doorways into time itself. A huge surge of power made his whole body tingle as he protected himself with a shield of blue light. His face become stern, almost granite looking in his determination.

In one fluid movement he drew his sword and held it aloft, a blade of shimmering blackness, almost like a living creature. His power shot forth in all directions.

'I am Lord Karl of Castle Tezz. I am the Wizard of Wind and Water. I am your master and I say, abate'. The blue shielding light began to flare; huge balls of blue fire shot forth as though in attack. The wind became stronger still, although the rain had eased. Karl forced himself to search for hidden strength; he brought his will to bear once more.

'ABATE I SAY'. His voice seemed to echo into the firmament.

With what seemed to be like one last defiant stand the wind grew even stronger causing the earth to shudder.

The sky was filled with blue fire-balls as Lord Karl stood statue-like, defiant, his sword still pointing to the heavens as he fought for control. The surrounding blue light, already glaring in its intensity, grew brighter as Karl's determination to succeed heightened. For almost an hour Karl stood motionless, locked in this strange battle of minds with an unseen enemy.

Suddenly the wind dropped. It was as though there had never been a wind; the rain had also ceased its torrential downpour. There then was a kind of calm that suggested it's not over yet. From out of a clear blue sky and without warning, a terrifying whirlwind advanced towards him. He did nothing but remain in the posture of Knight Rampant staring at the oncoming danger. Then it disappeared and Karl fell to one knee, he was completely exhausted.

Torran was soon by his side with a beaming smile. He explained that as the wind had grown stronger and stronger, he realised that this was no ordinary condition. It was a direct challenge to Karl and so he had sat in a hollow, pulled a canvas over his head and waited. This was one event that he could not interfere with even if he had wanted to.

'I salute you Karl, you have beaten wind and water, and you are now the master'.

'I feel worn out', said Karl.

As he rested he heard a voice speak in his mind. *'I am indeed pleased with my earthborn'.* 'And I with my Master' whispered Karl.

They rested for some time while Torran played nursemaid to the exhausted Karl, he told him that there would be no more tests but to remain strong. Before long, however, Karl had recouped his strength and the two continued their journey. Karl now felt like the master of his elements and that he had triumphed; the ordeal was over.

On the morning of the next day, the sun played its warmth on the travellers as they sat motionless in their saddles, their line of sight fixed as they gazed down upon the battlements of Castle Tezz. Memories flooded each mind; both hearts were beating a little faster in anticipation of a long awaited meeting.

Torran unstrapped the poles and, after dismounting, he began to arrange the standards. On one pole he fixed the colours of Ice and Fire, a red sunburst on a background of glittering white. On the other he fixed the colours of Wind and Water, a white lightning bolt on a background of equally glittering blue. Torran remounted and the two friends rode with colours flying toward castle Tezz.

During the years as a guest of Lord Torran, Lord Karl's features had dissolved from boyhood and matured into manhood; his physique had developed too. His once narrow body had become broad and powerful. He wondered as he approached the castle whether or not he would be recognised after so long.

'Sergeant of the guards' shouted a very nervous sentry.

The sergeant, veteran of a hundred battles, analysed the nervousness of the sentry and came running.

'Two riders in strange robes approach and they carry even stranger colours, sergeant'.

The sergeant climbed the wooden ladder that led up to the duty post and sighted the oncoming visitors.

'Beautiful horses', remarked the sergeant who had a love of the animals.

'Who are they?' Asked the sentry.

'I don't know lad, but I'm going to find out'. He cupped his hands to his mouth and shouted down to them. 'Hold strangers! What business brings you to the gates of Castle Tezz?'

The sergeant saw to it that the guards were ready in case of trouble. Karl had pulled up the hood of his robe and looked quite mysterious, so Torran, continuing his slight deception, answered.

'My good man, do you not open the gates when two passing nobles visit? It used to be the custom of this castle but it seems to have died like the brain of your fat, pompous lord. Tell him that a better man stands at his gate'.

'Oh no', whispered Karl.

The reply was as swift and as sharp as a rapier. 'My lords' shouted the sergeant. 'I shall convey your insult to the Lord Brin of Castle Tezz and having said this I fear for your safety. I would strongly advise you to flee, my lords. I wouldn't exchange places with you when the Lord Brin comes to return the insult, I like life too much'.

'We shall wait here for the sloth', replied Torran.

The sergeant went bright red in the face and turned away. Climbing down the ladder again he marched purposely towards Lord Brin's chambers. 'I'll take the big one' he thought. His footsteps echoed like canon fire as he marched through several corridors, finally to arrive at a huge double door. Two armed guards stood outside. 'Out of my way', he commanded as he pushed past and opened the doors.

Lord Brin, a huge thick set man with jet black hair and a short styled beard like his father, Lord Tezz, was writing in his diary when the sergeant burst into the room.

'Forgive the intrusion upon your privacy, my Lord', said the now perspiring sergeant.

'Why, you look all flustered, sergeant. Of course I forgive the intrusion. What seems to be bothering you?'

'Sire, we have outside the gates, two riders. They wear strange robes and declare standards the even I do not recognise'.

'That's not a crime sergeant. Perhaps they are travelling players or dealers in the exotic'.

'No sire they come for combat, they insult the name of Brin. One of them, forgive my repetition sire, but he called you a fat, pompous, brain dead sloth or words to that effect'.

Lord Brin pondered for a moment, and then a smile appeared on his face. 'Then let them in', he ordered.

'But my lord', said the astonished sergeant who had expected Lord Brin to order that the two visitors be brought before him to answer for their insults, or at worst be slain and be left for carrion.

'My dear sergeant, there is only one man I know who dare insult me thus, Lord Torran. This is going to be a good contest. Let them in'.

Hearing the word, contest; the sergeant cheered up a little. Quickly he travelled back along the corridors that led to the courtyard. 'Open the gates', he shouted.

The huge oak gates swung open on well-greased hinges and Torran led the way over the already lowered drawbridge. They halted in the courtyard as soldiers lined the area not knowing what to do. A man shouted from a distance.

'Fat and pompous? Brain dead? Sloth? Is it that mounted cripple who calls me thus?' called Lord Brin as he almost ran down the steps that led to the courtyard.

'Yes', replied Torran, and don't be impertinent to your elders you young squirt'.

The soldiers were totally confused and wondered when the real fight would begin.

'If I were a younger man', continued Lord Brin, 'I would have you horse whipped you, you ragamuffin'.

'Stuttering eh? Well that's the first sign of senility'.

'Nonsense, dogs-breath'.

'Hunchback'.

The game of insults continues for almost an hour. The guards and local dignitaries had now become seated. Heads moved from side to side as each took turn to insult the other; it was like watching a tennis match. Never had anyone there witnessed such an unusual event; no-one wanted to miss the finale.

'And get off that horse when you speak to me, Philistine'.

Philistine eh?'

The guards became slightly nervous when Torran dismounted and began a slow walk towards Lord Brin. Murmurs ran through the crowd and there was a clatter of armour as the soldiers stood up; several had already moved to the side of Lord Brin. Torran's black bladed sword came out of its sheath and into the position of Knights Salute in one living, fluid motion. The crowd gasped; never had they seen such speed. Lord Brin never flinched; slowly he drew his own sword and replied in like manner. The two faced each other as they put away their weapons, their faces asking so many questions. Eyes began to water as Lord Brin threw himself into a warm embrace with Torran. They kissed each other's cheeks as only brothers would and the guards let out a sigh of relief. The sergeant walked away mumbling to himself. 'I could have taken the big one'.

'Friends' shouted Lord Brin to the large crowd that had assembled during the unusual spectacle. 'Soldiers, people, members of my most trusted household. Let it be known that this day I receive once again my champion'. The crowd were visibly stunned because they had heard stories of the strange happenings all those years ago, but this man was young. 'And fiend'. He looked at Torran. 'My dear twisted fiend'.

'Don't you mean trusted friend?' Said Torran.

'I know what I mean', said Lord Brin, continuing. 'Lord Torran, Wizard of Ice and Fire'.

There was a general whisper throughout the crowd that seemed to confirm that this was indeed the same Lord who had visited all those years ago.

Torran was just about to address the crowd in reply to his friend when suddenly, the crowd parted. Heads bowed and people knelt as an elderly gentleman and his lady walked towards him. Torran drew his sword and kneeling, offered it, pommel first to the Lady of Castle Tezz.

'Still as gallant my young knight?' Said the Lady of Tezz.

'I am at your service, my lady', replied Torran.

He kissed her outstretched hand and she in turn stooped and kissed the pommel of the black bladed sword.

'Stand up my friend', said the Lord Tezz. 'Tell me, who is your travelling companion?'

'I shall introduce him momentarily', said Torran as he prepared to address the crowd once more. 'People of Castle Tezz, I raise my sword to my friends. Never will this family mourn death while I have the power to prevent it. I am by their side in all things'. A great cheer arose from the crowd. Torran continued as Karl came forward, head bowed. 'Furthermore my friends, I would present one other who would stand at the side of this family in times of danger'. Karl threw back his hood, drew his sword in one movement and stood erect in salute to his father.

'Lord Karl of Brin of Tezz. Wizard of Wind and Water. Earth born of Eqwin. Son and heir to the Lord Brin. Keeper of the Realm and defender of the right'.

'Windbag' said Lord Brin as tears of happiness began to roll down his cheeks.

'Cry baby'.

Lord and Lady Tezz were also weeping tears of great happiness as they met and embraced Lord Karl. Torran gave a sign to the soldiers. Slowly and quietly they cleared the courtyard. This was a moment when some people needed to be alone and even Torran made a tactical withdrawal during this family reunion.

To hold a feast that day would have been nothing but an anti-climax to the main event, but the following day, a great celebration was held to honour the home coming of Lord Karl, and great family friend, Lord Torran. The feasting and merriment lasted well into the evening as court jesters performed to the giggles of children. Musicians played a lively tune and people danced until they could dance no more.

'More wine. I feel like getting drunk', said Lord Brin who had had more than enough already.

'Would you like ice in your drink, my friend?' Asked Torran. He produced two round balls of ice and dropped them into an already overflowing tankard of ale. The guests exploded into laughter at the puzzlement on Lord Brin's face.

'Now listen here you mobile ice maker', shouted Lord Brin.

'Oh no, here we go again', said Lord Karl who eventually left the two to their games.

The barrage of insults and the encouragement offered by the remaining guests was left behind. Karl, after escorting Lord and Lady Tezz to their rooms, retired to his own. It had been a long and happy day. Karl was tired and soon fell to sleep.

A shallow mist clung to sand covered ground and vision was limited. Rows of eyes watched from high peaks as a solitary figure ran, almost in slow motion across a wide open space. The figure turned, it was a man, a young man. Fear showed in his eyes and worry on his face. Beads of perspiration rolled down his youthful features. Karl ran towards him pleading, trying to make him understand. The mist suddenly vanished revealing a dry barren landscape and the sun beating down made Karl uncomfortably hot. The figure turned again and Karl felt a gathering of power. He felt the earth tremble; it opened and began to swallow him.

Karl awoke in a cold sweat. He sat up and realised that he had been dreaming. It was a disturbing dream, one that asked many questions. He lay down again to try to sleep but it was a troubled sleep that came. He dreamed again. He dreamed that he called upon the God Eqwin. A mist appeared followed by lights of such intensity that Karl had to close his eyes. Eqwin appeared.

'My Lord Eqwin, I have had a dream such as I have never dreamed. I know not its meaning'.

'*Karl, my earthborn*', began Eqwin in a quiet, reassuring voice. '*I have come to answer your questions in the best way that I can. However, bear in mind that I am forbidden to change that which follows, nor can I tell you the road you are to take. All I can say to you is, be strong. Do not venture forth hastily, and deliberate on what you may find. It is all the help that I can give*'. Eqwin disappeared and Karl slept.

When Torran eventually retired to his bed, he was also plagued with disturbing dreams that night. He dreamed of fire with all of its destructive power and he dreamed of five knives. The dream was an enigma full of confusion. He was being pulled down into a web after which the five knives appeared, each one bearing his name in old-style script; each one wanting to embrace him and revel in his death throes. Dreams are wide open spaces of a reflective imagination, but these dreams appeared to be interlocked with reality.

The morning slowly raised its sleepy head, the sun banishing the darkness for another day. The sounds of the changing of the guards nudged the sleeping in to a state of awareness. Karl slipped out of his comfortable bed, washed and dressed, then made his way to the dining hall. Torran was already there, standing by an open log fire. He was watching the flames as they sent bright images across a worried face. The occasional *crack* of burning, knotted wood, launched miniature missiles across the emptiness of the hall, only to be scooped up by ever vigilant servants. Torran and Karl, after greeting each other, sat by the fire. Each related to the other the content of their dreams; neither knew the answers. The only agreement they reached was that the dreams were important and this meant that it was time to continue their journey.

On entering the dining hall the cheery attitude of Lord Brin disappeared as he read the faces of Karl and Torran. To have friends and family visit, even for a short time is a joyful occasion. For them to leave again on an unknown and possibly dangerous journey is a sad one. Lord Brin could not hide his emotions; they showed through as he spoke.

'It's time, isn't it?'

'I'm afraid so father', said Karl.

'Can't that thief-in-the-night speak for himself?' Said Lord Brin in an attempt to mask his heartache. 'If I was but a few years younger'.

'Oh that I wish you were' interrupted Torran. 'To play hide and seek just one more time'. For once Torran was serious.

'Perhaps a race around the castle walls?' Suggested Lord Brin.

'Well, I for one will not leave until we have; to horses'.

Like two youngsters the two lords ran for the stables. Lord Brin told the guards to open the gates and lower the drawbridge as he passed the guard house.

'I wonder what they are up to now.' Said one of the guards.

Moments later, two riders left the castle at full gallop. The conversation between them was not for the ears of young ladies as they exchanged insults en route. Torran was well in the lead at the first corner, but Lord Brin with an all-out effort was closing at the second. By the third corner both horses were neck and neck and remained that way until the fourth. A small crowd had gathered as, on the last stretch, Torran purposely slowed his stallion to allow Lord Brin the winners place.

'I'm too old for this', said Torran with a smile.

'Don't worry, I'll let *you* win one day', said Lord Brin with a knowing wink.

The two men dismounted and threw themselves into a brotherly embrace.

'Take good care of my son, my friend'.

'My life before his'.

'Come then, I will give you a letter of authorisation that you may be given access to the Border house. It lies about two days ride to the north. There you can rest, refresh yourself and obtain further supplies for your journey'.

'I am indebted my friend'.

'And it has been paid many times over', replied Lord Brin.

Karl had gone to the kitchen to arrange supplies. From there he called on his grandparents, the Lord and Lady Tezz, to say his farewells. As he returned to the courtyard where his father and Torran stood waiting, he felt a great sense of loss.

Something told him that he would not see his grandparents again, it troubled him. Soon Karl and Torran were sat astride their mounts facing a small crowd that had gathered and almost in unison; the black bladed swords were drawn.

'With honour', called Karl and Torran as they both saluted Lord Brin.

Swords were then sheathed and the two riders galloped out of the gate and away from Castle Tezz. Lord Brin watched for a long while, wondering if he would ever see them again. Images of happier times floated across the windows of his eyes. 'Take good care' he called, and raised his hand in salute.

CHAPTER THREE

'THEY ARE COMING FOR *you, Lord of the Rock. They are all powerful and yet, crafty in their will to succeed. They come to destroy you, Lord of the Rock, I know because I have seen them'.*
'*Who are you?*'
'*I am the God Zelfen, but fear not for I am also your friend. I bring you this news Lord of the Rock'.*
'*But I am not a Lord. I don't understand. I don't understand'.*

Edmund sat up in his little cot and viewed his sparsely furnished cell, the bare walls and narrow window, nothing had changed. Shadows caused by a single candle's light played on the thatched roof as the solitary flame danced to an imaginary tune. He climbed out of his cot, which was more like a low pallet with straw base, and tried to wash away the dream with cold water. Me a lord, he thought as he dressed in his leggings and half coat. The thought made him smile as he prepared for his daily duties. The sandals he wore made little sound as he walked along the cold, draughty corridors of Dronecet Castle. Each morning it was his duty to rise early and build up the castle fires. When he had completed this task he would labour at whatever his seniors ordered.

Edmund, a sandy haired youth with a freckled but clean complexion was well liked by his immediate superior, Secc. Secc knew that if he asked for work to be done by Edmund, it would be done and a good job made of it. Often, after all the daily work had been completed, Edmund and Secc joined in conversation about local events, the next day's workload and on one occasion, about the dreams.

'Is there any truth in dreams?' Asked Edmund.

This was a topic never discussed before and Secc pondered a while before answering. 'Is there any truth in dreams?' He began. May be sometimes, but in your case I would say definitely not. Dreams of grandeur, we all have them. I dreamed that I lived in a house made out of money once'.

'What happened to it?'

'Someone stole it'. Secc burst out laughing and even Edmund saw the funny side.

'But my dreams seem so real', said Edmund still laughing.

'Well let me see if I can better explain' said Secc. 'Dreams are only an extension of you. What goes wrong when you are awake is usually put to rights when you are asleep. What we cannot achieve in normal day to day living, we act out and successfully achieve it in our dreams. It's escapism to the happy land. A person with little or no money becomes rich and famous. It's each individuals own little world of being whatever they want to be and it keeps us from going mad I reckon'.

'But it's always the same dream'.

'And you are always the same person. Now get ready to serve the masters breakfast and don't tell him of any dreams. He'd probably call you a blasphemer and have you drawn and quartered'.

This he certainly would have done. Dronecet castle, a northern stronghold, was a stone built monstrosity which seems to reflect the feelings and actions of its lord. He was a hard, ruthless man with no thought for others; no fear of others. He wanted and demanded no less that to be the lord over all lands and all peoples. Numerous times he had sent mercenaries across the borders to loot and to kill, but he had always been thwarted by the guards from the border house. Ever vigilant they watched for, and repelled the numerous attempts to invade the south. These, however, were only small raiding parties compared to the army that had been slowly building in size over a period of time.

Lord Barek, the lord of Dronecet castle was sat up in his bed; his dark, almost hawk-like features showed no emotion as Edmund carried in his breakfast. As Edmund placed the breakfast try on a small table next to the bed and with lightening reflexes, Lord Barek grabbed him and twisted his arm to his back.

'Are you frightened of me, pretty boy? Does the thought of my power make you tremble?' Said Lord Barek with an evil grin on his face.

'Yes, my lord'.

'Good. Now get out', said Lord Barek as he pushed Edmund away.

Edmund, his arm slightly painful, left the bed chamber and hurried back to his cell. This kind of treatment had been his lot for some years but he was bonded and there was no escape except for death. Apart from the brutality which invaded his day to day existence, there were times when he actually enjoyed his position. One of his favourite duties was to look after a flock of sheep. Every two weeks he stood in for the permanent shepherd while the shepherd went to market to buy and sell livestock.

It was quite early the next morning that Edmund set off once again on the half-day journey to where the sheep were grazing near the Ketan. The River Ketan not only provided water for the castle, but also for its livestock. It flowed through rich pastureland before joining the River Powle on its journey to the south. Numerous times had Edmund been tempted to escape via this route, but he knew that to try would be futile. He would be caught and severely punished by Lord Barek and may even be killed depending upon his mood. He cast the thoughts from his mind and continued his journey. After arriving at the designated place and after exchanging news with the shepherd, the shepherd left Edmund to tend the sheep while he travelled to market.

It was a bright day but after the deluge of the day before, the river had swelled to almost twice its original size. Its normally clear waters were a muddy-brown and threatening. Edmund sat on a rock that overlooked the valley where the sheep seemed to be abnormally restless.

He thought that it was probably due to the unsettled weather of the day before; even so, he scanned the area for any signs of predators of which there were many. As he turned again to look into the swirling waters of the Ketan, a face appeared, half hidden in the murky depths. It was a timeless face with huge black eyes that pierced through the mud and grime. Edmund stood and took a few paces back.

'I am the God Zelfen. Hear me and obey'

It wasn't a spoken voice, but it echoed in Edmunds mind. It was the same voice that he had heard in his dreams. He tried to turn away but he was held by a hypnotic gaze. The voice came again, loud in his ears.

'They come for you Lord of the Rock. Two strangers come to destroy you. Hear my words and destroy them before they get the chance. Use your powers against them'.

The face disappeared; the river had risen again as though by design. Edmund did not know what to make of this vision; his dreams and the voice, it was too confusing for him to understand. He began walking down to a small hollow where the sheep were grazing; the river was higher still and he noticed that the banks of the river were becoming unsafe.

He looked towards the sheep and then back again to the crumbling river bank. Suddenly, large pieces of earth began to break away and were swept away by the torrent. The sheep started to show signs of nervousness as the river burst its banks and sought a pathway towards them.

Edmund was also worried, mainly about the safety of the sheep, but also about his own safety but then, as he watched the river, he felt a strange sensation overcome him. He felt as though he was growing although he remained the same size.

Mental images filled his mind, images of how to remedy the situation. A tingling sensation began to affect his feet and then his legs and then his body. Finally it felt as though his head had exploded. His hands shot forward as though controlled by some external force. A green light of octane brilliance shot forth from his outstretched fingers and surrounded the river bank. All was silent except for a low groaning sound. It became louder, louder until it was as though thunder itself was being conceived upon the land. The earth shook and stone trembled, it had no resistance against the awesome power unleashed to control it.

Edmund opened his eyes to find that he was lying on soft grass; he ached from head to toe. Never before had he felt like he did and he came to the conclusion that he must have blacked out. Sitting up, his mind once again became alert, he remembered. He turned quickly to look at the river banks and his eyes widened. From one end of the hollow to the other, a great mound of earth and stone held back the swirling waters. The sheep, contented, continued to graze on the rich green grass as though nothing had happened.

Karl's head was pounding. 'Did you feel that?' He said to Torran. 'Did you hear it?'

'I heard it'.

'What on earth was it? It made my head spin'.

'That Karl, was the Wizard of Earth and Stone. He has found his power, or been shown it'.

'Do you mean to say that's what it sounds like? I remember you telling me that we can hear powers being used when they exceed a certain level. It seems to me that wizards go around with a permanent headache during the hunting season'.

'It's not normally so loud. He must have been upset for some reason so we must find him'.

'Well the sound seemed to come from the north'.

'North it is'.

The black and the white stallions moved forward at a gallop, sending clods of earth flying into the air as horse shoes dug deep into the soft ground. Kinetic shapes of sunlight flashed past, reds and yellows screened in the hedgerows as the huge ball of fire rested in the west. As they crossed a section of grassland, a mist appeared before them causing them to slow their mounts. They halted as small red and white lights appeared to hover in the mist.

A grumble of the earth combined with flashes of lightening announced the arrival of the image of a man; a tall white-haired man. His wrinkled face and deep-set eyes were beyond age; his robes could only be described as red, white, and alive. Lord Torran dismounted; he walked towards the figure and knelt. This was the image of the God, Frezfir.

'*It has been a long time, Torran my child*'

'Indeed it has been too long Sire', replied Torran.

'*Does not the babe on yonder horseback show fealty to Frezfir?*'

Karl clumsily dismounted, drew his sword, knelt and saluted. 'My pardon, Sire, your presence enchanted me', said Karl.

'*Silver tongued too. Truly the earth-born of Eqwin*'.

'Sire?'

Frezfir smiled the kind of smile that would cure any sickness, calm any storm or tame any beast. '*My children*', he said. '*I have appeared to you this day the bearer of ill tidings. Jealousy and envy rage within one of our elders. He has taken leave of our haven and seeks to undo that which we have achieved upon this land. Such is the mind of Zelfen. Even we are not perfect, we have argued and are undone. For our part we have taken his godly powers from him and sadly he now stands as a mortal. Nevertheless, he still remains a most powerful sorcerer, intent on sewing nettles and thorns in our garden. However, we are excellent gardeners are we not?*'

When Karl looked up again Frezfir was gone, the mist had cleared and the lights had been extinguished. It was as though nothing had happened. Karl felt infuriated, and Torran had that determined look upon his face. The news was grave indeed, it meant another obstacle to overcome, or was this part of some larger plan? For a time after the two had remounted and continued their journey, silence filled the air. It was no ordinary silence, but the kind that clings and threatens before a storm. At last Karl spoke. It was like the snapping of an elastic band.

'This is a game, isn't it?' He voiced angrily

'It might appear that way to those who do not fully understand' said Torran. 'But you must realise that our benefactors cannot, under any circumstances, interfere with what we say and do. They have to, for the want of a better word, manipulate, no, help us indirectly to do what is right and just. At the same time they will try to protect us'.

'But that is manipulation; it's a game for them'.

'Perhaps it would be if the gods were the only ones to receive reward for our actions. But, Karl, we as occupiers of the land are the ones who benefit, we reap the rewards. Yes I will agree that if all goes well 'the garden will be free of nettles and thorns'. It's what the gods want, but isn't that what we want too, to live peacefully, to enjoy life. We have to be the instruments of the gods because there's no-one else. After all, we live here, they don't'.

Another silence followed as they rode into a bush covered valley. Karl eventually accepted the explanation and his anger flowed away. Things were back to normal as the evening drew to a close; a clear night lit only by the moon's soft glow encompassed them as they searched for a camp site. Suddenly Torran called for a halt after seeing something rather odd.

'That's funny', he said.

'What is it?' Asked Karl.

'I've just seen a Bemal bird run across our pathway'.

'Do you mean one of those delicious fat almost featherless things? What's so odd about that?'

'Well, it doesn't belong here. Under normal circumstances they can only be found on the Isle of Witches. A small experiment that went wrong, you understand'.

'Something to do with rabbits and chickens, I heard'.

'Something similar to that'.

A movement to Karl's right bought both riders to full awareness; their hands rested on the pommels of the black bladed swords.

'Hold your weapons', a voice called.

A flash of crimson light streaked past them; it was followed by the sweet smell of roasted meat.

'Ha! At last. I ordered that one already cooked but it came to me alive and kicking', continued the voice.

'Is it customary for you to speak from the shadows?' Called Torran.

'Damnation', replied the voice.

A cloud of miniature stars appeared; sparkled for a moment and then out of the half-light appeared a man of untold years. His uncovered head yielded a mass of snowy, white hair that rested at shoulder level. A long beard was complimented by an equally long moustache that interwove at breast level. His robes, jet black, were smothered in ancient runes with the insignia of Master Magician in silver thread situated centrally. He looked at Torran and Karl with pale blue, hypnotic eyes; his rounded and wrinkled face beamed a smile.

'Wizards both, I greet you'. He gave a long sweeping bow without a sign of discomfort. It seemed a feat for one so old.

Torran was stunned. 'Elio?' He Said.

'At you service, Lord Torran'.

'It was thought that you had perished hundreds of years ago'.

'Never believe the tabloids, Lord Torran. That is exactly what I wanted everyone to believe. I was tired of all the bickering between the gods over who should eventually have this land and for what purpose. No, I found a nice comfortable dwelling on the Isle of Witches which is the only place that the elder gods cannot see into. Of course the younger gods knew; it's still our only secret. They have asked me to join you as a sort of rear guard to the front line, if you understand my meaning. I understand that Zelfen will try his best to destroy this land by fair means or foul. He will wage war through the evilly intentioned, even try to turn the elements against you, but I am wise to his plans. This time we are on equal terms. Now, oh! I almost forgot. Greetings to you Lord Karl of Brin'.

'I am honoured, Master Elio'. Replied Karl.

'It is my privilege', continued Master Elio. 'Let's eat before supper gets cold'.

In the light of the night sky, the three friends sat on blankets, a blazing fire was warming strong mead; the flame's reflection dancing on the skeletal remains of the meal.

'Tell me Master Elio', said Karl as he wiped his greasy hands on a damp cloth. 'I have been instructed in the use of my powers in that I can control what is already here. How is it that your powers provide you with the ability to conjure things from nothing?'

'But the Bemal bird was real, Karl, I don't make things. Oh yes, it is possible I suppose, but all sorts of things must be taken into consideration in the making; it's too much trouble. Basically I am the same as you but with a little cream on top'. He smiled. 'For instance, the meal that we have just enjoyed came from the Isle of Witches, I just transported it here. I'm sure; well I hope that it won't be missed. The mead that we drink comes from the finest cellars and it's something of a devilment that I enjoy, It's also rather fun when I listen to all the explanations of why things around the land disappear. Lord Penste of Castle Penste firmly believes that a ghost haunts his milking sheds and drinks at least a bucketful every week. Do you know, it's delicious'.

'But that amounts to theft', said Karl.

'Mm, I suppose it does'.

Torran began to grin.

'Have you never felt guilt about these thefts?' continued Karl. 'Have you no conscience?'

Master Elio began to search his robes. 'I don't seem to have any at hand'. He replied.

Torran erupted into uncontrollable laughter and Karl, seeing at last that Master Elio was merely playing with him, also began to see the funny side. Master Elio attempted to explain magic in simple terms.

'First of all let me say that raw magic is a very dangerous thing to play with, unless of course you are extremely knowledgeable on the subject. Most magicians, wizard's etcetera, only used to specialise in one particular field of magic. From small enchantments, illusions, they advanced into, necromancy, sorcery, and some became theurgists. Some experimented to such a degree that they became, like me, Masters of the Art. Unfortunately it also has its dangers, even for a Master. One such person, the last magician apart from me tried to unmake one of his own creations and perished. Magic is everywhere. If you planted a small seed, and a tree appeared in seconds, you would think of it as miraculous. Consider then, that the normal growth of a tree is simply magic in slow motion'.

'You said that someone tried to unmake a creation', said Karl.

'Yes, he had created something that was not to his liking. He could have changed it, altered it; but without a thought he tried to unmake it. Once something is made through magic, it cannot be unmade. You see, when a magical spell is used, I hope that I am making sense; it draws energies from all around. From rocks, from trees, the earth and sky; a whole host of different parts come together to make the whole. As they are removed, other parts are waiting on the side-lines so to speak and fill the gap which is left. It follows that what is taken cannot be put back because there is no space for it to fit. If anyone tried this as in the case of our dearly departed, the energies sort of rebound and consume the spell-caster. He acts as the earth point for the stray magic.

He may of course try self-protection, but it wouldn't hold for long, and it could cause a catastrophe of immense proportions if someone with greater power was not available to calm it down. In fact stray magic could, in effect destroy the whole land. It's a question of action and reaction. Each time magic is used it creates minute changes elsewhere; not enough to notice sometimes, but changes nevertheless. Let me explain another way. I wave my arm and a slight breeze is created which moves a seed from its intended path from a tree to the ground; a tree still grows but not in its intended place. I walk through the forest and tread on that seed and a tree doesn't grow at all. The seed is the magic, I create the changes but I cannot undo the seed. I much prefer to transport things; it's much more fun and more easily explained'.

'Have you ever used magic in its raw state?' Asked Karl.

'Indeed, and on many occasions throughout the years, but they were necessary occasions. I did not bathe in its sensations as many did. It can become like a dependent drug if you let it get the better of you. Still, I must not bore you further; rest now for we have a long journey tomorrow'.

Master Elio's words floated around in Karl's imagination as the three friends rested for the remainder of the evening. Soon they slept, deep and peaceful.

The dark sky that was beginning to show streaks of sunlight heralded the morning. Stars winked out as though switched off and the moon, a seemingly transparent disc, paled into nothingness. Warmth flooded the land as the sun appeared over the eastern horizon.

Karl and Torran awoke to the aroma of bacon and mushrooms. Master Elio had, by the smug grin on his face, been transporting again.

Karl and Torran simply smiled as they sat down to eat 'Which way do we travel?' Asked Master Elio as he mopped up some bacon fat with a piece of dry bread.

'Mm', said Torran with a mouth full of food and waving a mushroom in a northerly direction.'

'The north it is my friends. Ajax'! Master Elio twiddled his fingers and miniature stars appeared followed by a huge grey charger. It stood before them, striking the ground with its front hoof. A black and silver blanket covered its wide back. 'Not exactly what I wanted; a little energetic for my old bones but it will do', said master Elio.

Torran and Karl were trying to supress another fit of laughter as they, along with the Master Magician, mounted and began a slow trot northward. Elio had without doubt ridden the grey on many occasions; it showed in Elio's handling and the way in which the two seemed to fit together.

'In case you two are wondering', said Elio, breaking the silence. 'I have 'er . . . borrowed Ajax for a number of years. He has served me well and in turn I have given him a few years of youth each time'.

'How many years of youth?' Asked Karl.

'Well, let me see now. There was . . . . mm . . . . And then also there was . . . mm . . . about six hundred'. Replied Elio without a flicker of emotion and without the crafty grin showing through his bearded face.

'Methinks that you jest, sir wizard', said Torran light-heartedly.

'Methinks that I do', replied Elio. 'To be truthful, Ajax has been with me since I was about your age, Karl. I couldn't let him grow old, why, we're practically kinsfolk'. Elio lovingly stroked Ajax's broad flank and Ajax nodded his approval. 'See', said Elio. 'He agrees with me'.

Edmund sat shaking in his cell; his mind going over and over the earlier events that he had obviously created. He stood and paced the floor several times before coming to a decision; he confided in Secc. Secc listened intently to Edmund's story; he did not interrupt or make comment. After Edmund had concluded his tale, Secc was shown to the part of the river bank indicated in Edmund's story and was shaken;

it was as Edmund had said. Following this, hours of contemplation brought no satisfactory conclusion for him and so, rather than make a fool of himself, Secc made light of the situation saying that it was probably just coincidence. It was suggested that perhaps an earthquake had occurred at the precise time of Edmund's thoughts.

'The land moves all the time, Edmund, but to think that you were the cause of it, that you have the powers to move earth just by thinking about it, is ridiculous. For your own sake, Edmund, let no-one else hear this story lest you be branded a heretic and a liar'.

The conversation faded, a shadow watching from one of the many spy-holes in the wall, moved quietly away. A voice reported to senior officials, who in turn told the story in an exaggerated fashion. Advice was given to the listener, Lord Barek.

During the morning of the next day, Secc was summoned to appear before Lord Barek. This wasn't unusual as he often made reports on the progress of the bondsmen. He thought nothing of the summons until he sensed the mood of his master.

'My Lord Barek, you summoned me', said Secc. He walked towards where Lord Barek was sitting and prostrated himself as was the northern fashion.

'How long have you been in my service, Secc?' Asked Lord Barek.

'My entire life, my Lord'.

'And during this time have I treated you fairly'.

'Without a doubt, my Lord', he lied.

Lord Barek walked over to where Secc was now kneeling; his face was a mask of anger.

'Then why may I ask do you keep from me the fact that someone in my castle claims to be a sorcerer?'

Secc realised that someone had overheard the conversation between Edmund and himself, and had informed Lord Barek; he could not hide his fear.

'My Lord, young Edmund is but a dreamer of dreams; he would not dare masquerade as something that he is not'.

'Young Edmund eh?'

Secc realised his mistake. The spy had not known who he was talking to, he had been duped into a confession and so he pleaded for leniency. Lord Barek shouted an order.

'Bring Edmund to me'.

'At once, my Lord', answered Secc. He hurried away after being dismissed, not sure of what the outcome of this would be for himself, or for Edmund. Lord Barek turned to his advisors who had been waiting in a side room and had entered the minute Secc had departed.

'Well', said Lord Barek.

'As I see it', said a shifty-eyed man as he stepped forward. 'If this Edmund truly has the powers of the ancient, he would indeed be useful in a war against the south. If, however, he hasn't?'

'If he hasn't?' Interrupted Lord Barek.

'Well my Lord you just cast him out. Let his magical land look after him. I can't see him lasting for very long'.

A broad grin creased Lord Barek's face at the thought of someone dying of hunger and thirst and casting imaginary spells'.

'And what about Secc?' Asked Lord Barek.

'Well, as he has failed to inform you of this, not only has he failed in his duties, but he has betrayed your trust. I am sure that we can devise a suitable punishment for him'.

'Indeed, I'm sure we can'. Agreed Lord Barek.

A short while later, a nervous Secc arrived back with Edmund in toe and Lord Barek asked him to repeat his story which nervously, he did. When he had finished, Lord Barek pondered over what had been said before consulting his advisors again. After some whispered exchanges Lord Barek turned to Edmund.

I'm inclined to believe your story, Edmund. In fact I am going to give you a chance to prove it to me, Guards'!

Two uniformed officers entered the room and a sign from Lord Barak told them to escort Edmund and Secc to the outer walls of the castle; Lord Barek followed with several of his staff. When they arrived, and after another sign from Lord Barek, stablemen brought forward four battle horses.

'Now then Edmund, show me of your skills at moving the earth'.

Some castle employees who had gathered to watch began to mock and laugh as Edmund tried in vain to move the earth with his mind.

'I am becoming impatient'. Shouted Lord Barek after several minutes had passed and cold anger began to replace mild interest.

'My Lord, I don't know how I did it but I know that I did'.

'Having stated that you have achieved a miracle, I expect you to show me another one. Would you not do this small thing for your Lord and Master? Something, it seems that you would readily do for a flock of sheep. Try again'!

Again Edmund tried to summon the power but failed in his attempt. He did not know how to reproduce his experience.

'So'. Continued Lord Barek. 'What do we have here then, a usurper, a liar and a blasphemer?'

'But my Lord', pleaded Edmund.

'You will not interrupt me, Edmund. Let me show you a little magic, the miracle of being in four places at the same time'.

At a given signal, the four horses were brought forward and Secc was bound, one limb to each of the horses. He was terrified; his eyes bulged, his lips moved as though in silent prayer; a prayer of pleading for intervention by the gods.

Lord Barek laughed. 'So all perish all who betray my trust. Mark this lesson well, young Edmund, it is your last'.

Secc was virtually paralysed with fear as leering soldiers raised their whips; lashed out mercilessly at the battle horses. Secc's arms came away from his body quite easily; the rest, amid screams of terror, took a little longer. Death came slowly for Secc and Edmund could only turn his head from the torn body of his friend. He began to tremble as Lord Barek cast an eye in his direction.

'No, Edmund, this will not be your fate. For you I have planned a more interesting ending. I have no room for dreamers in my employ, Edmund. You will be cast out. Go from here as you are, without food or water, without clothing and without aid of any description. See if your pretend magic will help you.

With those parting words, Lord Barek led the jeering soldiers and officers back inside the castle. The gates were closed leaving Edmund alone. He stood for a while, looking at the lifeless form of someone who had been his friend. Tears left narrow trails of dampness before falling, making dark patterns in the dry earth. His mind filled with happier times, the long discussions, the mild chastisements, and the laughter.

'Sleep well, my friend'. He said.

Edmund now had to fend for himself against enemies in many guises. Being a young man without experience and not knowing a great deal of the outside world, he tearfully started walking westward. Hours passed; the night crept slowly in and he sheltered in a small hollow away from the cold night winds. He was hungry, he was thirsty, and he felt alone for the first time in his short life. Birdsong welcomed the morning, and after a night of troubled half-sleep where images of Secc haunted him, he still felt tired He breakfasted on a few berries that satisfied his hunger in the short term, and then continued walking in the hope of finding more food and fresh water.

The uneventful day passed into night, the night into day and back into night. Each day was another day to survive, to learn to live using his wits, to eat whatever could be found and that would sustain life. Each night dreams told him of pursuing enemies; that only the God Zelfen could help him in his hour of need. Each time he rejected all but his own thoughts but slowly, he was being manipulated, moulded. After a while he began to accept that maybe, just maybe the dreams were the truth, and if he welcomed them, everything would right itself.

The Goddess Calia was furious, but could not intervene until Edmund had realised his power and called her by name. All she could do was to send dreams that would give him knowledge, to enlighten him, and persuade him that Zelfen was just an evil wizard bent upon the total destruction of all things good.

Calia pleaded with Frezfir and Eqwin, telling them what the already knew. That should the three earth-bound wizards not be united, havoc would soon become the master, and all their work would come to nought. 'We would have to start all over again'. Pleaded Calia.

It was to no avail; rules were rules, even if they did seem to be unfair. Eqwin stood on the dais. 'Dear sister, we have done what we are able to do, and we have sent forth Master Elio in the hope that if anyone, he will settle Zelfen's spite and cast him out'. The gods sat watching, waiting, each day a man's lifetime in their eyes.

After four days, Edmund neared a mass of barren land. He was hungry and thirsty, but the last four days had been a trial, and nothing would compare with what was to follow. There were no berries, nothing grew and he began to weaken. The young girl appeared from nowhere carrying a large roasted fowl. Edmund's mouth began to water at the sight and the smell and he wiped his mouth with his sleeve in anticipation. It was then that a thought crossed his mind. Where did the young girl come from? There were no villages in sight, no sign of an encampment or settlement. He quickly scanned the area only to find that the girl was seemingly by herself. She came closer and Edmund could plainly see her beautifully rounded face and deep blue eyes. Her long black hair hung down to her waist in plaited style. Her appearance was clean and well proportioned, almost like a serving maid at a castle. Edmund was spellbound, he rubbed his eyes to make sure that he was not seeing things; the girl was still there.

'Would you like to eat with me?' Said the girl, whose voice sounded like a peal of bells in Edmund's ears.

'But I have no payment', said Edmund.

'Follow me and I'll think of something', said the girl, lowering her eyes and blushing.

Edmund began to move towards her, but something did not seem right. After a few paces he noticed that the ground beneath him was becoming softer, his shoes began to sink deeper in the soft earth. He looked questioningly towards the girl. It was at that point, and to his horror, that he noticed that the girl had left no footprints. He turned quickly and ran back to firmer ground. When he looked back again to where the girl had stood, there was no sign, she had disappeared. His mind raced, not quite understanding what he had seen; where was the girl? He began to question his own sanity when, as he looked again in the same direction, a man stood there, it was his father.

'Edmund, my son', said the man in a deep voice that seemed not to come from him, but from all around.

'Father, how can you be here, you are dead'.

'No, my son, but you were told it was so. The fact that you appeared parentless helped you gain a position at the castle. It was all that we could do to give you a start in life. Come, eat with us, there is enough for all'.

'No, no. This is but a dream, a nightmare, you are but visions of my own imagination; you are not real'.

'Of course we are, do you not see us with your own two eyes, and do we not look real to you?' Said the girl who had appeared again with two others of similar appearance. 'The soft earth is there to fool our enemies, it is but an illusion'.

Edmund stood still for a moment, but although hesitant, he began to walk towards the smiling face and the figure of his father. Edmund showed no emotion, only wonder as the girl came forward to greet him, to embrace him. Suddenly she froze, her smile replaced by a worried look.

'Hold', commanded a voice.

The figure of Edmund's father urged a reunion and held out his arms to embrace his son. Edmund stood rigid, not knowing what he should do, undecided whether to continue towards his father's open arms or to wait. He turned to see who it was that gave the command; the next order followed quickly.

'Be gone vile creatures, there will be no victims this day'.

A thin streak of blackness flashed past Edmund and wrapped itself around the figure of his father; then around the girl and in turn, the two other figures. It was as though someone had taken a strip of night and placed it in daylight.

Slowly, the figures began to show signs of distress. The girl began screaming, it was not a human scream. They struggled in vain, trying to escape the powerful blackness. Their features began to melt away; began to reveal what could only be described as a hideous nightmare. Edmund began to retch at the reality, and at the stink that emanated from it.

Zelfen walked towards Edmund. 'Do you not know where you are?' Said Zelfen as the evilness appeared to sink into oblivion. He was inwardly pleased that he had arrived in time to save Edmund, because he needed him, for now.

'I'm afraid not' said Edmund feeling somewhat embarrassed.

'You', continued Zelfen, 'are at the side of the Swamp of Souls. Had you weakened and followed those creatures, you would now be one of them, and bound to remain here for all eternity or at least until you had caught an unsuspecting traveller. Only then, if you ensnared him, could you be released to rest in peace.

I have now proved to you that I intend you no harm. I am the god, Zelfen. You have seen me in your dreams and you have seen me in the waters of the Ketan. I have helped you in your hour of need and so I ask; will you now believe in me and follow me?'

'I will', said Edmund, prostrating himself before his new master.

'Good, good, good. I have sent dreams to Lord Barek telling him of his mistake in casting you out. I have also included in his dream the false wizards that come from the south. He will surely hide you and help you escape from those who would do you harm'.

'Thank you, Sire. I am in your debt'.

'I must be away for a short time, Edmund'. A grin of satisfaction spread across his evil face. 'Stay here until I return'. Zelfen waved a hand

and supplies of food and water appeared before him. 'For you, Edmund', and then he disappeared amid a haze of black particles.

In the large hall, a crowd of people, mostly important people had gathered to take breakfast with Lord Barek. He sat smugly at a high table watching the assembly, who in turn were wondering what Lord Barek had to say. He waited until breakfast was almost over before waving his hand to indicate silence. Within seconds the room was hushed as the crowds waited in anticipation of their lord's announcement.

'I have had a dream', declared Lord Barek.

A murmur passed through the crowd like the wind carried leaves; thoughts were being implanted by a hidden stranger.

'A dream, my lord?' Asked one of his barons.

Lord Barek stood and walked among his guests. He was like an actor upon a stage. 'Yes', he said. 'It was more than a dream, in fact it was an omen. He allowed the revelation to sink in as the crowds drew close to him, his face beamed with a radiance that appeared almost holy. After making sure that he had everyone's attention, he continued with his speech. 'My dream, my omen told me of false prophets, evil demons and people masquerading as wizards. Those who had advised this of course will be reprimanded. I also dreamed of the corruption in the south, and the evil there which was feeding from the very souls of our brothers'.

'Stamp out this disease', called a uniformed member of the crowd as though on cue.

'Declare war', shouted another.

The two speakers did not realise that they had spoken, or what they had said. They had no idea that they were just the puppets of a smiling stranger.

'My friends'. The crowd went silent except for the occasional whisper. 'I, Lord Barek of Dronecet Castle will not stand idle against the blasphemy of the south. I will not tolerate idolatry and anything evil produced by the south. Send word to the Bay of Wolves, to the coastal townships of Leith, Miland and Knie. Call my men to arms, let the fleet sail; we go to war to rid ourselves of ths southern vermin'.

Much to Lord Barek's pleasure, the crowd in the hall erupted with shouts of agreement. The noise died down as one of Lord Barek's generals came forward.

'Begging your leave to speak, sire. What if the stories are true and there are real wizards, wizards bent upon our destruction?'

'Nonsense', said Lord Barek. 'There hasn't been a wizard in these lands for hundreds of years. They don't appear out of the blue; they have to be trained, and if this was the case I would know about it. Furthermore, I have longed for an excuse, as have we all, to have these slimy southerners bend their knee to me for years. Discipline is what they lack, and we are going to show them what northern men are made of'.

The cheers rose again like deafening thunder, and as Lord Barek left the room, swords were drawn in salute, and officers rallied round him in the hope of a command.

The main forces of the north were always kept in battle readiness; Lord Barek demanded no less of his captains. Within a week, ships filled with men at arms sailed from the harbour port of Powle, their destination, Penste.

Secondary troops massed and were soon ready to ride southwards. Carpenters were kept busy in the building of assault machines, slings and giant crossbows. The smithy's forge grew white hot as the bellows worked overtime, and the rhythmic beat of metal upon metal heralded the making of swords, arrow heads and armour.

In other areas of the castle, canvasses were being woven and stitched together to make tents, water carriers and numerous other items needed for the war effort. Not a solitary person remained idle; each had his or her allotted task to complete, and completed it was.

Lord Barek was pleased at the speed in which his secondary forces were made ready. Ships were under sail, men at arms ready to march into battle, provisions loaded; he felt as though he had already won a victory. He called together a meeting of his Chiefs of Staff, his Generals and his advisors. Some advisors, however, were missing due to earlier bad advice; no-one cared to notice.

A small hall had been set aside for use as a war room in which, situated on a central platform, was a model of the land with markers indicating possible war zones. Other markers indicated fleet positions and landing areas; the assembled officers marvelled at the fine detail, but the artist was never mentioned, in fact he had mysteriously disappeared.

'Trusted advisors and friends' began Lord Barak. 'A short while ago I told you of my dreams; today I will show you the reality.

A low rumbling, not unlike thunder, shook the room causing those attending to cower in fear. A grey, swirling mist appeared, and small black particles that appeared to glow, darted, danced around like atoms in a chamber. Apart from Lord Barek, those in attendance pressed together against the furthest wall with eyes wide. Mouths moved but were unable to speak, and minds were unable to comprehend the strange occurrence. Lord Barek stood impassively, watching the mist as it began to disappear, watching as it began to reveal a tall figure dressed in black and gold robes. It was a timeless figure with eyes that could only be described as pits of hell. The assembly fell at once to their knees and pleaded to be saved.

'Gentlemen', called Lord Barek. 'Kneel as well you might, even as I do before the Earth God, Zelfen. A short while ago I told you of my dreams, of certain false wizards. I told you of their plans to invade the north. This will come to nothing as the Earth God Zelfen who stands before you, will aid the north in our quest to crush them'.

Amid whispers and nods of approval, Lord Zelfen stepped forward; a black nimbus surrounded him. 'The Lord Barek speaks truthfully. Already I know that you have foiled one attempt at infiltration, a man by the name of Edmund was possessed by these evil spirits and sought to spread fear amongst your ranks. In so doing he had hoped to aid the south in a victory over you. Alas, I had to dispose of him. It was against my better judgement, but there was little else that I could do under the circumstances'.

Slowly, the still puzzled assembly stood up. Murmurs of agreement passed between them as they rallied around Lord Barek. Lord Zelfen told them that in times of trouble, all that they would have to do was to call his name and he would come to their assistance. Then, without another word he smiled, then disappeared amid an array of sparkling lights.

CHAPTER FOUR

THREE STANDARDS COULD BE seen proudly held against the sky-line. They consisted of the Red Sunburst on a back ground of glittering white; the White Lightning Bolt against a background of equally glittering blue, and the third standard was a Lion Rampant on a black and silver background, the emblem of a master Magician. A snake curled around a staff set in silver decorated the centre of the lion. Three stallions, one black, one white and one grey, kicked up the dust as they maintained a steady gallop towards the Border House.

'Captain of the Guard, three riders approach from the south'.

Captain Dac'ra, a veteran of many campaigns, looked toward the watch. 'What colours do they fly?' He asked.

'One's I've never seen before, Captain, but they look important'.

'Lower the bridge', commanded the Captain.

On well-greased gears and chains, the draw-bridge fell almost silently to the ground, and came to rest spanning a wide moat. Captain Dac'ra walked to the end of the draw-bridge and stood, legs apart with his hands on his hips awaiting the visitors. Being frightened of strangers was never one of his shortcomings, but his scarred tissue and deaths-head looks warned strangers to be frightened of him. As the three riders approached, Karl lowered his standard in salute. Torran and Master Elio followed Karl's lead.

'Who approaches the Border House?' Boomed the Captain.

'Lord Karl of Brin', shouted Karl.

'My Lord', said the Captain softening his stance. 'We are indeed honoured'. He bowed as gracefully as a military man could, and allowed the party to enter. His military training then reasserted itself with more than the usual vigour. 'General salute'. He bellowed in an over-loud voice.

The command almost deafened Master Elio who was quite near; he stuck a finger in his ear and wriggled it about a little to emphasise the point. The Border House immediately became a hive of activity.

Men at arms seemed to appear from every doorway, crack and crevice. Not unlike ants from a nest they swarmed into the vast courtyard. It was a fact that the Border House was larger than most castles for military purposes, and housed more than five battalions of Lord Brin's fighting men; men that kept a vigilant watch on the north-south divide. The metallic sounds of armour, chainmail and shuffling feet filled the air as soldiers formed neat lines.

As trumpeters sounded the salute, Karl, Torran and Elio were equally as impressed by the speed and the precision of the soldiers drill techniques. They dismounted and immediately, stable hands led away their mounts. Captain Dac'ra shouted more orders, and in unison the men at arms opened ranks in readiness for an inspection; Master Elio unblocked his ears again. Then in softer tones that would have charmed the spots from a leopard, Captain Dac'ra advised Karl that the Border House was ready for inspection.

Soft music, provided by an adequate band, played in the background as four figures strolled between the ranks of immaculately dressed soldiers. Master Elio was positively enjoying himself. Lagging behind the others, he occasionally used his skills to pull a coin from behind one of the soldier's ears. He tried, mostly with success to make the iron-rigid soldiers smile; a smile that would instantly disappear the moment that the Captains eyes scanned the lines. For their part, Karl and Torran exchanged polite banter with one or two of the soldiers, at the same time admiring the uniformity and the discipline of the display.

When the inspection was over, Karl handed Captain Dac'ra the letter from his father. Master Elio had already seen the contents of the letter and had altered it, with Karl's permission, to include himself. It read:

To captain Dac'ra,

My dear friend and comrade. Today you bear witness that my son and heir, Karl, son of Brin, son of Tezz has indeed returned. However, he journeys still and my heart is heavy. For

him and his companions I ask for food, shelter and supplies in
plenty, for he is my hearts blood.
Blessed be you who are also my friend.

Lord Brin of Tezz.

'I am at your service, Lord Karl of Brin, and your friends?' Said
Captain Dac'ra.

'Captain Dac'ra, I apologise. Please welcome with the same
enthusiasm, Lord Torran'.

'My Lord I am honoured. I was but a boy when I last saw you. I
believe that you melted someone'.

'Well met, Captain. It was a long time ago'.

'Indeed, sire'.

Karl then introduced Master Elio hoping that he would behave
himself; he had not missed Elio's antics during the inspection.

'Master Elio, we are honoured by your presence', said the captain.
'But where are my manners? Come, let me show you to your rooms
where you may refresh yourselves'.

Captain Dac'ra led them into the main building which, as a military
establishment, housed no fancy decorations. It was a functional place
and when inside, another hive of activity greeted them. Soldiers involved
in administration duties moved about carrying paperwork; scribes were
busy at long tables. The only inactivity came from two sharp eyed and
nervous looking men; they were wearing long robes and were sitting by
a log fire.

'The best spies in the business', commented the Captain.

He led his guests through busy halls and corridors, and after
climbing four flights of stone stairs, the appearance of the establishment
changed dramatically. Here were situated the living quarters of the
Lords and visiting nobility. Woollen carpeting stretched the length of
the corridors. Walls were draped with fine linens, and coats of arms
decorated many doors. Eventually they arrived at a set of double doors
which displayed the White Dove emblem, the emblem of the Lord of
Tezz. Captain Dac'ra led the way into the room.

'My Lords, two more rooms lead from this one. I hope that you
will be comfortable. I will have guards at your door both night and day.

They will serve you with anything that you require'. He bowed slightly from the waist.

'Have you ever thought of becoming an actor?' Asked Master Elio.

The captain looked puzzled whilst Karl and Torran collapsed into fits of laughter. Realising the jibe a little later, the captain was heard laughing as he walked back to his duties.

The rooms had not a single military look or feel about them. All were softly furnished with low beds and cushions. Fires burned brightly in large open fireplaces, bringing warmth to a cooling evening. Clean robes were provided, and although their own didn't appear to attract dirt or stains, they changed to be polite.

After refreshing themselves, they spent a quiet evening with Captain Dac'ra and a few chosen officers. It was explained to Torran and Elio, that a fortress of the size of the Border House would normally be commanded by a higher rank than that of Captain. However, Captain Dac'ra admitted that he had in fact been appointed to the position of General, but had refused the offer on the grounds that he would rather be with his men than behind a desk in a stuffy office somewhere. Administration, he said, was for pen-pushers, not soldiers. Not losing touch with the men under his command had earned him respect from both his men and his seniors and, as a result, he was given command of the Border House.

The evening was a welcome break and was enjoyed by all, and after a wine tasting competition which was won by Master Elio, no-one knew how, the three companions retired for the evening.

They all slept soundly that night and awoke refreshed as guards admitted servants with their breakfasts. After re-joining Captain Dac'ra, the day was spent inspecting the fortress. Torran and Karl asked many questions relating to the architecture, defence systems, and how quickly could the army to be ready to march in times of trouble. It was explained to them that the whole fortress was in constant readiness and could leave, taking everything with them including the rubbish, within two days. Even Master Elio was impressed, and noted that it would take him at least that long to think up a spell to do it.

The three wizards stayed that evening, but advised Captain Dac'ra that they would have to continue their journey the following morning on urgent business. The Captain passed the order that supplies were to be made ready and a messenger hurried away to deliver it.

The morning came too quickly; the sun, a soft red ball on the horizon. A fresh morning breeze greeted Karl, Torran and Elio as they walked to the stables to collect their mounts. Guards in full dress uniform were gathered for the farewell salute as was customary for parting dignitaries.

After thanking the Captain for his hospitality, the three wizards prepared to leave, and with a wave to the troops, continued their search for the third wizard.

For this part of their journey, a dangerous stage as they were heading north, they had changed into the garb of merchant librarians; plain grey robes and cloak. Karl even removed his ring, the seal of the House of Tezz, and placed it in his pouch away from prying eyes.

As the stallions galloped side by side, lush pasture lands gave way to a hilly region that supported little plant life. On several occasions Karl, Torran and Elio tensed; they became more alert as strange sounds filled the air; sounds that were only audible within the mind.

'Someone is using magic', said Master Elio.

'Yes, I can hear it', said Torran. 'The thing is, it's not directed at any one person; it's too wide a band'.

'By the gods, he's raising an army!' Exclaimed Elio as he dismounted.

'Could he do that using a wide band of magic?' Asked Karl.

Master Elio was slow to answer. He mumbled a few words under his breath, and a fire appeared complete with roasted meat. Karl and Torran took the hint and dismounted. The horses wandered away to munch on the hillside grasses. The evening was beginning to close in. Already the sun was low on the western horizon, and small twinkling lights appeared like diamonds in the early evening sky.

'In answer to your question, Karl', began Master Elio. 'Yes he can. His power enables him to put suggestion into a lot of minds at the same time. Methinks that we have more trouble than we bargained for'.

'We could be wrong, of course', suggested Torran.

'Let's hope that we are', replied Karl.

Master Elio was mumbling to himself again as the three retired for the night. The Border House guards had supplied them with strong woollen blankets to keep them warm through the cool evenings; they were soon asleep.

Daylight crept over the hills bringing warmth, and casting shadows into shade, the land into full colour. Karl and Torran awoke to the sound of birds twittering in the clear morning sky, the constant buzz of insects, and the sound of someone counting.

'No, no, no, no, no. That's two diamonds for me, and of course, one ruby'.

'Then I should have two diamonds', said another voice.

'Of course you should my friend; there's plenty for both', said the first voice.

Torran sat bolt upright and stared at the two people sitting by the remains of the fire. They were counting pebbles and naming them after the names of jewels like sapphire, ruby and diamond. Master Elio stood a little way from them with a huge grin on his face. Karl also fell into watching this strange game.

'We can always come back tomorrow', said the other.

With pouches full of different sized pebbles, they departed. They didn't seem to notice that two wizards and one magician were watching them.

'Two unfortunate thieves', explained Master Elio. 'I had set a little, shall we say, protective screen around the camp last evening. Those two will probably think that the pebbles are diamonds and precious stones for quite some time. I wonder what the result will be when they try to spend them.' Another huge grin spread across Elio's face. 'A sight to behold'.

'It will serve them right', said Karl as he began to pack his blankets.

The day passed without any further incidents. It was a pleasant ride where worries seemed to drift away, and the happiness of being alive prevailed. By the early evening when the sun was low on the horizon and the air had begun to cool, the three friends descended a hill that led them to the village of Yani.

The village of Yani was a collection of wood-built structures sited by the river Powle. Its occupants, mainly families, had a tradition of rock carving as its main source of income. Fishing and boat building were also included but to a lesser degree. It was quiet as the three companions entered the village, and this was due to the fact that most of the menfolk were away working. A small gold strike had encouraged many to the hills, and they were not expected back until late that evening.

As Karl, Torran and Elio neared what appeared to be the only inn, a slow trickle of workers began to arrive back from the hills. They cautiously eyed the three men on horseback as they passed. Conversation had its chance later that evening when, after settling the cost of two nights' board and lodging, Karl, Torran and Elio made for the common room.

The conversation that evening was a mixture of: 'Who's made the best rock carving', to the angry debate on the uses of iron pyrites, and the 'I'm sure it was gold', lobby.

Master Elio explained to an interested crowd, and most convincingly, that he and his companions were merchant librarians. That some of the time they collected tales of mystery, sometimes odd happenings in rural villages, and at other times they searched for rare jewels with a history attached.

'I had a rare jewel with a bit of history attached', said an old man who was standing by the fire. 'But I married her'.

There was a roar of laughter from the locals, and even Elio had to smile. The old man who stood half-bet facing the fire, suddenly staggered backwards, his face took on a troubled expression as he turned around to look at the visitors.

'I think there is going to be a war'. He didn't say it like a thought that had passed through his subconscious mind, more as a statement of fact.

Torran's ears pricked up. Karl walked leisurely over to the fireplace and stood by the old man. 'Why do you think that?' He said, and began to stoke the fire.

'Well', said the old man after a pause. He straightened up as much as he could and placed a clay pipe in his mouth. 'I sort of know these things', he said. 'It's like the weather, I can tell if it's going to rain, or snow. Yes, I think there's going to be a war'.

The common room became deathly silent. People began emptying their tankards and leaving; worry was written on all of their faces. Not another word was spoken as the last man, the old man, vacated his fireside position and wandered off into the night. The three companions looked at one another and shrugged their shoulders. The innkeeper suggested that they retire for the night.

'What ails these people?' Asked master Elio.

The innkeeper looked at Elio, and after what seemed to be unspoken questions, he answered. 'The old man was born, and has lived in these parts as a man and a boy for all of his life. Quite often he sits and mumbles to himself. It's as though he is speaking with an imaginary person. Some say that he speaks with spirits. Some say that it's just old age and others say that he is mad; but when he says that he thinks something will happen, well I've never known him to be wrong. The strangest thing that he ever said was many years ago. He said that he thought that the Miller's wife would have a baby'.

'What's so strange about a woman having a baby?' Asked Karl.

'I was just coming to that. First of all she didn't have a husband because the Miller died some years previously. Secondly she had no callers, and thirdly, she was eighty-seven years old. She called the boy-baby, Birch.

'What happened to them?' Asked Karl.

'No-one knows. One morning when the village came to life she was gone. Of course there were rumours and wagging tongues, perhaps this was the reason but no-one has seen her since. Anyway gentlemen, tomorrow is another day and we should have news from the outlying areas by then. Most of the smaller settlements send representatives to our market; it's a chance to catch up on events. There's plenty to be purchased if you have a mind, and there is feasting and celebrations in the evening. I hope that you will join us in the happiness we hope to share'.

'We would be honoured', replied Master Elio.

The rooms they were given were comfortable but small, with an open fire, a basin filled with fresh water for washing, and a wool-filled mattress on which to sleep. Karl didn't get much of that luxury; he found it difficult not to think about what the inn-keeper had said. '*I've never known him to be wrong. She was eighty-seven*'.

Karl chuckled to himself about the story of an eighty-seven year old woman giving birth, and as for the man who was never wrong, may be the inn-keeper was stretching the story a little.

He did concede that some people did have a gift, for the want of a better word, and can predict the weather for instance, but eighty-seven? He chuckled to himself again at the thought of it, and eventually he drifted off into a less troublesome sleep. Except for the sounds of Master Elio's snoring, nothing could be heard until the sounds of many people welcomed a new day. Torran and Master Elio had both slept well, and awoke refreshed. They greeted a red-eyed Karl in the small, but adequate breakfast room.

'What, no sleep?' You look terrible', remarked Torran.

Karl was slow to reply. 'I had something on my mind'.

'About what the innkeeper said?'

'Eighty-seven?'

'Well I thought of that. What?'

'Having a child at the age of eighty-seven'.

'Oh, that. I thought you were going to mention about the war or the possibility of it'.

'That too'.

'Well it didn't keep me from sleeping'.

'Nor I', said Elio as he sat at the table. 'A most comfortable night's rest. Not many inns can boast of such comfort.'

'Good morning gentlemen', said the innkeeper who had overheard Elio's comments about the comfort. 'May I thank you for your words of praise? I trust that you will tell your friends of this establishment'.

'The praise is well deserved, Innkeeper', said Master Elio.

The innkeeper was full of pride as he laid platters of bacon, eggs and a jar of honey on the table. He went quickly away and returned with a bowl of fruit as an added extra.

'What a delicious little place', said Elio as he dipped his finger into the honey jar. He was about to add further comment when a man came running into the inn and commanded everyone's attention.

'Lord Barek has mobilized his forces!' he shouted.

'I knew it', said Karl and the innkeeper in unison.

'How come you by such ill news?' Asked Elio.

'Who asks?' demanded the man in a challenging tone.

The breakfast and common rooms went suddenly quiet. Master Elio stood up and wiped his hands and mouth with a damp cloth supplied by the innkeeper. He composed himself before speaking.

'Master Elio asks. I am, along with my friends, a merchant librarian. A war could, and most probably would alter our plans. You will no doubt see the importance of factual evidence'.

Master Elio's tone was soft and enquiring. Only the messenger could see the pale blue pools that were Elio's eyes show the hidden menace of unparalleled wrath should he chose not to answer. The messenger began to tremble; it was as though some inner consciousness had told him to be wary of this, this merchant librarian. After what seemed to be an age, Elio sat down again and the messenger recovered.

'My apologies, Master Elio', said the messenger. 'I have it on good authority from traders and the river people, that Lord Barek has mobilised his forces. Men at arms are marching forth from Dronecet Castle, and he has ordered his fleet to sail.

The traders tell me that about ten fully prepared battle ships have sailed from the port of Powle, and their intention is to attack Penste Harbour in the south. The land forces are said to be marching this way'.

After the messenger had told all that he knew without being able to stop himself, Elio smiled. 'Thank you for your news young man', he said.

The messenger looked around a little puzzled; not quite understanding what had just transpired. He left as quickly as he had arrived.

'By the gods, I'm glad that I am not on his side', said the innkeeper. 'I'd have to sew up his mouth'.

'People just like to tell me things', said Elio. He winked at Torran and Karl before dipping his finger once more into the almost empty honey jar.

'You said that you were glad not to be on the messenger's side. If sides there must be, who's colours would you fly, innkeeper?' Asked Torran casually.

'I would fly the colours of the south and be proud of it', said the innkeeper. 'Furthermore I would defy anyone to argue the point. I've done good business with the southern Lord of Castle Tezz. Lord Brin is his name, a gentleman if ever there was one, and he always pays for his wine. Although I've never actually met the man in person, I would rather serve him than a regiment of northern lords'.

The crowd that had gathered innocently resumed their daily gossip of business and war as Karl approached the innkeeper. 'What if you were attacked by northern forces', said Karl in a hushed voice. 'Your words are brave, but I doubt that you could hold off a regiment or two all by yourself'.

'Oh, I've got a way out if I need it', smiled the innkeeper who suddenly realised that he was being asked an awful lot of questions by someone who might be an enemy. 'You ask rather a lot of questions for a merchant librarian my friend', said the innkeeper suspiciously.

Karl took out his pouch, and putting his finger to his lips to indicate silence, showed the innkeeper the seal of Tezz.

'By the! His words drifted away as he moved closer to Karl. 'If you would have a need to escape from here at any time, there is a passage under the inn; it leads directly to the river. We use it to take the wine barrels and other orders to rafts. From there we travel downstream for two days where we connect with another tunnel. That tunnel lead to, and directly under the Border House. There is only myself and my workers who are aware of this tunnel, and not only are we alert to any danger, we always have boats ready in case of emergencies. Forgive me for asking, but who are you, and who are your companions?'

'Surfeit it to say innkeeper that my father will hear of your loyalty. Could you get word to him that the northern forces have taken to arms?'

'It has already been sent. Early this morning I sent one of my most trusted friends with a note for the captain of the Border House'.

'By way of the tunnel, I presume?'

'Indeed sire'.

'Good man. Keep the fires built up in our rooms. We will be back'. Karl turned to Torran and Elio. 'We must split up and try to find out what the enemy is doing on all fronts, and to search for the last wizard. Torran, will you travel north to the village of Spard? Master Elio to Holb and to Arvel. I will go to Turns Wood and the surrounding areas. We will meet here again in seven days, agreed?'

'If I live that long', said Torran.

'Is that a joke?' Asked Elio.

CHAPTER FIVE

Edmund was still waiting by the Swamp of Souls when Zelfen returned. Although he believed in Zelfen there was something, he wasn't quite sure what it was, that was nagging at his inner mind and told him to be wary. He had no idea where Zelfen had been; no idea that in fact he had been to Dronecet castle, and no idea that he had gone to consult with, and cast charms over Lord Barek and his army. They were also pawns in Zelfen's devious plans.

His ambition was to create chaos and bring destruction to the land and its peoples. One of the first things on his list of plans was to bring down the House of Torran, the only earthly place where the gods could appear in person. The destruction of that place would restrict the gods to only appearing in spirit, or in dreams, and would prevent them from wielding any great power themselves.

If he then could destroy Torran and Karl, he would be able to make Edmund into a powerful puppet; to use him until he became of no further value. He would then be the master. All would bow down before him, or suffer immeasurable agonies under his torture.

Edmund, who by now had regained his strength, was refreshed. Zelfen called for him to follow and obediently, he did. For two days they walked in a southerly direction along the edge of the Swamp of Souls, suffering its stench of rotting vegetation, and the continuous calling from the occupants for then to join them. They did not stop, for to do so would have given the occupants of the swamp another chance to ensnare them. By the end of the second day the stench and the calling had subsided, but Edmund was again exhausted.

'Can we rest now?' Asked Edmund.

'A little further. There!' Edmund looked up to see a mass of trees in the distance. 'There is Turns Wood', said Zelfen. 'There we will rest'.

It was late in the evening by the time that they reached Turns Wood, and the change in the atmosphere was dramatic. It was not unlike walking into a house to shelter from a blizzard and closing the door. Edmund looked back and saw the shimmering air that was the Swamp of Souls; he sighed with relief.

Although the darkness of the night had drawn in, the area was illuminated by the light of a full moon. The trees proudly displayed full blooms; little white and yellow flowers that reflected the moon's glow as they danced about in the light breeze. Full ripe fruits looked inviting, and were almost breaking the branches with their combined weight.

Edmund ate heartily of the sweet offerings, then without further words, he lay down beneath the trees and slept. He dreamed again of happier times. He dreamed of Secc and his many conversations with him. He dreamed of the barbaric way in which Secc's life had been terminated, and the laughter of the court officials during the process. He dreamed of the sadistic manner of Lord Barek; the mental as well as the physical torture. In his dreams he swore revenge. Several times a beautiful lady appeared and tried to speak with him, but could not make herself heard apart from the mention of her name; Calia.

The chill of the night rapidly disappeared as the morning sun played its warmth on the tree tops. Edmund struggled out of his sleep; he felt good. While he picked more fruit and made a light, sweet drink from the juices, Zelfen busied himself by collecting ground nuts in an attempt to show his friendly domesticity toward Edmund. The ploy to show concern for Edmund's welfare seemed to work.

'I am indeed fortunate to have you as a friend Lord Zelfen', said Edmund with a slight nod of his head.

'It is nothing', said Zelfen who, in the quietness of the morning, was smug with satisfaction. 'I like to help where help is needed. Did you sleep well?'

'Yes, I dreamed of a beautiful woman'.

'Don't we all, Edmund. Don't we all'.

'I suppose so. Her name was Calia'.

Zelfen dropped his bowl of ground nuts. He was visibly shaken but recovered quickly.

'What ails you, my lord?'

'Oh, nothing. It's just that I had a friend once with a similar name, but that was before your time. I will have to leave you for a short while because I have some important business to attend to. While I am gone, continue journeying on this path by the sea's edge. In two or three days you will come to a great desert. To your left will be the Dete Beacons, a small mountainous region. Wait for me there and be careful. Heed no strangers and take little notice of dreams, especially about women. Remember your experience by the Swamp of Souls'.

Edmund agreed, then, as quickly as Zelfen had appeared, he was gone again. Although he was alone again, he felt happier as he gathered ground nuts and stored them in his sack for future use.

As he packed away his other supplies, he thought of Zelfen; never before had he known such a friend. Secc was the only other person who had treated him with kindness, with respect and with consideration. His face saddened at the memory. He set off again just before midday. The sun was hot, but the cool breeze that came in from the sea made walking bearable. Lost in thoughts of the past, present and future, the day passed quickly, and evening arrived as the dull red ball that was the sun, rested on the far edge of the sea.

Little woodland creatures made their final preparations of the day, as the soft murmur of ocean waves played their everlasting melody. The last of the sea birds closed their wings and settled in the sandy dunes.

Edmund camped close to the water's edge, his small fire of driftwood sending sparks to illuminate the sky with minute red and yellow dots. He drifted off to sleep with the sea whispering hidden messages, sending visions of a beautiful woman named Calia, looking sadly down at him. In his vision he spoke to her.

'What do you mean; you can only come if I call you? Zelfen is my friend and I need not call after a woman. Besides, it is undignified. I will not call. I will not!'

After the strange night of dreams, Edmund awoke to the dampness of the early morning sea mist. He looked about him. He was still alone with the exception of the sea birds that dived and swooped in search of their first meal. 'Funny dreams', he thought. He stood up and stretched the last of the sleep away, then after a satisfactory breakfast, he gathered up his sack of supplies and set off once more. He made good progress, for late that evening as the trees began to thin towards the edge of the wood, he sighted the Dete Beacons. A large expanse of desert lay before him, and he shuddered at the thought of the cold night to come, but he was reassured as he looked at his sack of supplies. He found a suitable location, and after lighting a fire to keep away the chill, he settled down to await the arrival of Zelfen.

One minute Master Elio was in the village of Yani, and the next minute he was standing just outside the village of Holb in the east. Holb was a tidy village with raised wooden walkways and fashionable wooden buildings mounted on stilts.

Being a main river village it supplied most districts with building wood, which was shipped down the River Zarh, and collected for storage by the side of the Lake of Dreams.

On more than one occasion, the river had burst its banks after a deluge, and had flooded the village. The raised walkways and stilted houses were necessary measures, to ensure that no further damage was caused during times of flooding. Master Elio wriggled his fingers in some secret sign, and a large grey horse appeared at his side.

'Let's go and meet the natives, Ajax', he said.

He mounted the horse's huge back, and then urged him into a steady canter across a small open space. Being almost midday, the village was at its busiest; new buildings were being erected, children played on the streets, and then it all went quiet. Master Elio had entered the village and, as always, people were immediately suspicious. Strangers, especially ones who had a look of nobility about them, normally meant trouble.

The normally difficult task of getting known came easy for Elio, especially after he had thrown a handful of coins to some playing children. 'Plenty where they came from', he thought. He didn't consider thinking of the difficulty that some distant accountant would have in balancing his books.

Eventually he came upon a well-constructed lodging house, and after seeing to the needs of Ajax, he went inside.

The owner of the lodging house, after looking at Master Elio's pale blue eyes, let him have his best room for a very low price. Elio was extremely grateful, but the owner could not understand why he had done it; his best room for a pittance? After a short rest on an over-large feather bed, Elio washed himself and then ate a sumptuous meal, unknowingly supplied by several estates throughout the land.

'My, my, that was tasty', he said to himself. 'Now to go and listen to some gossip'.

At that time of day the lodging house was quiet, so Elio, feeling a little restless, decided for a walk through the village to take in his surroundings. The majority of the buildings were solidly built, obviously the work of craftsmen, and of them there were few shortages. The area was without doubt, a place for the well-to-do. For the whole of that day, and the following morning, Elio had heard nothing of interest. It was during the late afternoon that he heard something that made his ears prick up. He was sitting in one of the local taverns sampling some of the wines made there, when he overheard a group of carpenters having a heated discussion.

'I tell you that he is possessed. He turns himself into a cat', said one man.

Elio moved a little closer so that he could hear the full conversation.

'I wouldn't go as far as to say that the boy was magic', suggested another.

'Well my workers are afraid to go near the place', said the first.

'What is this I hear of magic? Said Master Elio, trying to show as little interest as possible.

'Well', said the first speaker. 'It appears that there is a boy, or young man living in the forest. It is reported that he changes himself into a cat to frighten away my work-force'.

'What, a little pussy-cat? Said Elio. 'I find it hard to believe that such a creature would frighten a full-grown man'.

'Have you ever seen a Timber cat?' Asked the man, sarcastically.

'Oh! One of those ... mm ... I think I will have to go and have a chat with this young man', said Elio.

'Be careful my friend. Those cats are evil, and the young man has magic on his side'.

'No he hasn't', said Elio. 'But I have'.

Everyone suddenly burst into fits of laughter, and then Elio promptly disappeared along with Ajax who, at the time, was being washed down by a stable hand.

The young man had been abandoned as a child. His only possession being a scrap of parchment on which was written his name. His mother having lost her husband several years before the birth, and had not had a man to lie with since, considered that she had been bewitched. She felt like an outcast, unclean.

It was late in the evening that she had gathered what belongings she could carry, and with her baby in her arms, she left the village where she had lived in for most of her life, and had headed for the coast. Age, however, was the prime motivation for her decision to abandon the child. With much reluctance, the old woman took the child to the Timber Wood and placed him on the doorstep of a cottage that lay deep within it. She hoped that whoever lived in the cottage would give her son the life that she could not give him.

'Goodbye my son'.

It was all that she could say, as tearfully she walked away. It was with much heartache that she travelled to the village of Powle in search of employment with the fishing fleets. She could mend nets, bake bread; it was not difficult to obtain employment, and so she worked.

Many times over the next few years she had thought of making the journey back to see her child, or hope to see her child again. But as the years passed and she became frail, such thoughts of a search dwindled. She died never seeing the child again.

In the Timber Wood the owner of the cottage, an aging herbalist, found the child covered with the morning dew. The little droplets reflected the soft glow of the morning sun, and appeared like pearls of silver upon the child's bare face and arms. The herbalist carefully picked up the child and cradled him to his chest. It was then that he noticed the scrap of parchment, it read: BIRCH.

'Well', said the herbalist. 'Whoever left you on my doorstep meant for you to be looked after and gave you a name. You shall keep that name, Birch; it will ever remind you of the little bundle of silver that some unfortunate woman, for whatever reason, had to part with. Oh! What agony she must have suffered to leave such a treasure. What mental torment does she still suffer? Still, I shall look after you until such times as she might return. I have never married you know, but it is every man's dream to have a son. What am I talking to you for? You can't understand. You can't even speak yet!'

The child's penetratingly deep blue eyes stared at the face which was hidden by a large white beard; made a typical baby sound and smiled. 'Well, perhaps you do'.

That day passed, the months passed and the years passed, all in the twinkling of an eye. The early years were filled with great happiness and wonder for both Birch and his new found father. Birch's insatiable appetite for learning bordered on the astonishing. He easily remembered the art of administering herbal medicine, and knew all of the secrets before he reached the age of seven.

The herbalist was amazed at his learning capabilities, But Birch just used to smile when he was asked how he managed it. In fact he was unlike any child that the herbalist had ever known to have been born, even in the way he controlled his emotions.

'I was under the impression that all children cried at some time, Birch'.

'Haven't I ever cried, even as a baby?'

'No'.

'Well I must be happy then', was all he would say.

During these years, Birch learned the ways of small animals, to respect the larger ones, and even learned to converse with some of them. His talent for understanding animals further amazed the herbalist who, as a reward on his eighth birthday, gave him a tiny kitten whose mother had died during the birth.

'It's a Timber Cat', said Birch excitedly.

'Yes; a rare animal and should be looked after', said the herbalist. 'It should be handled with care and treated with respect'.

'Oh I will. I will', said Birch as he rubbed himself on the Timber Cat's fur so that his scent would be known. The kitten responded in a like manner. They were friends.

More time drifted past as the years melted away, years of joy, of learning, of happiness. Birch entered his fourteenth year and was developing both physically and mentally. It was a result of the dedication his adopted father had given him.

The Timber Cat had grown too! It was a huge beast of feline supremacy; proud and without equal, but the happiness they shared was not to last.

For Birch, happiness gave way to immeasurable grief on one cold winter's evening. The herbalist, the man that Birch had grown to know as his father, passed away peacefully in his sleep. Birch had not known sadness. He had never cried, and he was lost for understanding when tears formed; left damp traces down his face, then fell to the ground.

Like a dormant volcano reactivated, his emotions crashed through his outer defences. He ran through the trees shouting his grief for all to hear. He ran until he could run no more, then limply, he fell to the ground and cried. When he eventually returned to the cottage, the Timber Cat in its own way offered him comfort. She too felt a great loss. She spoke soft words of comfort in the language of the cats.

'We are indeed as one', said Birch

To Birch and the Timber Cat, the Timber Wood became a sacred place. It was where his father had raised him, where he had walked in life and now walks in spirit. It was both a happy place and a sad one. It was where his father was buried. For two years Birch, along with the Timber cat, frightened anyone who dared venture into his part of the wood, so much so that people began to think that an evil had settled there and made a home amongst the trees.

Rumour quickly spread amongst the smaller villages and settlements.

'The wood is bewitched. There's an immense black cat which sometimes changes into a boy'. These words were on everyone's lips.

Elio materialised at the edge of the wood along with Ajax. He climbed on the horses huge back and began a slow walk through the trees. A pathway of sorts lazily wound its way along a leaf covered floor picked out by the last of the day's sunlight. Elio was humming to himself a low chant, a spell of discovery so that if anyone, man or beast lurked behind a bush or tree, he would know them before they knew him.

As the light began to fade, his senses alerted him to another presence. He looked into the darkness of the wood. A pair of green eyes watched his every move. He spoke softly to Ajax and calmed him, for he too felt the presence. They continued to walk slowly and the eyes followed. It was during this cat and mouse game, that a voice came from the general direction of the green eyes.

'Who are you, Stranger?'

Elio pondered for a while before replying. 'I am Master Elio'.

'What do you want of this wood?' Asked the voice.

'I seek only the owner of that voice I hear, and it doesn't belong to that Timber Cat. I have spoken to cats before and they sound somewhat different to that of a human voice'.

'You have spoken to cats?'

'Of course, doesn't everyone'.

'You mock me, Master Elio'.

'On the contrary, most people speak to their pets. The difference is that the pets don't answer them back, and I mock the voice, I cannot see the person'.

This was a tiny untruth. Master Elio could see in his mind's eye anything that he wanted to within a vast area. The green eyes began to move closer to him, slowly, cautiously. After a few minutes, the Timber Cat came within eye contact, the darkness of the wood still camouflaging its long black body although it was close. Elio spoke to it in the language of the cats and it came to him, sat by his side and purred. A moment later, a young man clad only in a simple green robe, appeared out of the dense undergrowth.

'I am Birch', he said.

'I am pleased to meet with you Birch. What a fine cat you have as a friend'.

'She has been with me as my companion and friend for a long time, Master Elio. You are the first she has accepted, and therefore I know that your intentions are only good ones'.

'I spoke to her in her own language to reassure her of this fact. I also spoke with Ajax here, for he too has a fiery temper when possible predators are close. I believe that they understand each other'.

'How is it that you can speak with animals? Are you a magician, a wizard?'

'I am much, much more, Birch. I am the Master'.

'Then tell me, what brings a man of power to my wood?'

Elio again pondered over the question. Birch had some hidden power, but he had not the knowledge or capacity to use it. Furthermore, he was not the one that he was looking for. Fate had decreed that they should meet, but why? Then, as Elio concentrated, the answer came to him. 'I was seeking someone but you are not he'.

'Then I bid you farewell, Master Elio'. He began to walk away, back to the cover of the trees.

'Wait! Called Elio.

Birch stopped and turned around. Elio saw then the deep penetrating eyes, the latent power that was stored just waiting to be released. He knew that he was right.

'Do you not ask a traveller if he would like refreshments before he leaves?'

'Forgive me, Master Elio, I do not normally encourage visitors, but on this occasion I will make an exception. Please follow me'.

Elio followed Birch through the trees. Ajax showed his disapproval at the Timber Cat bringing up the rear, but was calmed by a word from Elio. The night was closing in fast and the wood was getting darker, but Birch knew every inch of the wood. He had lived there since his birth. Elio had certain memories of the Timber Wood too, and it wasn't long before, when they came to a small clearing, they came back to him. The cottage still stood to one side, a small fire that burned within lighted the windows with glowing shadows, and looked like so many eyes searching the darkness. A mound of earth on the other side of the clearing was decorated with fresh flowers, a testimony to the long departed herbalist.

'I see that the window is still broken', said Elio.

'Do you know of this place?' Asked Birch.

'Indeed I do. I have been here a few times. As I remember there was a herbalist living here, a young man. I take it that he is now deceased and has been for some time?'

'A little over two years. He was my father.

'He married then?'

'No, I was abandoned and left on his doorstep. He adopted me and my heart still weighs heavy with his passing'.

Birch and Elio sat by the warm fire. The Timber Cat lay on the edge of sleep by the door. At the slightest sound, inaudible to the human ear, her eyes would spring wide open, then, satisfied that no danger approached, her eyes would slowly close again.

Birch told Elio of his life in the Timber Wood, the learning, the happiness; the joy when he was given the kitten, and the inconsolable sadness when the herbalist passed away.

He explained his decision to keep strangers away from his part of the wood. Besides it being to him a sacred place, it was also a place of beauty and wonder that should not be destroyed by inconsiderate men.

Elio quietly sat listening to the tale, and when Birch had finished, Elio spoke to him of his own thoughts.

'Birch, let me first of all thank you for your hospitality and your company. I must travel forth soon and I would like it very much if you were to accompany me'.

'Me?'

'Yes. It might be hard for you to understand what I am about to say, but please bear with me. You are not as others. True that you are not the one that I had originally sought, but he will be found no doubt. I believe that you, Birch, will be my successor, the one that I have been searching for these past two hundred years. The one that is god blessed with ancient powers yet to be discovered'.

'What!'

'Please bear with me a little longer. You were born of a woman who was considerably advanced in years. You were not born of a man's love but of someone much higher. It shows in your learning, your understanding. It shows deep within you. I can see it in your eyes.

When we first met I saw the beginnings, but you lacked knowledge. I can teach you. I am very old, much older than you could possibly imagine and I will not last forever in this form. I will add that the road I travel will be fraught with danger. It might even be the last road that I will travel. Will you follow it with me? Will you indent yourself as my apprentice?'

'Forgive me, Master Elio, but how can I be sure of your intentions? Who will look after the wood and tend my father's grave? I have heard of magicians but I have never seen one. There are many questions'.

'Birch, come with me', said Elio, a little angry because of the doubt. He took Birch out into the night and to the grave of his late father. Birch stood back whilst Elio approached the grave. 'Come, Birch; see the power that is rightfully yours'. Elio's voice echoed through the trees as he raised his arms and began a chant, a slow chant that sounded soft like silken thread but no less commanding than a lord's commands to his armies.

A slight wind appeared to blow through the trees; it became stronger as miniature lights began to weave about in the current. Birch pressed hard against the cottage wall as the Timber cat paced restlessly within.

The lights seemed to gather above Elio's head, and then enter his body causing a dull, pulsating glow to emanate from the whole of it.

Elio pointed towards the grave and a bolt of white brilliance shot forth from his outstretched fingers. 'Come forth', he commanded.

A voice that was not spoken filled the air. Birch recognised it, knew it, and tears began to form in his eyes.

'Who calls me from my rest?' Said the voice.

'I, Elio. The master calls you forth'.

By the side of the grave the air began to shimmer and form itself into a figure.

'Father', cried Birch as he ran toward the apparition.

'Come no further, my son, for you are not of the spirit and I am not of the flesh'. Birch fell to his knees, sobbing like a small child. 'My son, go you with Master Elio, for your destiny is with him'.

'I will go, father', said Birch.

As quickly as Master Elio had used his powers to raise the spirit of Birch's father, he gave the spirit leave to return to its rest. The wind dropped, the lights disappeared and everything returned to normal.

'Come, Birch, we will rest', said Elio.

'What will happen to Timber Cat?' Asked Birch.

'The Timber Cat is part of you, Birch. She will accompany us. Have you given her a name?'

'She is Cat', said Birch.

Elio mumbled something under his breath which sounded like; 'Well, it would be, wouldn't it'.

Chapter Six

KARL HAD KEPT OFF the regularly used footpaths and had stayed in as much cover as possible during his journey to Turns Wood. Occasionally he saw lone riders scouring the terrain, but he paid them no heed. It was generally thought that no-one would bother a merchant, but in times of impending war, anything could happen.

It was during his first nights encampment, that he heard the sounds of someone approaching. A sign of genuine friendship, or the complete opposite?

Karl remained in a sitting position by his adequate camp fire. He tried to look as innocent as was possible, but was ready in case of trouble. After a while, two riders wearing plain robes came into view at the edge of his campsite. They appeared nervous, and as Karl suspected, not entirely with a vision of friendliness.

'We seek warmth by your fire and friendly conversation', said one of the riders rather unconvincingly.

'I am but a merchant, but you may share what I have', said Karl, shifting his position to face them.

With falsified groans of tiredness, the two riders dismounted and walked towards the fire.

'The night is cold. We thank you for your hospitality. Where do you travel, merchant?'

'To the Dete Beacons. I hear of rare ores amongst the rocks'. Karl tried to sound as genuine as was possible.

'You must be careful, merchant. These are troubled times, and we hear that the north has taken to arms. Have you come far?

Karl noticed that the other man had started to edge around and toward his blind side. He stood up, his readiness a coiled spring. 'From the south', he said.

'Then we must consider you to be an enemy, for we support the north'.

The man had his sword only half way out of its scabbard when Karl's black bladed sword entered his chest, took flesh and bone out through his back. The man blinked twice and jerked a little as he sank slowly to the ground and into death's estate. The other man stood transfixed, trying to speak words that would not form when a blue octane flame shot towards him from Karl's outstretched hand. He was caught in a circular wind that carried him high into the air. After pulling out his sword from the lifeless body of one assailant, Karl cancelled the wind. The scream was followed by a dull thud as the other embraced death. Karl wiped his sword.

After making sure that there were no others and that he was quite alone, Karl sheathed his sword, gathered his things together and continued his journey. He rode fast, his stallion easily responding to the demands made of him as no other horse, with the exception of maybe two others, could do.

By the late evening on the second day, Karl's stallion had carried him a great distance to arrive at Turns Wood. He camped there for the remainder of the night, allowing the stallion to rest and to refresh himself. He made a satisfying meal of fruit and bread, and then sat down by his horse to eat. When he had finished he slept, a peaceful, dreamless sleep.

He awoke to the sounds of birds fighting over an uneaten meal and smiled. A light breeze played amongst the trees and toyed with fallen leaves as Karl prepared a light breakfast.

It wasn't long before he was continuing his journey through Turns Wood, the wide spaced trees making the pathway easy to follow. Little white and yellow flowers fell like snow in slow motion, collected in the folds of his robes, as his stallion set a steady gallop. It was nearing the late afternoon when Karl saw a spiral of smoke and headed towards it.

Edmund who was sitting by a small camp fire instinctively knew that someone approached. He looked up to see a rider in the distance heading towards him. Heeding the warnings he had been given by Zelfen of strangers, Edmund began to walk into the desert, and was some distance away when Karl arrived at the camp site and dismounted. The stallion wandered away from the heat and the smell of the camp fire, and began chomping on the tufts of grass, while Karl took in the sea air as he looked around. It was only a few moments before Karl sighted Edmund crouching in the desert. He had a feeling that this was the person for whom he had been searching.

'Hold, friend', shouted Karl as he began to move towards him, but Edmund hesitated, then began to run. His fear of the unknown took over from his better judgement. 'Wait, I mean you no harm', called Karl.

Edmund sensed that this person running towards him may be one of the wizards. Had not Lord Zelfen warned him of such people, people who were intent on taking his life? He remembered the cruelty that Lord Barak had administered and continued in his effort to escape.

Karl continued to run towards him. It was then that he felt the ground begin to shake. A thunderous sound filled the air as earth and stone began to move. Karl called again but to no avail. Suddenly Karl remembered his dream, the dream of a frightened youthful face in a barren land.

The first small stone struck Edmund on his right leg, he winced as another sent a pain through his left.

'What do you want of me?' He cried as Karl moved closer.

'Only to be a friend'.

Another stone caught Edmund on the side of his head causing him to momentarily lose his balance.

'Do people who come in friendship cause stones to injure the person they want to befriend? You are one of those who would bring me death. I have been warned of your coming and you shall not succeed'.

'I do not desire to harm you', pleaded Karl.

The sands of the desert began to shift, to heave as more stones rained down on Edward. He began to sink.

'Use your power. Gather your will to fight against it!' shouted Karl, his voice almost lost in the rumble of the earth.

'I don't understand you', called Edmund who was now bleeding from several small wounds.

'It's a test Edmund. It's a test'. Karl's voice was almost lost again as the ground rumbled like thunder.

Edmund started to panic as he sank deep into the sand which now was at his waist and slowly creeping upwards. Karl could not directly intervene with this test by using his powers so he tried to help him verbally.

'Listen carefully, my friend, before it's too late. Think of the earth as a small child, a mischievous small child who has spent your patience. Think of what you might say to that child. Think of how angry you would be. Think of what you might say or do to a person who had killed your best friend. Think of years of hatred held back, then suddenly allowed to flow out of you in a few words'.

Karl was doing his best to find a trigger, something to release that which was held within Edmund. He didn't realise that the winds and the seas were awaiting his commands; a bright blue nimbus had surrounded him. Huge boulders now began to roll towards the half buried Edmund. Karl remained unable to help, but protected by his own powers.

Seconds passed, and Edmund saw death approaching as the huge boulders came closer. He began to get angry at the futility of his attempts to free himself. Then, when all hope appeared gone, Edmunds fear disappeared. 'I will not die as a result of a magical spell! He shouted. 'I will overcome this'.

He again thought of Secc and the way in which he had been treated by Lord Barek. Another small stone found its mark and Edmund screamed out his frustration.

Suddenly, when all seemed lost, it was as if some key had just opened a lock, some piece of a puzzle had fallen into its place, a great enigma solved in an instant. A green nimbus surrounded him, and Karl's worried expression turned to one of great joy as Edmund spiralled out of the sand to stand hovering just above it.

'Rest', he commanded. The larger boulders ceased to move instantly, but some of the pebbles kept up their attack. 'REST I SAY'. A green octane light burst forth from his outstretched fingers and reduced the offending pebbles to dust.

'Overdid that one a little, didn't we', said Karl.

Edmund's feelings were still riddled with doubt and caution as Karl approached, but he stood his ground.

'I am Karl of Brin, Wizard of Wind and Water'. He held out his hand in a gesture of friendship.

'I am Edmund', he said, taking Karl's hand lightly.

'Wizard of Earth and Stone', said Karl.

'I thank you, Karl of Brin, for if it hadn't been for your prompting, I would have been swallowed by the sands or been crushed by the rocks. I would not have understood the power that is within me'.

'You are not complete in your powers yet, Edmund, and I cannot tell you why. It is not allowed for me to help really. For this reason I could not physically help you during your ordeal with the elements, but I am overjoyed at your successes.

'I wonder why Lord Zelfen didn't appear, to help me as he promised'.

'Lord Zelfen?' Karl looked genuinely surprised.

'Yes, he saved me from the Swamp of Souls, and has guided me this far with constant promises of help in times of trouble. He said that he would meet me here'.

'But Lord Zelfen is the one who has been causing chaos in the land. He has joined forces with Lord Barek against the south'.

'What!'

'Yes, he has been cast out by the gods for his actions'.

'It appears that I have arrived too late', called a voice from a nearby hill.

Karl and Edmund looked up to see Lord Zelfen and four armed guards looking down on them. Karl was again reminded of his dream. He remembered the rows of eyes looking down from high peaks, and knew that he had lived his dream. The green nimbus that surrounded Edmund grew intensely bright.

'You made to deceive me!' He shouted at Lord Zelfen. Green light flashed from his hands and the earth beneath the soldiers opened. They fell screaming to their deaths. Lord Zelfen remained standing in mid-air for he had anticipated the attack. He did not, however, anticipate the actions of Karl who sent a flashing blue light towards him. Wind as hard as rock caught Lord Zelfen unawares and carried him to the farthest side of the Dete Beacons where he landed in an undignified heap.

'Come, Edmund, let us make good our escape. He is stronger than us in the magical arts. I will try to explain things as we travel'. Karl gave a shrill whistle, and wasn't surprised when, accompanied by his own stallion, was a brown one.

'You thought to bring me a horse!' Exclaimed Edmund.

'No. He sort of came by himself'.

When Karl explained that they now faced three day's hard ride to reach their destination, Edmund expressed his concern for the horses.

Karl laughed. 'You don't know these horses, Edmund, they are sort of special'.

Lord Zelfen, although speedily creating a spell of protection against Karl's attack, was knocked out by the tremendous force of the blast. He burned several patches of earth in his temper before transporting himself back to Dronecet Castle. 'I will have my way', he said during his transportation. 'Even if I have to summon the hounds of hell to achieve it. I will have my way'.

Meanwhile, in some far distant place, a beautiful woman let out a sigh of relief and smiled.

----×----

Master Elio started to instruct Birch in the ways of the wizards on the following day. He was amazed at the boy's power of understanding in that Birch remembered immediately everything he was taught and craved more and more knowledge. Master Elio could hardly keep up with his demands for instruction.

The faster he chanted and described spells, the faster Birch learned the ways of the Master.

They travelled to the village of Arvel on the east coast, Master Elio on Ajax, and Birch on a grey mare that Elio had borrowed from some unsuspecting stable. The Timber Cat followed at a discrete distance, so as not to frighten the horses. She thought it courteous although Master Elio had, to be safe, cast a calming spell on the mounts. They made camp about one days ride from Arvel in a small hollow that sheltered them from the cool night's breeze.

After a light meal the teaching continued for most of the night. It was as though there was some urgency about Birch gaining the knowledge of the ancients. Eventually, being too tired to continue, and with a head full of new spells, he drifted off into a deep sleep.

Master Elio, however, not needing as much sleep as mortal men, spoke softly to the Timber Cat. His mind formed the words and they were heard.

'Guard him well, my friend. I will return shortly'.

'Although he is human, he is like my brother. I shall look after him'.

'And he is like my son'.

Small multi-coloured lights briefly flickered in the air and Elio was gone. The Timber Cat settled down into her usual half-sleep. It was early the next morning before Elio returned to the camp, and although he made no noticeable sound, as he turned he saw the Timber Cat poised and ready to strike. Elio smiled, the Timber Cat relaxed, and then came to him sniffing at his robes just to make sure.

'One cannot be too careful, Master Elio'.

'I am thankful, my friend'.

Birch awoke to find Elio preparing the morning meal. Well, not so much preparing, more like acquiring.

'We might run into a few problems this morning', said Elio.

'What sort of problems?' Asked Birch.

'The kind that comes in uniforms. I scouted around a little last night, and there were armed men everywhere'.

'Should we not go back to safer ground?'

'Not yet, I have a few things to check on first'.

'Don't you mean, we?'

'How careless of me, yes, we'.

It began to rain as they set off once more towards the village of Arvel. Elio spent much of the journey scanning every inch of the road, and its surroundings for hidden dangers. The Timber Cat, also feeling the tense atmosphere, scouted the dense grasslands that bordered the area. Both knew that danger lurked, they could feel it, sense it. Even Birch began to feel uneasy.

The village of Arvel was more like a small town. Indeed it was referred to as such by most that lived there. It was also quite disorganised. Low stone built structures were erected, it seemed, wherever the builder decided to put them. There was little or no regard for environmental planning, and as a result, the streets were an unintentional maze.

Birch was passing away the time, trying to solve, with little success, how people found their way about in such a tangle.

The rain became heavier, which diverted people's attention away from the two travellers with an unusual pet. Those who did notice gave a wide berth and crossed themselves disbelievingly. They would forget, because Master Elio would make sure of it.

What are we looking for?' Asked Birch.

'We have to look seaward first of all. Ships have sailed and I want to know just how far they have travelled'.

They made their way to the village harbour, Birch taking a mental note of the streets as they passed them.

Elio made enquiries of men's minds, and learned that a fleet of warships had already passed, and were travelling at a phenomenal speed.

'Sorcery', said Elio, as he edged Birch under a small but adequate shelter. 'We have not much time'.

'Can I use a spell to dry myself?' Asked Birch.

'It wouldn't work, well not yet. You have been receiving the knowledge, but the power to use it is being withheld. Someone with a higher authority will know when to release it. It will be there when you need it, probably sooner than you think. Now, we must find somewhere to stay for the night, and then we can join the others'.

'Others?

'Yes, there are two others. There is Lord Torran and there is Lord Karl of Brin. Both are gifted wizards who are on a quest to find a third wizard appointed by the gods. I hope that they have found him, and that no harm has befallen them. I have been hearing the use of magic for quite some time'.

'Look, there is an inn by the wharf'.

'Right, let me do the talking'. They ran over to the inn.

Elio cast a spell of invisibility to others over the Timber Cat as they entered, and after a short bargaining session, Elio secured a room at virtually no cost.

'How do you get away with paying so little?' Asked Birch.

Master Elio just smiled and tapped his nose. The room that they were shown was adequate, but a lingering smell of fish was only enjoyed by the Timber Cat. She immediately secured herself a position in front of the fire and fell into another half-sleep. This meant that she could be alert at all times, and yet fail to hear words like move, excuse me, and shift your fat arse.

Elio and Birch dried themselves and changed their clothing. Elio wore his robes of a Master Magician.

'Wow, its alive', said Birch.

The jet black robes played host to a number of ancient runes of silver thread that appeared to move. The emblem of master magician took up a central position.

'No Birch, it's not alive. Our eyes can sometimes deceive us when we look at magic. It's like looking into a mirror at a reflection of ourselves. If we bend the mirror we see a different reflection but we are still the same.

'Will I have a robe that appears as magical as yours?'

'Well, let me see now. I think that you deserve one, don't you? Elio stepped back and looked Birch up and down trying to get the measure of his build, and then began a chant of making.

His fingers twiddled in secret signs, he raised his arms and little light of silver and black began to circle the room. Streamers of red, blue and white intermingled with the silver and black lights. A mist then appeared; a green tinted mist that encircled the lights without dimming them.

Birch sat on a low stool, amazed at the display. Never had he seen such an array of coloured lights.

After a while the mist thinned to reveal three figures, and Birch saw for the first time, Frezfir, god of Ice and Fire. Eqwin, god of Wind and Water, and the beautiful Calia, goddess of Earth and Stone.

'My Lady, my Lords', began Master Elio. 'I call you to this place, although it is unbefitting of your presence, to ask you for your blessing upon Birch. I have chosen him as my successor'.

There was no discussion amongst the gods. It was as though the announcement was expected.

Calia stepped forward. 'Your choice pleases us, Master Elio. Teach Birch the chant of calling, for he must only be given the power when the time is right. You will stay here in this place until the knowledge is complete. We are aware that you fear for the safety of your companions, but the means will justify the end'.

The mist began to move once more, and the images of the gods faded. The display of multi-coloured lights hovered above Birch, and then, as though passed through an hour-glass, the lights poured down upon Birch's knees, where the robes of a master appeared.

'My work begins', said Master Elio.

Unaware of events in the north, and preoccupied with matters pertaining to his own household, Brin of Tezz hummed to himself as he thumbed through the pages of correspondence. He was interrupted by his personal attendant, who informed him of a messenger from the Border House. 'Admit him', said Lord Brin as he collected his paperwork and placed it in a drawer.

The messenger, a soldier courier in uniform, was ushered into Lord Brin's office, and after an awkward and hurried bow, he informed Lord Brin of the recent uprising of the northern forces. He explained that, even at that moment, armed forces were preparing to march, and that battle ships had already set sail for an unknown destination.

Lord Brin handed the messenger two gold pieces. 'For your family, soldier. Times will be hard in the coming months'. Lord Brin had always been generous to his troops and their families.

They in turn responded with unwavering loyalty, and clutching his reward, the soldier looked into Lord Brin's saddened face. 'If it pleases you my Lord, I would remain and serve you here'.

'This is what the southern fighting men are made of', said Lord Brin to his personal attendant. 'It pleased me greatly, soldier. Bring your family to the safety of Castle Tezz. You will serve with my personal guard'.

The over joyous soldier hurried away to tell his family of his good fortune, that he would be in the front line of any battle, and probably be the first to die.

Lord Brin sent messages to the Border House, and to all the outlying districts. Like a well-oiled clockwork mechanism, the soldiers of the Border House and castle Tezz geared themselves for war.

The messages were carefully worded and emphasised that no blow be struck in anger; that no shot is fired unless severe provocation in the form of an attack be made. This was to ensure that no blame for the impending war could be attached to the southern forces.

He sent letters to Lord Barek of Dronecet Castle, urging him to cease hostilities and withdraw his forces. Every diplomatic channel was investigated, and the long wait for answers followed.

Torran had ridden towards the village of Spard at the gallop, his stallion easily coping with the demands made of him, and he made good time, arriving there during the evening of the first day. The villagers, who were frightened at the prospect of war, were making preparations to leave. They glanced nervously at Torran as they collected what things they could carry, and hurried off into the darkness.

Some were heading north to join Lord Barek's army, and some were heading south. The vast majority, however, comprising of young and old alike, were heading west and to the possible safety of the woods and hills. The few that had decided to remain, about one third of the population, had businesses or material wealth that could not be carried.

Carts, wagons and horses were being sold off at ridiculous prices, and robbers and cut-throats were in abundance. A frightened and disorganised village to a robber was like a jar of honey to a bee. Many unsuspecting travellers met with untimely deaths on the roads out of the village.

Torran rode at a slow pace along the main street. It was littered with all manner of discarded goods. Houses were being ransacked, gleaned of all that was valuable.

A few priests still remained there in the make shift temple building. They prayed for peace and urged people to remain calm; words that fell on deaf ears. Friends became acquaintances, acquaintances became strangers as doubt and suspicion, worry and self-preservation became foremost in people's minds. Torran picked his way through the street until he came upon the local inn.

He bedded down his stallion before he entered. He knew that no-one would be able to steal his mount. It would be a lucky man indeed to escape with his life for trying. His stallion had definite ideas about who should, and who should not climb on his back, and took an instant dislike to strangers as did the other stallions.

Once inside the inn, the choice of rooms was numerous. The original occupants had fled to less troubled areas. He chose a pleasant room that overlooked the main street, and paid in advance at the owner's request. Although feeling a little weary after his long ride, he decided to settle in the common room. He was hoping to hear news of recent events. After three days he had heard nothing. Each day he would sit in the same position in the common room, listening.

The innkeeper kept Torran's tankard full and delivered meals to his table. There were no pleasantries, no questions asked, and no other words passed between them, but the innkeeper felt that he had to look after this stranger. Besides, he had plenty of ready cash and he always paid in advance. Furthermore, anyone who was travelling towards a possible war zone was either mad or dangerous, either way the innkeeper thought it best not to interfere.

On the fourth day, Torran had settled into a routine and was feeling comfortable in his surroundings. He could have easily forgotten his quest had it not been so important. That evening, tiredness crept up on him and he retired to his room early. He lay on the large, straw-filled mattress, and drifted off into a dreamless sleep.

The bright yellow ball that was the morning sun peeped over the eastern horizon, and shone its warmth over the land. The new day also welcomed new dangers as the sound of marching feet and war drums broke the silence.

Torran was abruptly woken by the sounds of shouts and screams. He leapt from his bed and rushed to the window.

Down on the street, people were running in every direction as an advance party of skirmishers raided the village. He picked up his robes and then thought, 'Why not'. From a small casket he took out his wizards robes.

'What's happening innkeeper?' He shouted from the emptiness of the upper part of the building.

The innkeeper mopped his brow with a much used cloth and hurried upstairs to Torran's room. 'There's a war coming', he said. The innkeeper's words suddenly died as in a mixture of fear, surprise and amazement, he stood transfixed.

Before him stood not a merchant, but a figure of noble bearing, clad in red and white robes. Upon the robes were ancient markings that moved as though alive. They were alive, alive with power.

'You were saying?' The words jolted the innkeeper.

'I was saying that a small band of skirmishers have arrived in the village. They are seeking out supporters of the south. They are also helping themselves to supplies, and they will be here shortly, I suppose to raid my cellars and demand free lodgings'.

'How many are there?'

'Five I think. Are you worried?'

'To answer that truthfully my friend, no'.

'Friend?' Questioned the innkeeper.

'Yes, innkeeper. If you had been the opposite, then your position would have been the opposite, more or less. Instead of standing you would be laying down, and instead of breathing, you wouldn't be'.

'Who are you?' Asked the innkeeper swallowing hard.

'I answer as Lord Torran, Wizard of Ice and Fire'.

'But you are supposed to be a legendary myth, my lord'.

'I am? Well this legendary myth would like to know where these skirmishers are at this moment in time'.

There was a crash from below. 'Downstairs', said the innkeeper.

The innkeeper hurried away. Torran slowly walked the narrow corridor that led to the top of the stairs. He made no sound as his senses heightened; a faint red nimbus surrounded him as he gathered his will. In the common room, five tough looking individuals who were more mercenary than trained skirmishers helped themselves to wine. They were laughing and joking and making fun of the innkeeper who was doing his best not to upset them.

As Torran entered, there was a surprised silence for a few seconds, then one who appeared to be the leader began laughing. 'What is this then, fancy dress?' He said with a beaming smile and a mocking tone.

Torran didn't alter his serious expression.

'He'd look good in a cage', said another.

A net was suddenly cast, a perfect throw that landed where Torran should have been. However, no account was taken of the speed and agility of the intended prey as he dodged the net with ease. Torran stood once more facing the five would-be captors. Not a flicker of emotion was showing on his hardened features

'So, not only do we have someone in fancy dress, we also have an acrobat. He jumps like a bird', said the leader.

'I'll have a leg', said one.

I'll have a wing', said another.

'And I'll have his guts for a bow string', said the leader as they all drew double edged daggers and spread out in attack formation.

The red nimbus that surrounded Torran began to glow brighter.

'I wonder how you manage to create the lighting effect', said one of the skirmishers as he attacked. He said nothing more. Only his eyes told of the horror that his body and mind were experiencing, as the red octane light of death from Torran's fingertips, burned him to a crisp.

The look on the faces of the remaining skirmishers ranged from anger to surprise, to worry, and at last to pleading. He showed no mercy as those who were left met the same fate. Another living dream. A net, five knives, and five burning figures.

A white stallion awaited Torran on the road near the inn. Three would-be thieves lay in agony around it. The innkeeper could only stare open-mouthed as Torran departed with a farewell message. 'Have a nice day'.

———◆———

Lord Karl did not yet have the confidence in Edmund, because although Edmund had realised his powers, he had had no real practice with them, nor had he any experience of swordplay. These facts played slightly on Karl's mind as they galloped at speed towards their destination; the meeting with Lord Torran and Master Elio. It was accepted that their horses would not tire during the journey, but Karl thought it best if they halted to refresh themselves when they were but one days ride from their destination. 'We will rest here', said Karl.

Not being used to riding great distances, Edmund dismounted and rubbed his sore parts. Karl smiled, remembering when he too had had similar ailments. The way his instructor had laughed at him and the way his instructor had suddenly become drenched with water. No-one ever knew where the water had come from, but Karl knew where the small pebble that struck him on the rump came from. 'Cut that out', he said.

Both laughed as Karl told Edmund of his instructor's fate. Throughout the early evening, Karl helped and guided Edmund in the use of his powers, told him about the sword he would receive, and of the training that he would undoubtedly enjoy. Edmund asked many questions relating to both subjects, and for the most part they were answered. As the darkness began to fall, small splinters of firelight could be seen in almost every direction.

'Get some rest, Edmund. We will have to travel early'.

'Those enemy fires?' Asked Edmund pointing north.

'Yes, and we can't afford to get involved at this stage'.

They only rested that night; sleep did not come easy because there was a tension in the air that seemed to forbid it. It was the small droplets of rain that introduced them to the morning. The air was fresh, but the tension was still there. It lurked behind every bush and tree. Every outcrop of rock became an ambush point for imaginary assailants. They didn't break their fast that morning; they headed at full gallop towards the village of Yani.

CHAPTER SEVEN

I T WAS A COOL night; the rain tapped its rhythmic tune on the slated rooftops, and then ran down to the earth to join already formed puddles. A mist hung in the air like so many grey blankets, with little or no wind to push it on its way. Through the mist, a lone rider on a white stallion appeared at the village borders. The mist swirled and gave way as if by silent command. The rider was dressed in a red and white cloak and robes. They seemed to be alive with movement.

This was Lord Torran, Wizard of Ice and Fire, Champion and Protector of Lord Brin of Castle Tezz. His piercing blue eyes passed over the village scanning every corner, every dark place as he edged his mount forward. His whole body was tense, and was like a coiled spring that would trigger at the first sign of hostility. Although unseen by the naked eye a faint nimbus surrounded him, a soft glow which could be charged for protection, or used as a weapon with catastrophic results.

As he moved forwards towards the first wooden constructions, he found the village alive with people coming and going. Frightened people, worried people, refugees from other towns and villages all with one hope sustaining them: survival.

Torran accepted the open-mouthed stares at the way in which he was dressed, the nervous giggles and the open ridicule, for the people did not know him. Had they known him, they would have been in awe of his presence.

He came eventually upon the village inn where he and his companions had stayed some days before. He dismounted, and after removing a small casket and a wrapped sword from his mount, he entered the inn. Inside it was unusually active, but after a short while he was noticed by the continually busy innkeeper and ushered into a private room.

'My Lord Torran, it pleases me that you return safe', said the innkeeper.

'It pleases me to be able to return, my friend'.

'Knowing that you would return, my Lord, I have kept your room vacant', said the innkeeper with his fingers crossed.

Torran looked at the innkeeper with a quizzical smile. The innkeeper grinned sheepishly back. 'Well, almost vacant, my Lord'.

He could not help but laugh at the little man. 'Bring some wine, innkeeper and I will toast your good health'.

The innkeeper hurried away, and after shouting instructions to his hired help, he returned with two tankards of hot spiced wine. 'What of your companions, my Lord?'

'I await them'. He lifted his tankard. 'To the south!'

'And all who dwell there', replied the innkeeper'.

'Now, what about that room and some hot water?'

'I'll just be a moment, my Lord'.

The innkeeper rushed away again, this time to a different area of the inn. Several moments and a few lost tempers later, he returned. 'I told you that I had kept your room vacant, my Lord', he said with an innocent smile.

'So you did, my friend, so you did. Now, tell me of any other news'.

'Well, my Lord, I sent the message as the other gentleman instructed. A servant, one that I can trust, took it by way of the tunnel to the Border House. There has been no fighting around here yet, well, none that I've heard of, but a lot of refugees are entering the village. This can only mean that it is but a matter of time before the conflict follows'.

'If the worst comes to the worst, my friend, escape through the tunnel and make your way to Castle Tezz. The river I think would be the safest way to go'.

'My Lord, I have never been to castle Tezz in person. They might not admit me'.

Torran thought the problem over for a few minutes, and then he whispered in the innkeeper's ear.

'What!' Exclaimed the innkeeper.

'Do as I say my friend. I will guarantee that you will be safe and they will let you into the castle'.

The innkeeper wondered away mumbling to himself. 'I can't say that to Lord Brin of Tezz. He'll have me horse-whipped. I'd be in the dungeons. There again, if Lord Torran guarantees it, I suppose it will be alright, I hope'.

For most of the night Torran sat in his room watching the street from a conveniently placed window. Rain still fell, but tapped a slower tune; the vertical rivers on the windows reduced to mere streams, and the mist had risen to form low clouds that hovered above the village.

The human tide of refugees seemed to be never ending as they slowly surged through the village like sheep. Some were hampered by oversized sacks that contained their belongings, others tried to comfort their children who wept in the confusion. Very few were fortunate enough to have a cart. None owned wagons which would have afforded them a certain amount of comfort, especially for their families. Each one followed the other until, as they left the village, they parted to go their separate ways.

They trudged on not knowing their destinies, not knowing the final outcome of their travels. Lost, blank stares haunted every face. Only the fear of the unknown kept driving them onwards. Occasionally in the half-light, a fight would break out over rights of way, possessions, or because some unfortunate wretch had become overwrought and confused of mind.

Torran felt empathy for the younger ones who in their innocence did not understand what was happening. He felt for a young child lost and weeping for its parents, and for the mother of that child searching through the waves of misery.

From the vantage point of a hill just outside of the village of Yani, two riders watched in silence. As the outgoing masses passed them by, suspicious looks were cast over the riders who didn't appear to take notice of the exodus.

'Do you think anyone's arrived yet?' Said Edmund breaking the long silence.

'Let's find out', said Karl. He began to gather his will. A bright blue nimbus flared and surrounded him. Nearby people fell to their knees. Terrified they crossed themselves and began to pray to whoever might listen.

'Wind', he commanded. A bright octane light flashed from an outstretched hand; it circled and spread. Then came the whistling. Then the wind came. Like an express train, a wind of some considerable speed and force passed over the village. It caused some to cower. It harmed no-one.

Torran jerked upright out of his deep thoughts. He did not sense anyone close but he knew that it was Karl. He gathered his will and sent a red line of octane brilliance shooting towards the heavens. It was seen and they knew.

'Time for you to meet Lord Torran of Ice and Fire', said Karl.

As the two wizards rode towards the village, many offers of gold were made for their horses by people needing transport. They could have sold their mounts a hundred times over but politely declined. These mounts were not for sale.

They were threatened with violence only once. A cold stare from Karl soon altered the minds of the would-be aggressors.

As they entered the village they saw the extent of the human river. They were saddened by the sight of so many people young and old, and from a hundred different encampments.

Torran spied the two wizards from his upstairs window and hurried down to meet them. 'Innkeeper I have friends arriving. They will need refreshments', called Torran as he passed the common room.

'At once, my Lord', replied the innkeeper.

As Karl and Edmund arrived at the inn and dismounted, Torran ran out to greet them.

'Karl, my friend, it's good to see you', said Torran as he embraced him in a brotherly hug.

Edmund was startled at the sight of Torran's robes, as were many who were passing.

'Well met, Torran, and how went your journey?' Said Karl.

'Come both, let us eat and celebrate and tell each other of our travels'.

They entered the inn where the innkeeper was nervously waiting. He bowed stiffly to the three lords. 'My Lords, you honour my humble dwelling'.

Edmund had never been treated like a lord before and found it slightly amusing.

'It's good to see friends again', said Karl.

'Come my Lords, I have a table in my private rooms'.

The innkeeper led them through the crowded common room, past the enquiring stares, the open mouths, and into a well decorated part of the inn. The room they entered was comfortable; soft furnishings sat upon a woven woollen carpet, and a large open fire gave the room a homely atmosphere. A rectangular table in the centre of the room was laid with bowls of hot stew, goblets of spiced wine, and three tankards of ale.

'My Lords, are there any further requirements?'

'Thank you innkeeper', said Karl. 'Your hospitality already exceeds what is expected in the finest of dwellings'.

'Then by your leave, my Lords. I have other duties that need my attention'.

Torran acknowledged with a polite nod, and the innkeeper withdrew, leaving the three together. Karl was the first to speak. 'Edmund, may I introduce you to Lord Torran, Wizard of Ice and Fire'.

Both stood and shook hands. 'Well met, Lord Edmund of Earth and Stone'.

'Indeed, sire. I'm sorry; it's just that I'm not used to all this yet'.

Torran grinned and flicked a lump of ice into Karl's stew. Edmund's tenseness eased as the evening became night, and then the night became early morning.

Karl related the events of his journey which included the meeting with Edmund, the test, and the minor clash with Zelfen.

He told how Edmund had been deceived by Zelfen, and that good fortune had smiled upon them in their escape.

Torran emphasised how fortunate they really were to escape without harm. He then spoke of the events surrounding his journey. The journey to the village of Spard, and like Karl, his dream had also come true.

'There is but one last ceremony to perform before we retire', said Torran as he finished his tale.

Karl and Edmund looked up from their tankards with a puzzled look on their faces.

'We must dress our new companion', said Torran as he stood up.

Karl wiped his hands on a damp cloth which was provided by the innkeeper, and indicated to Edmund that he should follow. He told him not to be alarmed at what he might see, or hear. Leaving the room and heading for the stairs, they bid goodnight to the innkeeper and his staff. The innkeeper gave a polite nod and wished them a good evening.

Edmund was quite looking forward to a good night's sleep in a real bed. This was a luxury that he could not remember sampling. However, it seemed that he would have to wait a little while longer.

On reaching the landing, Torran invited them into his room which was at the front of the building. They both readily agreed. The first thing that Torran did upon entering his room was to go to the window and observe the scene below. The crowds still passed by, but a lost and lonely child sat crying at the side of the road.

'Karl'.

'Torran?'

'Will you ask the innkeeper to go and collect that child', he said pointing to the street below. 'Ask him to give the child shelter until his family return to claim him. Seeing this negligence, I cannot keep my thoughts on the business at hand'.

Karl left the room without further comment, and returned shortly afterwards. Torran still continued to watch from the window. Eventually he saw two servants of the innkeeper fight their way across the crowded street. He smiled in satisfaction as the child was taken up and brought into the safety of the inn. Turning only then to Karl and Edmund, he pointed to a small casket and a black bladed sword that lay upon a low table. 'These are yours, Edmund of Earth and Stone. Use them with honour as befits your title'.

Edmund walked towards the table, and as if fragile, he picked up the black bladed sword. He immediately felt the sword become part of him, and he marvelled at the sensation. Next he opened the casket and gazed in astonishment upon the robes of Earth and Stone. Torran and Karl watched, as like an infant with a new present, Edmund tried on the wizard's robes.

He was slightly afraid as the power of Earth and Stone flowed into him. He felt strange as a tingling sensation began to build up inside of him. He wanted to shout; he knew not why a green nimbus had begun to glow around him, and then:

'C-a-l-i-a', he raised his sword and shouted again. 'C-a-l-i-a'. Green octane light flashed from his outstretched hand, from the tip of his sword. Even his body seemed to be covered in a web of green mist which emanated from the very heart of him.

A moment passed; a pause of nothingness; a void in which there was no movement except for the movement of a green light that pulsated around him. Then, as if in answer, more green mist, and green and brown lights began flickering around the room.

A golden tinted mist appeared like a small ball which began to grow in size and density. It swirled around the room. White starlight flashed within it, and from within it stepped Calia, Goddess of Earth and Stone.

Edmund stared in wonder as he remembered the beautiful woman who had appeared in his dreams. It was she, it was Calia. He made a feeble attempt at a salute as Karl and Torran knelt in respect.

Calia smiled a warm open smile, and as she spoke, Edmund was complete. 'At last the three wizards join once more to engage in battle against a common foe. I am indeed pleased with our choices. Hear now a riddle, for it will be your destinies. It has been decreed that we can help no further.

Now the three are joined once more
against ill forces now do stand,
and calm the ancient into stone
to live again upon this land.
Edmund holds the know of three
the fourth the three's decision be.

Calia smiled once more before slowly retreating back into the mist. There was a large flash of green light that temporarily blinded the three wizards; then there was nothing. The room had returned to its normal state.

'What does the riddle mean?' Said Edmund.

Torran thought for a while. 'Well', he said. 'We know that there are three of us. We know that we will probably have to stand against evil forces, and Edmund knows what we know'.

'The fourth could be Master Elio', suggested Karl.

'Calm the ancient into stone could be something to do with Edmund, and I think that maybe he has a lot to do with this puzzle', said Torran.

'How does a stone live again? What decision do we have to make regarding Master Elio?' Said Edmund.

The debate continued for some time, each offering what he thought the riddle meant, but no definite answers were forthcoming. As tiredness began to weigh heavily upon them, they each retired to their own rooms and slept.

A black robed figure angrily paced the small room. A fire crackled and sparked in an open grate reflecting his mood. His tantrums showed in the table that was upturned, in the collection of fruit and wines in disarray upon the stone floor, and in the damaged goblets that littered one of the corners. 'Seven days! Seven days it has taken so far. The army should be marching towards the south. Why is it taking so long?'

The voice, cruel and uncompromising, echoed through the halls and corridors of Dronecet Castle.

'My Lord Zelfen, we have gathered our forces, we have sent out the skirmishers, but there are still preparations to be made', said Lord Barek apologetically.

'I have given you everything. I have used my power to speed up your ships, and still they have not arrived at their destination', stormed Zelfen as he threw another innocent goblet at the wall.

'Sire, I plead with you. These southerners, our opponents in this forthcoming battle, are not foolish. To march forward without preparation and planning, would be nothing short of taking our own lives'. Lord Barek was visibly shaking in the presence of such an angry and unpredictably dangerous Lord Zelfen.

'When the time is at hand I will demand nothing less', said a seething Lord Zelfen. 'Hear me now, Barek, for if you incur my wrath, I will torment you even after your miserable death'.

A shocked Lord Barek said nothing in case he angered Zelfen even further. Zelfen, who still liked to think of himself as an earthbound god, had been in a foul temper ever since his return from the Dete Beacons and his surprise encounter with Lord Karl. Being caught off guard by a mere wizard had definitely hurt his pride. However, after a short while, and having thought more of his words, moods and actions, he spoke once again to Lord Barek, but in softer tones. After all, and for the time being, he needed him, he needed the army.

'My dear Lord Barek, forgive my outbursts of the last few days. You will no doubt understand my concern in these troubled times. If we are to succeed in defeating the southerners, we must strike hard and fast. We must not delay. We cannot allow them time to prepare their defences, nor build up their strength'.

'Your apology is accepted sire, although there is no need of one. I quite understand that we all are on tender nerves at this time. Perhaps if we were to walk amongst the ranks it would serve to fuel encouragement. Gentle persuasion and a show of solidarity would be better an order for haste. I'm sure that you will agree. Meanwhile, I will send despatches requesting that my generals speed up the landing at Penste Harbour. Winter is drawing near, and it would be an advantage to gain a foothold before the hard snows of the season make it impossible'.

'I was forgetting about your harsh weather conditions. Well, if everything is in readiness before the winter sets in, I shall be contented'.

Lords Zelfen and Barek, the air now not so electric, joined several generals on a walk through the multitude of tents and makeshift huts that surrounded Dronecet castle. Soldiers sharpening weapons on wet stones, employing long deliberate strokes, eyed the procession as it passed. Some saluted and were acknowledged with a wave or smile. As the lords and generals passed a large open tent, carpenters could be seen making final alterations to vast war machines.

A little way from the tent, an open forge glowed with white-hot coals. Two scantily clad youths laboured at the bellows at the back of the forge. Shimmering red metal was being hammered into various shapes at the front by an overweight smithy.

Even the women were pressed to help by sewing tunics and leather. All smiled, showing rows of blackened teeth as the procession passed slowly between them. Towards the evening and as the sunlight faded, the air began to cool noticeably. Huge camp-fires that had been built during the day were lit, many gathered around them to ward off the increasing coldness of the night. Sparks danced towards the blackness of the sky, forming their own patterns. The red glow of the fires cast moving shadows on many faces.

After dismissing the generals, Lords Zelfen and Barek returned to the warmth of the castle, much correspondence needed to be answered; many decisions had to be made.

One letter was from Lord Brin of Castle Tezz. It contained diplomatic requests that he, Lord Barek, cease hostilities and recall his forces. Lord Barek answered the request with no more than six words.

DEFEND YOURSELVES IF YOU ARE ABLE

Barek, Lord of all Modania.

As the days passed by in the village of Yani, the long stream of refugees dwindled. The human tide of misery, the river of fear now but a trickle. A quiet had descended upon the village. Not the normal quiet of the country or the quiet of an evening, but a tense quietness, a quietness that seemed to penetrate the imagination of hidden things in the dark.

Hardly anyone moved anywhere at night without glancing from side to side, without constantly looking over their shoulder.

During this time, Edmund was taking instruction from Torran. He was a willing student, and learned quickly which pleased his tutor, as time was of the essence. Meanwhile, Karl took to investigating the village.

Absently, as though preprogramed in self-defence techniques, he noted weak spots where defence would be difficult. He investigated the approaches and possible defence lines; he left nothing to chance. Finally, taking in all that he saw into consideration, he realised the futility of attempting to defend such a small and easily attacked location. One flaming torch in the right place could, with unquestioned certainty, wipe out a village, especially one built out of timber, without one attacker being harmed.

The only defence as a temporary measure, or diversionary tactic, would be to lay traps. It wouldn't hold off an army for long, but it might afford a little time in the case of need. It was with these thoughts swimming around in his head that he returned to the inn.

A cooling sun was now in its zenith, and as usual the innkeeper had prepared a midday meal of cold meats, fruit, and hot spiced wine. As the three lords ate their meal, many discussions hovered around them. Defences, escape plans, the riddle given to them by the Goddess Calia. They were lively discussions that kept minds away from the worst eventualities, but they came; they came the following day. The morning dawned with an electric silence, the air felt heavy with an imminent danger that almost took form within the air itself.

A chill wind whipped around the wooden buildings. Autumn leaves made the only audible sound as they raced along the street like so many large insects. No birds sang their sweet morning welcome. No dogs barked, and no children played. Torran and Karl awoke simultaneously, their bodies like coiled springs, their minds alert. Something was wrong. They felt it, breathed it, and sensed it in every fibre of their being.

'Innkeeper!' Shouted Torran as he swung out of his bed and roused Edmund.

The innkeeper came running into the room, mopping his brow with a towel. 'My Lord?

'My friend, we feel that something is about to happen. Be prepared to leave at short notice. Better still, gather your family and your servants; go down the tunnel and make your way to Castle Tezz by way of the Border House. Remember the message that I gave you'.

'I may be small, my Lord, but I can hold my own in a fight as well as the next man, and I can handle a sword'.

'This may be so, my friend. However, should you be injured or worse, who would blend the wine for Lord Brin? Who would care for your family and friends?

'But, my Lord'.

'Go now, my friend, and with you go our blessings'.

'As you command, my Lord'. The small man hurried away, collected his family, which included the orphan who had become part of it, and made ready to leave.

Torran, in checking the inn for a final time to ensure that no-one remained, saw the innkeeper sitting on a stool polishing a sword. He gave him a stern look.

'Okay, I'm going', said the innkeeper.

He smiled as the innkeeper was the last to disappear along a well concealed tunnel. 'Give me an army of men like that and we would frighten the enemy witless', he said aloud, but to himself.

It was roughly midday when the first rider was spotted atop a hill overlooking the village. Others joined him, twenty in all, but these were no military skirmishers. These were mercenaries from the Bay of Wolves. The village folk that first saw the horned helmets and braided hair ran screaming into the main square of the village. A crowd gathered round, and as one body, they all turned around to look in the direction of a pointed finger.

Hearing the commotion, the three wizards ran out to join them. Some of the villagers had seen the wizards in their robes; others didn't quite know what to make of them.

Torran, Karl and Edmund viewed the scene for a few moments before Torran addressed the crowd. 'Good people of this village', he began. 'You know not who we three companions are, or what we are about. Be assured that we are indeed your friends. You see over on yonder hill your enemies'. He pointed to the distant riders. 'Mercenaries who would slay all and plunder your homes for profit.

Good people, I urge you to gather what possessions you are able to carry, and seek the shelter and safety of the southern borders. Those of you who would stay and challenge the enemy, I urge not to take any unnecessary risks'.

At that moment, another finger pointed to reveal that more riders had joined the group of mercenaries.

'Who are you anyway?' A member of the village gathering confronted Torran. 'How do we know that you do not deceive us?'

'You know because at the moment you are still alive. I am Lord Torran, Wizard of Ice and Fire', he said in an ice cold voice.

'Rubbish', said one of the villagers.

'Myths and old wives tales' said another.

At a sign from Torran, the wizards summoned their powers. The villager's eyes widened as they saw three figures begin to glow, each a different colour.

'Who calls Lord Torran a liar?' shouted Karl as octane light flashed between the three wizards.

The crowd gasped in disbelief. Some crossed themselves. 'Then the legends are true', said a woman as she fell to her knees.

'This', continued Torran, pointing to Karl, 'is Lord Karl of Brin, Wizard of Wind and Water. Our third companion is Lord Edmund of Earth and Stone. Now get up woman, you'll get your knees dirty. The last thing I need now is people falling over themselves to pay homage. There are people up there desperate to part our breaths from our bodies'.

The woman stood up, her face, flush with embarrassment. She attempted a smile, and then disappeared into the crowd.

'What do we do now, my Lord', said a villager.

'Those of you who wish to stay; in my opinion will be committing suicide. Even we three shall eventually have to make good our escape. We will hold the enemy back for as long as possible to allow you unhindered passage'.

'I'll stay', said a voice from the crowd.

'Me too', said another.

'And me'.

Altogether, ten men defied the odds.

'You ten are brave men. Foolish but brave, and what you are considering is madness', said Lord Torran in an attempt to have them change their minds.

'With respect, my Lord', said one of the volunteers. 'If we ten are considering madness, then what are you three considering?'

'Let's give it what we can', said Lord Edmund.

The remainder of the village folk began leaving quietly in ones and twos as instructed by Torran. The aim was to attract as little attention as possible. If the mercenaries suspected what the village folk were about, they would almost certainly attack straight away, and with catastrophic results.

To the relief of the three wizards, the evacuation went smoothly and without incident. Some took to the hills and a hundred different hiding places; others followed the river on a variety of sailing vessels, and headed south. Soon, unbeknown to the mercenaries, only ten volunteers and three wizards remained.

'When will they attack, my Lord?' Asked a nervous volunteer.

'If they didn't notice the other villagers leaving, they will probably wait a while in an attempt to unnerve us. They might expect a delegation to go and ask for peace, but that would be a waste of time. In a while they will discuss methods of attack, and then they will implement them', said Torran.

'Time to make some welcoming preparations', said Lord Edmund.

For the next hour, ten men and the three wizards discussed tactics. Pit traps were discussed but even with Edmund's powers, time would not allow the construction of such devices. Eventually, and because of the time factor, very little was achieved. The extent of the village defences amounted to barricades combined with trip ropes that were laid across the main roads, and at head height on the side alleys.

The hope was that the mercenaries, on finding no complicated defence systems, would be over confident to the point of being careless. The wizards agreed to limit the use of their powers, as to use them excessively would tire them too quickly. In the event that the mercenaries should gain the upper hand, it was agreed that all should meet at the inn where a possible escape route could be found. When all the words had been spoken, all objections considered, silence once again descended, and the wizards waited.

The air began to cool towards the late afternoon. Torran passed a flagon of hot spiced wine to the volunteers who were trying to occupy themselves in a game of chance to pass away the time. The game remained unfinished as a battle cry pierced the quietness, and the thunder of galloping horses filled the air.

'They come, my Lord', said a worried volunteer.

'To your positions, and don't take chances. Wait for our commands', shouted Lord Karl as he raced across the street.

One man looked for the second time in disbelief as the glowing lights around the wizards grew brighter. Octane flashes crackled as though trying to escape from Edmund and the ground beneath him moved with each step.

There was a lack of order in the mercenaries attack. Had there been a semblance of organisation, a different result might have been achieved. It began with two mercenaries riding into the village at full gallop, with battle axes swinging.

'I wish that Master Elio was here', said Lord Karl. 'Ropes', he shouted.

The ropes that he and others had laid across the road were pulled tight as the mercenaries approached them, and realising the danger too late, the two riders were catapulted from their mounts to land heavily on the hard ground.

The volunteers ran forward before the mercenaries could recover, and despatched them with ease.

The main body of the attack force followed a few moments later. They were yelling war cries and screaming for blood. Two inexperienced volunteers ran towards the oncoming charge swords in hand, but on foot they were at a disadvantage, they were felled by two expertly thrown axes.

'This is not going to work', said Torran.

'Let's give them one good blast, and then run', said Lord Edmund.

Lord Karl agreed, so the three wizards moved to stand in the open. It was almost peculiar that the mercenaries failed to notice the three strangely clad figures immediately, but then one pointed and shouted something in a northern tongue. For the longest while the mercenaries stared in disbelief. Then, with cries of vengeance for their two fallen comrades, they charged.

The scene was as if it was in slow motion. As the riders spurred their mounts into full gallop towards the three wizards, green, blue and red nimbuses appeared about them. The mercenaries took little notice and rode hard towards them, quite unprepared for the next turn of events.

Torran raised his hands and spoke. 'Fire', he commanded. Red octane light shot forth with pinpoint accuracy and with deadly results. Two riders were unhorsed and fell, burning, to the ground.

'Shall I put them out?' Said Lord Karl in jest.

'Don't be stupid! They're trying to kill us', said Torran completely missing the joke.

Green octane light then began to spread, like a web, over the ground. 'Stone', commanded Lord Edmund. A sound like thunder filled the air, and the earth vibrated making the horse's rear and the riders fall.

Rocks began to appear on the surface in front of the remaining mercenaries. Not being able to negotiate the new terrain, and being completely out of ideas, the riders turned and fled. The over joyous volunteers rallied around the wizards.

'They will be back', said Torran. 'Rest while you can.

'When do you think they might attack again?' Asked Lord Edmund.

'I think that they have had a little surprise, but that alone will not deter them. They will most certainly discuss new tactics and attack again tomorrow; we must be ready for them'.

As the evening drew in and darkness began to descend, Lord Karl ordered lights to be lit in all the remaining buildings. Some had been put to the torch earlier by the attackers. Without the exact knowledge of which buildings the defenders would occupy, or how many defenders there were, the mercenaries would probably not risk a night attack. After a meal of cold meats and fruit, Torran outlined plans for the next day. It was a short meeting, and when it was concluded, all but two retired. The remaining two had volunteered to take the first watch, and although through the night, shadows played a cat and mouse game, there was no enemy attack.

As Torran had predicted, and at first light, the thunder of hooves once again broke the morning silence. Each of the volunteers rushed to his allotted defence position as war cries sounded through the village, this time from two different directions. During the previous night, half of the mercenary band had skirted the edge or the village. The attack came from both directions at the same time.

'I didn't bargain for this', said Torran. 'To the inn', he shouted.

The volunteers came out from their positions and began a dead run to the inn. The mercenaries, having learned a lesson after the first attack, had dismounted, and seeing the defenders apparently fleeing, gave chase. Only one of the defenders fell, an expertly thrown axe embedded in his back. The remaining seven reached the safety of the inn.

Lord Karl was the first to unleash his power as he stood again before the charging mercenaries, his robes flapping in the wind. Coiled like a spring and glowing with a blue nimbus, he stretched forth both his hands. 'Wind', he commanded. As a son would come to his father, so the wind answered the command of Lord Karl. Blue octane light streaked through the air like miniature lightning bolts, and a wind of pure energy swept five mercenaries aside like rag dolls. When two others were almost upon him, the blue nimbus grew blindingly bright. 'Water', he commanded. His face showing the depths of his anger.

A deep rumbling filled the air. The two mercenaries suddenly stopped their attacks. Puzzlement filled their faces as water began oozing from their bodies. Their horror became evident as they dehydrated at an alarming speed. Their screams for mercy went unanswered and lasted but for a few seconds, before, dry as the sands of a desert, they fell to the ground in pieces.

Lord Karl fell to one knee utterly drained. He was weakened by the use of his power and was now vulnerable to attack. He stood up again to face the oncoming hoard, and although weak, in a movement faster that most could witness, the black bladed sword was in his hand and ready for work.

Torran had conserved his power and stood facing the mercenaries that had attacked from the opposite direction. Cautiously they approached, and then with blood-curdling screams, they charged. Torran's sword was in his hands in one smooth movement and through the body of the first attacker. Eager participants in the game of death became fewer, still, hopelessly outnumbered, the wizards fought on. A well-aimed axe missed its intended target by inches as Torran side stepped out of the line of fire. He began to weaken.

'We need a diversion, Edmund', shouted Lord Karl.

Lord Edmund, who had been guarding the entrance to the inn, reacted immediately. A green nimbus cloaked his body, and streaks of octane brilliance earthed from his fingertips. 'Cover your eyes and mouths', he shouted. The earth began to shift and dance. Fine grit from the road began to rise and spin to form small whirlwinds of detritus. Torran and Karl backed away as the whirlwind exploded, sending showers of small granite-like particles into the faces of the enemy. Temporarily blinded, the mercenaries fell into confusion.

'To the inn', shouted Karl, and they ran to join Edmund and the seven remaining volunteers.

'To me', called Torran as he entered the inn and made for the doorway that led to the cellars.

A narrow flight of stairs led them to the main storage area where the air was damp with the smell of stale wine and ale. Barrels of every description were stacked in neat rows, the older ones betrayed by gossamer webs that stretched geometric patterns from one to the other. The volunteers followed Lord Torran with Karl and Edmund keeping a guard at the rear.

After travelling along another narrow passage they arrived at a small enclosure. There, embedded in the rock that formed part of the foundation of the inn, was what seemed like a huge wine barrel, the end of which was easily the height of two fully grown men.

Lord Torran moved to the side of the barrel and released a hidden lever. Everyone moved back a few feet as the front section of the barrel opened up to reveal a spacious tunnel.

In the streets the mercenaries had regrouped, some still with sore eyes and minor cuts, but all with enraged tempers. 'We will burn them out', said the leader through clenched teeth. A moment later, and to the cheers of the mercenaries, burning torches were thrown into the inn. The fire caught and quickly spread throughout the building, and gleeful mercenaries gathered around to attack anyone who tried to escape the flame. No-one came out of the inn. Little did they realise at that time, that the three wizards, along with the remaining volunteers, were making good their escape by way of a well-constructed and concealed tunnel.

The tunnel was perhaps four, maybe five hundred yards long, and the stone floor gave added support to the many wide timbers that held up the roof. Along the floor at one side, were wooden rails which were used to roll the wine barrels back and forth from the entrance.

At measured intervals along the roof of the tunnel, holes had been drilled to act as air vents, and were disguised above by natural rock formations. Clean breathable air filtered in, cooling and refreshing the inner chamber which was fully the height of a man, and easily negotiated. It took but a short time to reach the end of this undetectable tunnel, an opening by the river hidden by reeds, and they quickly climbed into to the waiting boats.

A sudden commotion prompted Torran to climb to a vantage point from where he could see into the village. The inn had quickly burned, and with such ferocious heat, that it had already been consumed. The upper floors had collapsed and now the inn looked quite unrecognisable. Although burning rubble still crackled and fizzed leaving nothing to survive the heat, doubt played on the minds of the mercenaries.

The leader called for his men to gather round. 'How many went into the inn? Eleven? Twelve? No man or wizard could have withstood that kind of heat. They could not have endured that death without crying out in agony or trying to run; where are the bodies? No, I say that there must have been an escape route of some description. Perhaps like the ones that the smugglers use in the Bay of Wolves. Search the area. Leave no stone unturned'. The mercenaries scattered at the command of their leader.

Torran, who was joined by Karl, moved a little closer to allow a better view of what the mercenaries were doing. They watched as they began searching the village and surrounding areas. Some were heading in their direction and getting closer.

'To the boats', said Torran.

Both hurried back to the others who were standing by two large boats that were complete with sails and oars. A few provisions had been placed in each boat by the innkeeper before he left for Castle Tezz. Torran took the first boat with four of the volunteers, and Karl and Edmund took the second with the remaining three. Quickly they hoisted the sails, and with a small amount of power supplied by Karl, the wind responded, filled the sails and aided a speedy escape.

Within minutes the two boats were well down the river, much to the annoyance of the mercenary leader, who could only watch as the boats slowly faded from view.

CHAPTER EIGHT

THE INNKEEPER FROM THE inn at Yani, together with his extended family and servants, had made good progress. The river had been fast, taking them swiftly to the tunnel that led to the Border House. After being escorted to Captain Dac'ra, the innkeeper explained to him what had happened at the village.

'I will shelter your family while you go on to Castle Tezz', said the ever helpful captain.

A horse was supplied almost immediately, and the innkeeper, after a brief farewell, rode off at full gallop. The journey to the castle was uneventful. The innkeeper, with his mind on other things, didn't notice the two dark cloaked figures that shadowed him for the most part of the journey as a precautionary measure. It was early in the evening when he arrived at Castle Tezz and he made a request to see Lord Brin.

'A lone rider at the gates seeks an audience, my Lord. A commoner by the look of him, but he asks for you by name'.

'Does this person have a name?' Asked Lord Brin.

'He didn't give a name but he tells me that he is from the inn at Yani, my Lord'.

'These are troubled times. Has he any proof?'

'I will enquire, my Lord'.

The soldier hurried away, leaving Lord Brin with his own thoughts. The recent events were playing heavily on Lord Brin, and although he was an accomplished soldier on the field of battle, he hated the complete waste of life that it caused, not forgetting the destruction of crops and homes.

'The Lord Brin requests proof of your identity', said the soldier to the innkeeper.

The innkeeper hesitated before passing on the message given to him by Lord Torran. The soldier, after listening to what the innkeeper had to say, was red-faced with anger. He returned to Lord Brin's chambers, but not before he had ordered two guards to take charge of the innkeeper, with instructions that he should be watched carefully.

'My Lord', said a breathless soldier. The person at the gate says that he comes from someone who considers you to be an overgrown, pompous, ass. Please forgive me, my Lord, I am only repeating the message. I have also taken the liberty of having the person guarded so that he does not escape'.

'Well done. Admit him and bring him directly to me'.

'By your leave, my Lord'.

The soldier again hurried away and had the innkeeper escorted under guard to Lord Brin. Lord Brin was standing by the large log fire as the innkeeper was frog-marched into the room. He turned and made a mental decision before speaking. 'Release this man and leave us', commanded Lord Brin.

The guards obeyed instantly, but remained in the corridors in case further orders were issued. Lord Brin, who stood a head and shoulders above the small man, surveyed him for a while. 'What brings you to Castle Tezz', said Lord Brin, 'and who are you?'

'My apologies sire, I have never had the honour of meeting you in person, but I am the owner of the inn at Yani'.

'Ah! The maker of excellent wines'.

'I am pleased that they are to your liking, sire'.

'Indeed. Now tell me of the person who gave you this message',

'There were three all told, sire. One showed me a ring with the seal of Tezz on it'.

'My son. Is he safe?'

'When I left, sire, yes. I wanted to stay and fight the mercenaries that were gathering at the edge of the village, but the tall one who was wearing red and white robes, the one who gave me the message, commanded me to leave with my family'.

Lord Torran', he said, and smiled. 'Who was the third?'

'Well, sire, when the lords first came to my inn, there was an elderly gentleman with them, very good with words was he. Then they all left, and a few days later, the lords arrived back and in place of the old gentleman, there was a younger one. I don't ask questions, sire'.

'Well-spoken innkeeper, but come, sit and tell me of other news'. Lord Brin made the innkeeper welcome, and arranged for his family to be escorted from the Border House to the safety of Castle Tezz.

Lord Karl, Torran, and Edmund slept lightly as the boats rocked gently on the river. The volunteers, for the most part, also tried to sleep, but anxiety over what was to happen to them forbade the rest that they so desperately needed. Only two kept fully alert to guide the boats, and to keep a watch for any hostile movement on the river banks.

There were numerous hiding places along the river's edge; places that the enemy could easily be concealed and lay in wait to ambush the travellers. Long reed grasses and rocky outcrops were commonplace. Bushes and the occasional tree added to the potential danger of attack. However, fortune smiled upon them, and no attack materialised as the boats drifted slowly downstream, much to the relief of the two watchmen.

The night drew in, and it was an unusually warm night for that time of year. It was almost peaceful, a far cry from the yells and screams for vengeance and blood. The full moon reflected its brilliance on the gently moving waters, and the occasional fish splashed idly as it took a late night feast from the surface. The music of the night played by an orchestra of nocturnal insects filled the otherwise silent air.

The darkness with all of its mysteries gradually faded to make way for a new dawn which crept purposely over the horizon. Awake and refreshed, all hands manned the oars with the exception of the watchmen who attempted, mostly without success, to sleep. It was just before midday that they found what they had been looking for: the tunnel entrance to the Border House.

'Stand to the guards'. The order rang out across the river, and two score veterans rushed to their defence positions. 'Who approaches?' called the guard commander.

'Lord Karl of Brin'.

'And who travels with you, sire?'

'Friends of the south', replied Karl.

'Advance, Lord Karl of Brin, and be welcome'.

'My thanks to the guard commander', replied Karl.

With the help of the guards, the boats were moored, and the party moved towards the tunnel. Horses were supplied for the journey to the Border House.

'We only had five spare horses last night', said the guard commander. 'Three more suddenly turned up out of the blue this morning'.

'They will be ours. We sent them on ahead', said Torran who winked at Karl.

On entering the tunnel, Edmund was keenly interested in its construction. It was easily the height of three men and at least five in width. No roof supports were visible, just blocks of stone holding themselves together, and arched to support a roof. Long boats were stacked on top of each other and lined almost the whole length of the tunnel. 'It's fantastic', he said. 'Never have I seen such craftsmanship in stone'.

'And to think that to take just one stone away would result in the entire tunnel collapsing', said Karl.

Edmund ducked his head and spurred his mount. It was about four hours later that the party arrived at the Border House. They were greeted by Captain Dac'ra.

'Welcome, my Lords' called the captain.

'Well met Captain Dac'ra', called Karl.

'Come', continued the Captain. 'Refresh yourselves and tell me of developments'.

'Our thanks, Captain Dac'ra but first of all', said Karl, pointing to the seven volunteers, 'these seven are all that remains of a loyal band of fighting men. Treat them as your own, and by my order they shall receive acknowledgement of their services'.

'As you command, my Lord'.

Captain Dac'ra shook each of the volunteer's hands in greeting, which made them feel rather important. He then gave orders to have them accommodated, clothed and fed. It felt good to relax in a hot tub, the aches and pains melted away, and the seven volunteers felt like celebrities.

It was explained to them by the attendants, that a long standing tradition in the Border House, was to welcome with enthusiasm those returning from battle, and to offer what comforts could be spared. It was the least that could be done for those defending the south.

After refreshing themselves, Karl, Torran and Edmund met with Captain Dac'ra in one of his private rooms.

'What has become of Master Elio?' Asked the Captain.

'We have had no news of him at all. We had expected him to meet with us in the village of Yani, but things became a little too hot for us there', replied Karl.

'And your new companion?

'Lord Edmund of Earth and Stone', replied Torran by way of introduction.

'Well met, my Lord Edmund', said the Captain, warmly shaking Edmund's hand.

'Lord Edmund is not yet used to his new estate', said Torran.

'Ah! The subject of your quest, my Lord?'

'You are very perceptive Captain Dac'ra'.

'What of northern activities?' Asked the Captain.

'Unfortunately there will be war, but we will have to speak with the Lord of Tezz, Lord Brin before committing ourselves fully'.

'Will you be travelling to Castle Tezz today?'

'I think not. We will rest first and then continue our journey at first light'.

'I shall have your rooms prepared for an overnight stay then'. By your leave, my Lords'.

The Captain walked into an adjacent office and began giving out orders. Like a well-oiled machine, soldiers and servants hurried away to carry out their instructions.

Lord Edmund still could not grasp the reality of his new status. He felt lost when people bowed and curtseyed. He was not used to servants waiting on him. When he was eventually led by Torran and Karl to his room, he stood amazed by the obvious comfort and facilities, and that night he slept as never before under clean, wool-weave blankets. He awoke to the sound of a young bondsman who had accidently dropped a log whilst feeding the open fire.

'Good morning', said Edmund as he sat up in his bed.

The bondsman began to apologise for the disturbance, but was halted by Edmunds raised hand. 'Does your master treat you well?' He asked.

'Yes, sire, Captain Dac'ra is an extremely generous man, and very thoughtful towards his employees'.

The bondsman was plainly nervous, and it was obvious to Edmund that he was new to service.

'Then I shall be equally as generous. You shall take breakfast with me', said Edmund.

'But, my Lord, I am below your ranking. I could not presume . . .'

He was again cut short by Edmund's raised hand. 'We, my young servant, are more equal than you realise'. He called the guard and requested, to the astonishment of those within earshot, that breakfast be served; a large breakfast for two.

When the breakfast arrived, the bondsman had no idea where to start. A huge platter of assorted meats, eggs, and cereal topped with honey was set before him. A goblet of hot spiced wine was served to him by his puzzled superior. The bondsman's eyes were everywhere, trying to decide what to sample first. The expression on his face told of his utter delight.

During the breakfast, Edmund asked about the bondsman's duties in the Border House; his ambitions and conditions of service. The bondsman, beginning to relax, answered each question as Edmund would have done in similar circumstances: truthfully and without exaggeration. Noticing Torran and Karl enter the room, the bondsman began to rise from his sitting position.

'Sit, young sir, and enjoy your breakfast', said a bemused Torran.

'Is the wine to your liking?' Asked Karl, also smiling.

'It is excellent wine, sire', replied the bondsman.

'Good, good', said Karl, winking at Edmund and smiling.

After the breakfast the bondsman, being granted leave to continue with his duties, took away the breakfast dishes. He agreed at Edmund's request to return once his work was finished.

'Why the breakfast invitation?' Asked Karl when the bondsman was out of earshot.

Edmund explained that, until quite recently, he too was a servant, and that he had often dreamed of being treated as an equal and sitting to breakfast with his masters. He explained that he thought that he would give this bondsman his dream.

'A truly noble gesture. Why don't you take him as your squire?' Torran jested.

'Do you think that Captain Dac'ra would release him from his bond?' Said Edmund, not realising that Torran was jesting.

'Of course he would', said the Captain as he entered the room and bowed.

'Why don't I shut my big mouth', said Torran.

'But how did you . . .' began Edmund, looking questioningly at the Captain.

'My young Lord', said the Captain. 'With respect to your privacy, there is nothing that happens within the Border House that escapes my notice. It's my job and my duty to know these things. If a mouse has babies I know about it, and I send a bouquet of flowers to the mother'.

'Do you really?' Asked Edmund.

Torran, Karl and the Captain burst into laughter, and Edmund joined them when he realised the joke.

The morning had turned cold as winter approached. Icy winds took advantage of a cool sun to further the advances of the coming season, and the ground was hard with a white frost that sparkled like a million diamonds in the suns light; trees pointed bare fingers to the sky begging for new growth. Clouds of steam blew from the horse's nostrils, as the wizards, together with Edmund's newly appointed squire, departed the Border House en route to Castle Tezz.

Although this time the journey was a relatively safe one, the wizards were continually aware of their surroundings. During the first days ride, parties of allied soldiers were spotted surveying the area, making notes and discussing possible danger areas in case of an attack from the north.

The wizards made camp at the [place where Master Elio had first appeared, and half expected a Bemal bird to come flying out from the undergrowth. The thought made Torran smile and wonder where Master Elio was. Why hadn't he joined them in the village of Yani? Karl built a huge fire to ward off the chill of the night, and shadows danced as the four ate a small meal before retiring. Missing the comfort of the Border House, they slept.

The following morning, an even colder spell of weather greeted them. The fire was quickly built up, and wine, hot and soothing, made a difference to the way they felt. Soon they were mounted again and heading for Castle Tezz.

When almost in sight of the castle, the banners were raised: A red sunburst on a background of glittering white, a white lightning bolt on a background of glittering blue. The newly appointed squire held proudly a banner of brown diagonals on a background of living green.

Lord Brin of Castle Tezz was making his rounds of the castles defences when word came of the approaching lords.

'Open the gates and lower the bridge before he starts calling me names', commanded Lord Brin.

Several bemused guards hurried to obey their lord's orders, and as well-oiled machinery began to move, the gates opened and the drawbridge slowly descended. It had not quite reached its lowest point when the wizards arrived. As usual this gave an opportunity, and a reason for a barrage of insults from both parties, before warmly, they embraced as only true friends do.

'Come, tell me of your new companions and of your journey, horse-breath', said Lord Brin.

The name calling had to be explained to Edmund, who was wondering when the fight would start. The explanation amused him, and he wanted to know when the second round would begin. Over a tasty and well prepared evening meal, Karl, who sat at his father's right hand as befits the heir apparent, related the events of their journeys. He told of the meeting with Master Elio, and if anything were to mysteriously disappear, especially wine or food, Master Elio would be the cause of the disappearance. Edmund was seated to Karl's right, his squire stood behind him as was the custom.

Torran was seated to the left of Lord Brin, a favoured position at the court of Tezz. All listened and occasionally added to Karl's story, and Lord Brin promised to build a new inn for the one burned down by the mercenaries.

Much wine was consumed that evening, so much so that the squire had to help Edmund to his quarters. Not being used to so much, he quickly lost control of his arms, his legs and then his head. This led to much laughter, intermingled with insults, and the occasional threat of a beating.

Lord Brin stood up and steadied himself. 'Gentlemen, it pleases me beyond words that we are united as a family once more', his voice slightly slurred as a result of too much wine.

'It pleases me to belong to such a family, my fiend', replied Torran.

'It pleases me to correct my family member. Friend is spelled with an 'r' as in rat face', said Lord Brin.

'And it pleases me to say that no correction is needed. Fiend is spelled, f-i-e-n-d'.

'Well, if it pleases you both I shall retire. I feel that shortly, the language will be unfit for tender ears', said Karl. 'By your leave, father'.

"Sleep well, my son', said Lord Brin.

During the early hours of the morning, a routine patrol of the castle guards noticed Lord Brin and Lord Torran. Their faces were flat on the table, their arms across each other's shoulders. Carefully, the guards helped guide the two lords to their respective rooms, and then summoned the necessary staff to tidy and clean the hall.

It was almost midday before the lords met again. Washed, shaved and with headaches almost gone they invited army commanders to a conference on the worsening situation. It was a lively but serious debate which covered the deployment of the army, attack strategies, and escape routes should events lead to a withdrawal. Enemy tactics were discussed, but this was a difficult subject due to the fact that there had been no major military action for some years and times and tactics change, as do military allocations in the way the armies are formed.

It was widely thought that the northern battleships might sail into the Messica Ocean, and from there they could attack Castle Tezz from the rear. This would undoubtedly create a sandwich effect, with the southern forces as the filling. All were agreed however, that the attack, if any, would not be mounted before the winter had taken a hold and before spring had brought warmth back to the land. To attack during the harsh winter period would not be impossible, but militarily speaking, it would be foolhardy. The winter could be extremely cold, and with no canvasses to protect them, the soldiers would perish before they had a chance to fight.

It was during this discussion that Lord Brin received a message from the northern commander, Lord Barek. Lord Brin called for order and the room was silent.

'My friends, I have this day received an answer to my request from Lord Barek of Dronecet Castle and the northern forces. It saddens me to inform you, gentlemen, that from this hour we are at war with the north. May the gods look with kindness and mercy upon us all'.

The room suddenly became one full of kneeling figures, each with swords drawn and with blades touching every face as a sign of loyalty. 'Death before dishonour', they cried.

'Gentlemen, I am moved by your support', said Lord Brin, and with that he left the conference to be alone.

It was hoped earlier that the northern displays of force were just a sham designed to intimidate, that it would not escalate into a full-blown and bloody war. Still, the now inevitable conflict would have to be faced, and so it was that the word spread.

Although the southern forces were already on alert status, Torran and Karl advised the commanders to prepare further. To place both the Border House and Castle Tezz on war footings. The commanders respectfully bowed and left to make the necessary preparations.

'Thought you'd like a tankard of my excellent wine', said a small man who had entered the room carrying a tray.'Innkeeper!' exclaimed Lord Torran. 'It's good to see you again my friend'.

'The one and only, my Lord', replied the innkeeper as he placed the tray of drinks on a low table.

Karl shook the innkeeper by the hand and thanked him for the knowledge of the escape tunnel, a secret that even he was not privy to, and without it events would have been disastrous. He also had to apologise, and told the innkeeper that the inn had been burned to the ground during their escape. However, Lord Brin had set an order that when this strife was over, the inn would be rebuilt at no cost. Meanwhile it was understood that the innkeeper was working in the castle winery at the request of Lord Brin.

While the three raised their tankards and drank to each other's health, the castle was fast becoming a hive of activity. Messengers were sent fourth to Goston, to Hib, Caspe and Nolle. Other messengers were sent to Penste Castle in the south east, and to the Lake people. Border patrols were being increased and scouts were sent to key places to keep watch on the northern movements. It seemed a reckless time with orders being shouted by the minute, but amid the confusion, there was a system that was slowly evolving to produce a masterpiece of strategic planning. Outbuildings were being constructed to house those who would fight for the south. Defence ditches and traps were also under construction should the enemy manage to reach the gates of Castle Tezz.

Besides all that was going on, the army commanders had given orders that training groups be organised to help those not accustomed to war. All was in readiness for when the first of the many volunteers began to arrive.

Local farmers gave willingly to ensure that the assembling army had plentiful supplies, and wives took to cooking, sewing, and making preparations for a room in Castle Tezz to be used as a hospital for anyone wounded in battle. All this was happening and more, yet Lord Brin had not issued one single command. He sat alone and wept at the undivided loyalty of his people. He was still weeping when Karl entered his room.

'Come, father, your people await you'.

Lord Brin stood up with tears in his eyes. Unashamedly he went into the courtyard to hear soldiers, merchants, farmers, fishermen, blacksmiths, and the people of a hundred trades and professions cheer his name. En masse they knelt in respect to the banner of Brin of Tezz. Last but not least, Karl, Torran and Edmund drew their black bladed swords and offered them handle first to he who would be lord over all during the coming conflict.

Edmunds squire carried three banners and placed them behind the banner of Brin of Tezz, to the cheers of the multitude.

Lord Brin raised his hands and silence followed. He spoke in a clear, loud voice to people who had already accepted anything that he might have to say without question.

'Many lords' began Lord Brin, 'many masters, indeed many kings throughout the ages, have at some time stood before an assembly such as I witness today. They begin by saying, 'my people', whether it is true or not. I will not begin by saying, my people, because you don't belong to me. You are not my property to do with as I please. You are free people. You are your own masters. However, I would be honoured if you will permit me to call you my friends'.

The cheers from the multitude were such, that no other words were necessary. Lord Brin had said exactly what the people wanted to hear; that they were united.

A man with a flute began to play a lively tune and before long, people were dancing and singing the praises of the Lord of Tezz.

'Do you have any warts?' Asked Torran.

'No, only people who practise the black arts have them', replied Lord Brin.

'You mean witchcraft?

'Yes'.

'I think you ought to check again', said Torran, smiling.

'Come on mighty mouth, let's get drunk. I have a barrel that might fit you'.

CHAPTER NINE

THE FIRST WINTER SNOWS like thin wafers of whiteness, began to fall. The sea was choppy and cold, and lines of white foam raced towards the coastline as ten battleships flying northern colours dropped anchor into the black depths. The sea winds blew an angry and icy gale that whistled through the lowering sails.

'Lower the boats'.

The order echoed along with the sounds of crashing waves, and the running of booted feet through the rolling mists of the morning: the enemy was preparing to land. Many times practised over the years, boats were lowered fore, aft and amidships, with the precision of a clockwork mechanism. The northern commanders would accept nothing less. Although each boat had the capability of carrying twenty men, they had to return to the ships several times over, to offload the human cargo and their supplies.

The first to land on the deserted beaches were the surveyors, engineers and builders. It surprised them that no opposition waited on the bleak shoreline to challenge their landing.

Immediately and full of confidence, the forward landing party built a huge fire to ward off the cold morning air. As more fighting troops began to arrive, tents were erected to accommodate them. The ship to shore operation lasted for most of the day, until an assault army of two thousand had amassed on the beaches. Although the northern army commander's first goal, Penste Castle, was only two days ride away, orders were given to rest; to get used to the land once more, and to secure a base camp.

Before long, several fires were burning, the lights of which could be clearly seen from both Penste Harbour and Penste Castle. Those living in the harbour village and who had not joined Lord Brin, began to flee to the possible safety of Penste Castle. Another human chain of frightened people fled into the night.

As the night gave way to a new dawn, soldiers of the northern force prepared for battle, and just before the day ended, with a slight change of plan, they attacked Penste Harbour. There were only a hand full of families remaining in the village, but their misguided hopes for mercy were as insignificant as a raindrop in the ocean. The invading army had no compassion for man, woman or child, all were put to the sword as the northern forces laid waste the little village.

A few buildings were saved from destruction, and these were set aside for use as the officers' quarters. The bodies of the slaughtered village folk were piled unceremoniously in one heap at the edge of the village, carrion for scavengers, and a reminder of the ruthless determination of the invading troops.

Food and accommodation were now in plentiful supply, and because of this, orders were given for the ships to return northward to bring more fighting men to the landing area, such was the confidence of the northern commanders.

No-one noticed the two figures clad only in black, as they viewed the proceedings through slits in their face masks. No-one watched or heard them as they slipped silently away to take the news to Castle Tezz. The sacking wrapped hooves of the two mounts made little noise, as silently, they sped away into the blackness of the night.

The report of the landing and the slaughter of the people at Penste Harbour was grave news indeed. This was a blatant violation of the rules of war, and as the northern forces had attacked first and had killed innocent civilians, Lord Brin felt that he had no alternative but to act. He issued orders that would send his troops into battle.

A message was sent to Captain Dac'ra at the Border House, that his troops were to mobilise, and occupy a position south of the village of Yani. Lord Brin would strengthen their position by sending three battalions of elite fighting men to join them on the eastern flank. A further four battalions, it was proposed, would set up a defence line along the River Zarh, and be commanded by General Xante, a hardened veteran and long-time friend of Lord Brin.

Engineers were sent forward to build bridges, dig traps and defence ditches. Small parties of skirmishers followed to harass the enemy, and to act as messengers between allied groups. It had started. Long lines of soldiers, some in uniform, and others in a variety of military and civilian clothing, began the march. Lord Brin sat astride his mount, his face set with determination.

Pride shone from him like a beacon as he watched cheerful and enthusiastic men at arms salute as they passed.

He drew his sword, an old and trusted weapon, and raised it high into the air.

'For the south', he shouted.

'And for the Lord of Tezz', was the voluminous reply.

Lord Brin sat astride his mount for a long period of time. Even as the marching troops faded into the distance, he watched. He wondered how many would return to share stories with their grandchildren. He wondered how many would fall and leave loved ones behind.

To reduce the possibility of death caused by illness or fatigue, Lord Brin gave an order that arrangements were to be made that every fourteen days; replacements would be sent for a section of the army. That section would then retire to allow rest and recuperation, warmth and good food to build up their spirits.

A small contingent of Lord Brin's personal guard was sent to Millers Hill. Although they would not be able to see what it was that they were supposed to guard, they were told that it was of the utmost importance that the hill was held against any enemy attack.

Other small groups were sent to the various villages to offer help, support and protection for the families of serving soldiers.

Captain Dac'ra, after receiving Lord Brin's message, changed from a soft gentle man into a born and hardened leader of men. The soldiers under his command recognised the serious side of the Captain's nature. They knew instinctively that the worst had arrived. At a meeting in one of his private rooms, and after a long deliberation, Captain Dac'ra spoke to his lieutenants.

'Gentlemen, the time for fun and games is over. Today we march for the protection and the good of the south, and for our Lord Brin of Castle Tezz. Let no man falter in his duties and we shall be victorious. I will not cloud the issue: we are at war. Many will not return. Those who do return will be known as heroes, and those who fall will be remembered as heroes. Their names will be written boldly in the great hall at Castle Tezz for generations to see, respect and admire. May the gods strengthen and guide your decisions'.

The captain then left to prepare himself for the coming ordeal. It was but a short time later that the trumpets sounded, flutes whistled, and the war drums of the south began a slow beat as the captain, with three of his battalions, slowly marched from the Border House towards the north. One battalion headed directly for the village of Yani, one to the east of the village and one battalion to the west, over the River Powle.

At Castle Tezz, Torran, Karl and Edmund sat with Lord Brin around a large table. A model of the land had been built upon it.

'Within five days the southern forces should be in place and ready to advance', said Lord Brin.

Karl asked about the possibility of the northern forces braving the winter and attacking in the hope of a quick victory. After all, this kind of manoeuvre is not uncommon in warfare but it would depend on the confidence of the northern commanders.

'It wouldn't be an impossibility', said Lord Brin after considering the question. 'I think, however, that it would be highly unlikely. The only other danger of course, is the northern force at Penste Harbour. If they come straight at us through Penste Castle, the advantage could be ours. For a start, laying siege to a castle takes time and provisions.

On the other hand they divide their forces: one half taking the coast road and the other travelling along the River Penste to the Lake of Dreams, we might have a problem. Firstly they will be able to gather provisions en route, and secondly, they will be able to attack us on two fronts before their main army arrives. We would have to recall the northern based army to give us protection, and this would leave the Border House open to attack. To put it delicately, we would be in a mess'.

'How can we help?' Asked Edmund.

'I would like you three to travel between allied armies. Use what powers you have at your command to thwart the northerners. Create havoc and disorganise them. This may give them the illusion that there are more than three of you, and weaken their resolve. I will travel to join our northern based forces at the village of Yani. Furthermore, I would be honoured if you three would escort me there'.

Without hesitation Karl agreed. Torran and Edmund also agreed, although Torran grumbled about having to ride alongside a windbag. With a smile, a suitable reply slipped from the corner of Lord Brin's mouth.

Over a light lunch, Torran discussed powers with Edmund and Karl. He told them in no uncertain terms, that to use their powers to the excess would leave them vulnerable. He referred Karl and Edmund to the small fight that had occurred in the village of Yani, when the excessive use of their powers had weakened them. He explained how, by using existing elements instead of creating them, their powers could, and most probably would last twice as long. The discussion lasted well into the evening, when the castle appeared almost ghost-like due to the absence of many staff.

There was no merry making, no music, and no dancing. The only sounds were those of women sewing, cooking, and the distant sound of the blacksmith's hammer as he laboured well into the night. A cold but bright moon shone its light upon the grey castle walls, and a lone rider was seen heading at full gallop towards them. On arrival he was taken immediately to see Lord Brin.

'My Lord', began the messenger. 'Northern forces have gathered along the sea reaches at Penste. They have taken the harbour and slaughtered the occupants of the village there. They now laugh and mock us from a distance. As you are aware, my Lord, Penste Castle is not a military estate in its ways; we have a few soldiers, but nothing near as many that would be able to withstand an invading force of this magnitude. The Lord of Penste Castle sends me, his envoy, to seek the protection of castle Tezz'.

'Well trusted, envoy. I think that you will be safe, well, until the end of winter at least. By then I will have approved a plan for your defence. Fear not if you see nothing for a while, but be assured that I, Lord Brin of Castle Tezz, confirm our support, and send our respects to the Lord of Penste'.

'Our deepest gratitude, my Lord'. The envoy bowed, turned, and then left as quickly as he had come.

Penste castle, although well placed within its borders, was smaller than most. Its main income was from farm produce with a small income from the guild of silversmiths.

'I do not relish the thought of northern forces taking root in Penste castle', said Lord Brin.

'Nor will they. Torran, Edmund, let us begin our work', said Karl.

The three wizards and Edmunds squire left almost immediately, and although the night was severely cold, it didn't appear to affect the four determined riders.

Stopping only once for a light meal, they reached the River Zarh by the following evening.

'Who approaches?' Shouted a nervous sentry.

'Lord Karl of Brin with friends of the south', answered Karl.

'Advance, Lord Karl of Brin, and be welcome', said the sentry a little relieved.

'Well spoken, sentry', said Karl as he led his party into the encampment.

A tent was put at their disposal, and after a tankard of hot wine, they slept. The following morning after a breakfast of army rations, scouts gave them an account of northern troop movements, and that at the present time; they seemed content to stay where they were. Only the occasional patrol had been seen surveying the land.

'How and when do think they will attack? Have you any thoughts on their methods?' Asked Karl.

'My Lord', continued the scout, 'I think that they will wait until the spring before laying siege to Penste castle. They will not try to destroy the castle, because in my opinion, they will want it intact so that they can use it as a base for their operations. The castle could easily be fortified to withstand even the largest army, my Lord. It is my submission that this will be their plan'.

'Good', said Karl. 'Do you think that our southern troops could, when the time is right, sneak around the sides of the enemy and catch them in a pincer movement?'

'An excellent idea, my Lord. They will not expect that of us. Perhaps if we could get some reinforcements into the castle under the cover of night, it would be the ultimate surprise. The northern troops could be attacked from right, left, and centre'.

'Are you forgetting that the moment any troop movement occurs, spies will be reporting the same to the northern commanders', said Torran.

'No, my Lord. If what you say is true and the northern army will not advance before the spring, it gives us plenty of time to organise a few farmers at a time. Who would notice farmers going into the castle, or wine merchants?'

'I see your meaning, and it's a good idea', said Torran. 'What do you think, Karl?'

'An excellent idea. Soldiers go in disguised as tradesmen. The aged, women and children come out . . . devious. Edmund?'

'I agree, and if we can prevent further landings as well, we might stand a chance'.

'Soon gentlemen we shall have iced northerners', said Torran.

'With added water', said Karl.

'On the rocks', said Edmund.

More snow was falling in the northern territories, and through the millions of white flakes came the sound of war drums, and of marching troops. Line upon line of northern soldiers marched towards the village of Spard. Cold soldiers with their faces set against the worsening weather conditions, and with hands tinted blue, they marched southward. Occasionally one would fall and be left to embrace the snow for the last time.

Before crossing the River Powle, the northern army had divided into three main battalions. Two battalions had crossed the river and had taken the eastern route that covered the central plain. One of those battalions had then advanced and crossed the River Zarh to the north of the Lake of Dreams, to take up a position north of the Timber Wood.

The remaining battalion had proceeded in a south-westerly direction, to take up a position covering the west of the village of Spard, and Turns Wood area. A further three battalions followed the leaders, and everywhere could be seen the remains of burned villages, crops, slaughtered livestock and people, all covered with the white of winter snow.

Very few people had remained in the village of Spard, and when the northern forces arrived there, those remaining gave no resistance. The skirmishers that had preceded the main force had crushed all opposition. This then was to be the front line of the northern attack force. Six battalions of some of the finest, but misguided fighting men.

What building that remained standing in the village of Spard, were quickly commandeered by the highest ranking amongst the northern officers. The foot soldiers and lower ranks had to make do with tented accommodation, which, when erected, could be seen stretching from Turns Wood to the village of Arvel in the east.

Black canvasses were silhouetted against the white of the snow, and soon, small fires in a dotted pattern of red and yellow, reflected their brilliance on a million small mirrors. The war drums kept up their slow intimidating beat for most of the time. Even during the hours of darkness, drummers were relieved by more drummers, as the slow continual beat sent out its almost eerie message.

Northern spies had reported the southern forces to be south of the village of Yani, but they were making no attempt to advance. What the southern forces had been doing was organising second and third lines of defence, something that the spies didn't see, and something that, for some reason, had not occurred to Lord Barek. The second line of defence for the southern forces would be the Border House, east and west from the River Powle to the River Zarh, and the third line of defence would be Castle Tezz.

As the blue-white of winter closed roads, and brought normal movements to a stand-still, only those concerned with the war effort continued to toil in the harsh winter conditions. Southern carpenters and engineers especially, were constantly active in the making of bridges to span the river Zarh. Finishing touches to huge crossbows were being carried out before being assembled. Long bolts that would be propelled hundreds of yards were being fitted with metal heads the size of two hands together.

Two months passed, two months during which Edmund continued to practise his skills with power and sword. Two months during which soldiers dressed as farmers, or were concealed in wine barrels continued to head for Penste castle. Two months just did not seem long enough to make the plan work. The snow did not relent. The winds dropped, and soon, snow drifts up to several feet deep were commonplace.

It was on one cold morning when the snow was knee deep the Torran called Karl and Edmund. 'Time to go hunting', he informed them.

After they had packed a few possessions and assured Edmunds squire the he would be well treated, for it was deemed too dangerous a journey to include him, they left the camp. To be clad in heavy winter clothes would have been too restrictive, and so each dressed themselves in their wizard's robes.

Although seemingly of thin material, the robes were remarkably warm and comfortable. The horses didn't appear to feel the cold either; in fact they looked as though they were enjoying the exercise. Only the faces of the wizards displayed any sign that this was the winter period. The icy winds had turned their noses a reddish pink, and this was something that Karl seized upon to joke with Torran.

All the fun and laughter suddenly stopped as the three companions crossed the River Zarh. From here they would have to tread with extreme caution, as northern spies, some in disguise as friends of the south, would be hiding in the most unlikely of places.

They travelled towards the south in the direction of the coast road. This, being wide, would in all probabilities be passable due to its constant use. In contrast, the narrow roads and country lanes that they were now crossing presented many problems: not only was the snow a problem, but there might have been traps hidden and snags placed there by the northern mercenaries. For this reason the horses were allowed to travel at a steady pace. Animals can sense hidden danger underfoot, and so all obstacles avoided, they arrived at the Watch.

The Watch was an immense stone structure rising some one hundred and fifty feet from the seas edge. Its purpose was obscure; some thought it to be a lookout tower, others thought it to be a building of mysterious magic from a bygone age. Whatever the case, no-one had entered the Watch for some considerable time.

Torran, Karl and Edmund would be the first as they dismounted, and cautiously moved towards it. It did cross their minds that the northern forces might be using it, but on inspection, it was decided that no-one had opened the door for some years.

Spiders had made webs that decorated each corner of the door, and although caked with rust, the bolts slid easily as though well oiled; the door opened with a slight groan. Before them, another door revealed that the walls were more than two yards thick which added to the puzzle of its use.

The second door also opened with comparative ease to reveal a gigantic staircase spiralling upwards.

'What's up there I wonder?' Said Edmund pointing to the staircase.

'Let's investigate. It might serve us as a lookout tower', said Karl as he moved towards it.

Torran didn't join in the conversation. He was too busy trying to understand the strange markings on the walls and floor. Ancient runes were in evidence throughout, and continually decorated the walls and the stairs, as the three companions moved slowly upwards.

It was a tiring climb, but when they eventually reached the top of the stairs, another door stood before them. It was larger than the other doors, and it was constructed out of black wood crossed with metal straps and studs.

More ancient runes decorated the door on both wood and metal. Torran brushed away the webs of gossamer that blanketed the writings.

'Have you never been here before?' Asked Karl.

'I've never been inside', said Torran as he tried to decipher the lettering. 'But the building has been here for as long as I can remember'.

'This stonework must be ancient then', said Edmund. Suddenly, as though a light had been switched on, he turned to Torran and Karl. 'That's it', he said.

'That's it?' Karl was confused.

'It's a prison', shouted Edmund triumphantly.

'A what?' Said Torran.

'Listen', continued Edmund. 'Do you remember what the Goddess Calia said; 'Calm the ancient into stone'. This is a prison for the ancient Lord Zelfen. The writings must have some sort of hold over him'.

'By the gods I think he has it', said Torran.

'Try to gather you will, Karl. Try to use your powers', said Edmund.

Karl tried, but it was as though he had never had power. 'I can't', he said.

Torran then tried but found that within the walls of the Watch; even he could not muster his power. It was quite a sensation for him, and one that he had yearned for many times over: to be mortal. He sat for a while and thought about the riddle. 'Of course', he said, making the other two look up. 'Edmund has the know of three. Edmund knows the third line which is, calm the ancient into stone. That's it, we have to get Lord Zelfen here so that he is powerless'.

'But what about the last line? It could mean the fourth wizard, but there isn't a fourth wizard. Whatever it is, it seems that we three have to decide about it', said Karl.

'Who would think of looking for a prison amongst farmlands and farmers', said Edmund.

'Come on, there's no time to study just now', said Karl as he began to descend the stone staircase.

Edmund and Torran followed, and when they had reached the bottom, they rested and ate a meal of dried meats and fruit before continuing their journey.

The coast road that they followed edged the Messica Ocean, and although covered by several inches of snow, it was easy to follow. The blanket of undisturbed whiteness appeared to continue endlessly and their tracks were soon covered by the intermittent snow fall.

Three more nights were spent in makeshift shelters around open fires before the first signs of troop movement were sighted. They were but a day's ride from Penste Harbour, and hidden by a high divisional hedgerow, when they noticed a group of ten northerners on horseback. It was obvious that eight of the riders were northern soldiers by the uniforms they were wearing, but two wore the distinctive black cloaks of spies.

Torran was sure that he had seen the two spies before, but that couldn't be, or could it? The northern troops continued to ride in the direction of the wizards. The two black cloaked figures were pointing to where the wizards were hiding. As the northern soldiers drew closer, the two spies held back. Then, to the surprise of the wizards and the confusion of the northerners, the spies attacked the soldiers.

"Come on', shouted Torran, and Karl and Edmund followed.

Three black bladed swords slid from their scabbards and were immediately put to use. The confused northern soldiers were totally bewildered as they tried in vain to counter the unexpected attack. The first to reach Torran had barely time to raise his sword before it fell from his unresponsive hands, the white of the snow now patterned with red stains.

Another soldier who was attacking Edmund began to bring down his sword in an overhead swing.

Edmund flipped his sword to change his grip, blocked with one arm, and then sank his sword dagger-style into the northerner's chest.

Karl had already dispatched two soldiers and was fighting alongside the spies; it was soon over. The heads of the spies still covered with a black mask to protect their identity, they knelt before the three lords.

'I know you not', said Torran which was almost the truth, 'and now is not the time for introductions because I'm sure that you have business elsewhere'. Torran was not being unkind, he was releasing them and allowing them to retain the anonymity that they preferred, and which came with the job. One of the spies looked up at Torran, his eyes betraying a smile of gratitude behind the mask. 'By your leave, my lords', he said.

'Best in the business, said Torran as the two black cloaked figures departed and were lost from view.

With Edmund's help, the bodies of the fallen northerners disappeared beneath the ground. Karl summoned wind to blow fresh snow over the area, and which completely covered all signs of a skirmish.

The three wizards continued their journey in the direction of Penste Harbour, keeping their cover as much as was possible, because any thoughtless move could, and most certainly would lead to further conflict. It would also give the enemy a warning of their presence. The wizards didn't want recognition at this time.

When they arrived, the wizards viewed Penste Harbour with a sense of loss. The village was, but for a few buildings, laid waste. Evidence of the northern occupation was not only abundant, it was horrifying: a mound of human remains was piled high on the outskirts.

Snowflakes fell on faces masked in death: old faces, young faces, men, women and children's faces, all were showing their brutal end at the hands of the northern soldiers.

As he looked at the needless waste of life, Edmund remembered his friend, Secc. He remembered the way in which his life had ended in the jeers, the sadistic laughter, as Secc's body was torn apart. A green nimbus suddenly surrounded Edmund; his anger reached the point of no return. Torran turned to see Edmund shaking with uncontrollable rage, as the green glow became difficult to look at in its brightness. 'No!' shouted Torran.

'Edmund!' shouted Karl.

It was to no avail. All that Edmund could see was the battle horses pulling apart the body of his friend, Secc.

The ground under the fallen villagers softened, became as quicksand and slowly, gently, the bodies disappeared.

Edmund stood rigid as his mood continued to blacken: green lightning fizzled and cracked all about him, his hands pointing forward.

Green octane brilliance, a light of pure energy shot forth.

'Earth and Stone', he commanded in a voice that none dare disobey.

There came a distant rumbling sound that gradually came closer, then louder, then louder still. It was as though the earth itself was crying out for vengeance. The air, the trees, the whole ground shook in angry reply.

Soldiers in the harbour village at first thought that a storm was gathering; it was. Then, as the sound grew even louder and the earth began to shake, soldiers started running in all directions.

Torran and Karl threw a protective shield about themselves as houses began to crumble. Stones flew about like catapulted missiles, and finding their targets, brought injury and death to the fleeing soldiers.

Screams of mercy went unheeded as the earth opened up in several places, swallowing whole groups of terrified northerners.

Suddenly, the green light disappeared, Edmund fell to the ground.

'Hurry!' shouted Torran. 'Help me get Edmund to his horse. We must get away quickly'.

Torran and Karl hurried to where Edmund lay in a semiconscious state. Gently they lifted him to his horse and secured him.

Northern soldiers began to rally, what was left of them, and Edmund was vulnerable.

The wizards rode with as much haste as would the circumstances permit towards Penste Castle. Travelling through fields proved to be hard going, and twice they saw the results of man traps: the victims lying in death's estate and partially covered with a veil of snow. For just over two days they travelled continuously until finally they saw the grey walls of Penste castle.

CHAPTER TEN

PENSTE CASTLE WAS DIFFERENT to most other castles in that it was more of a market that a military fortress. Accommodation and administration centres were built into the castle walls leaving an open space in the centre. This huge courtyard with evidence of small enclosures and make shift stalls, was the area where, and in which farmers and merchants conducted their business.

There was little in the way of defences other than a few soldiers, who acted mainly as a policing force. Accommodation, however, soon became of primary importance.

The problem presented itself due to the influx of soldiers from the southern defence force, and the Lord of Penste Castle solved the problem by turning the administration blocks into a temporary barracks.

When the three wizards arrived they were allocated private quarters by the Lord of Penste in his own chambers. There they rested until Edmund was fully recovered and had regained his strength.

Many conversations took place during this period of rest. Edmund, knowing how the power could control him, and how dangerous that could be, suggested that he would rather have had a life without the responsibility of power and wizardry. It was too dangerous in the hands of a novice.

Torran and Karl agreed, but with reservations. These centred on the fact that to defeat magic, magic must be used, otherwise all would be lost and chaos would rule. Torran promised to instruct Karl and Edmund in meditation techniques that would enable them to adjust to the force of the power they held, and to be able to have more control over it, especially for Edmund because of his uncontrollable temper.

Other conversations included the defence of Penste Castle, but the talk of war was limited, especially in public. The Lord of Penste, a white haired man of some considerable years, disagreed with the subject of war although it was virtually at his gates. It was one reason why Penste Castle became a market rather than a fortress. In conversation he said, 'When a person reaches a certain age, he gives up the fancies of the young and foolish. My dream is to live in harmony with my surrounds and my people. When people strive for power it creates flaws, and through these flaws they are always defeated so there is no point. Seek peace and harmony, and in that you will find successes'.

'Then what if, as now, a strange and warlike army comes to your gate in order to destroy you like they did the village of Penste Harbour?' Said Karl.

'What will they gain by their actions? They will not gain friends or comrades. There is no wealth to speak of in the castle. What would be the sense of such an action without gain or favour?'

'They would gain your lands and your castle'.

'And who would work the land? Who would tend the livestock, and who would take care of the castle if all within were put to the sword. Without working the land there would be no grain, no harvest. The army would starve and have to leave. They would gain nothing'.

Karl saw no point in continuing a conversation with a Lord who was plainly bonkers, although in one way he was right, in a wrong sort of way. What the Lord of Penste did not understand was the mentality of the northern soldiers and their commanders. He also did not understand that the person behind all the trouble, Lord Zelfen, was not interested in crops or livestock, or indeed the welfare of any community, he was only interested in himself.

Edmund was mesmerised, he listened intently to the Lord of Penste whenever he spoke. His commanding air and common sense, coupled with the wisdom of age, added poetry to his thoughts and rhythm to his words. However, this would have been perfect in any theatre, except the theatre of war where no common sense prevailed.

For a further month they stayed at the castle, and during this time Edmund and Karl received instruction from Torran, and words of wisdom from the Lord of Penste about the futility of war.

Winter was now almost at its turning point, heavy snow still fell in the high places, and cold winds still swept the plains, but there was a freshness creeping over the land. Penste Castle had been well equipped with man power and weapons, provisions and drinking water. All this achieved under the noses of the northern spies. Satisfied that all that could be done was done, the three wizards thanked the Lord of Penste for his hospitality, said their goodbyes, and then headed once more to check on the allied defence lines.

During the next three months the cold spell kept up its momentum as the wizards, after collecting Edmund's squire, journeyed between the allied armies to give words of encouragement to the troops. In conference with the commanders they discussed the possibility of attack rather than defence. This was not as Lord Brin had ordered, but if the advantage could be achieved by the action, it had to be considered.

The snow still fell as spring approached. It had been a harsh winter, and early sunshine that played upon the sparkling crystals, had little effect. The southern soldiers, however, began to feel tenseness in the air. Birds failed to sing their favourite morning melodies . . . the quiet had returned.

On the bleak shoreline of the Sea of Winds near Penste Harbour, things were different; great activity was in progress. Sea birds screamed their disapproval at the trespass upon their nesting sites as armour was removed from its wrappings and coated with preserving oils. Swords and knives were being sharpened, leather softened and supplies checked.

More ships had braved the winter seas to bring horses and supplies to the northern base camp. Five ships had begun the journey but only two had reached their destination. The remaining three ships had been beaten continuously by heavy gales in high seas and had sunk. The crews, supplies and livestock were given a watery resting place far from the battle preparations. Food for a hundred sea creatures, they waited without fear as they prepared to play their final role in the cycle of life.

The quiet of the following morning was broken by the sound of music; the shrill sound of the northern flutes coupled with the slow beat of war drums. A thousand pairs of booted feet began to march westward. Black Eagle banners hung limply in the still air. Spies and guides preceded line upon line of northern soldiers to forewarn of ambush . . . it had begun.

Behind the invading army were siege engines all pulled by teams of dray horses. There were catapults, great cross bows and rams. Penste Harbour village by contrast, was now deserted. It stood by the sea, a ghost town lost in dreams of past habitation, watching as two ships began their journey home in calmer waters. A hundred souls cried out from windows of ghost-like houses as they re-enacted their last moments of earthbound existence.

With the long period of rest without much exercise, the northern soldiers tired easily, and by nightfall they had only travelled a half days journey. The commanders were none too pleased, but allowed the army to camp for the night.

Soon, the orange glow of campfires had spread their light for all to see; the sound of war drums adding substance to the eerie glow. By the end of the second days march, the northern army was in sight of Penste Castle rising defiantly out of the distant plains. A lone soldier pointed towards it, and amid much cheering he shouted. 'Tomorrow we shall see'.

Reported by spies on the first day, news of the approaching army was dispatched by messenger from Penste Castle, and was received by General Xante, the commanding officer of the southern army encampment by the River Zarh. From there a messenger sped to Castle Tezz to inform Lord Brin of troop movements, and to request engagement.

Within the southern encampment soldiers were continually busy preparing for battle. Orders were being shouted, arms collected and sharpened, and horses saddled as the southern army at Zarh prepared to advance. Teams of muscle bound engineers began heaving at thick ropes and slowly, inch by inch, the wooden structured bridges began to edge out into the river. Four men stood on each structure ready to leap to the far bank to secure the bridges with ropes. All that remained was the order to come from Lord Brin, and the southerners would march forward in defence of their land.

The young men of the northern forces were in a joyous mood. They were convinced that the forthcoming battle would be an easy victory. Songs of ancient battles were being sung around huge campfires, and minstrels and fools lightened the mood even further.

Only the older soldiers, veterans of many battles were silent and slept little that night. Most sat alone carefully cleaning or sharpening weapons and reflecting their younger days. In their minds no battle was ever won; there were no victors, only better fighting men and a lot of wasted lives.

However, they would serve their chosen lord with all of their strength, even unto death: this was their vow of service.

A cold but fresh morning greeted both young and old alike as it eased itself over the land. A light wind swept loose snow into piles at the side of tents as long robed priests, some extolling the virtues of the north, walked between them giving rising soldiers blessings of good fortune and strength. Chanting the name of Lord Zelfen, they assured victory for those who would march to war in his name. The tempo of the war drums increased as soldiers rallied to the call of their commanders, and as musicians played on flute and trumpet, the order was given.

'We march for the north'.

Lines of soldiers in block formation began a slow march forward. Hundreds of faces displayed a variety of emotions: fear, aggression, shame, determination. The one thought that was common to all was that of self-preservation, the determination to survive regardless of cost. A massive trail of compacted snow marked the northern advance, as closer and closer they came to Penste Castle.

The sun was directly above them when they sighted the southern flags of Penste blowing high in the wind.

As orders were shouted the northern army separated into two sections, each section taking a different side of Penste Castle, and as they approached, the siege flags of Penste were hoisted on the battlements.

By the late afternoon the northern army had completely surrounded the castle, and an envoy was dispatched to demand that Lord Penste surrender in the face of an obviously greater force. As the envoy approached, and to make the castle appear as normal as possible, soldiers sent by Lord Brin concealed themselves from view.

The gates were opened and the envoy was admitted; a courtesy afforded to those who would seek a peaceful solution. He viewed the scene in the courtyard which was not unlike a market, and smiled. Then, in an arrogant manner, he addressed the Lord of Penste who had been waiting for him.

'My lord, I bear you a message of good intention. Surrender yourselves. Surrender your castle. We are not barbarians and we wish you no harm. We would not enjoy unnecessary suffering by north and south alike. Open your gates to us and let us be friends. I give you my promise that those who would wish to leave shall have safe conduct. Those who would wish to stay I give promises of fair treatment. What say you my Lord of Penste?'

The Lord of Penste Castle, clearly agitated by the envoys approach, paced the snow covered ground a little, and then looked directly into the face of the envoy: their eyes met. The Lords manner was soft, almost reassuring as he spoke in clear tones. 'Envoy, I have honoured the time served custom by listening to your words. I have listened to your arrogant manner with more than a little curiosity, but the northern army's reputation has preceded them. They trespass upon this land and without quarter they slaughter innocent men, women and children. These actions tend not to support your promises, envoy. It is my decision, and with a certain amount of reluctance that I ask you to leave this place as you came. I would add that when, and if we meet again, my ancestors would damn my soul if I were not to seek vengeance for the atrocities that have been committed by those who you would want me to call friend'.

The manner of the Lord of Penste clearly unnerved the envoy. He bowed, turned, and quickly left: the huge wooden gates closing noisily behind him.

'Apart from a few farmers and guards, there was no-one else', said the envoy when he had returned to make his report.

'I don't like this', said a northern commander. 'The Lord of Penste is either a fool, or he knows something that we do not. Did you notice any traps or hidden obstacles?'

'Not one. It's only a farmers market after all. I say we just go in and take the castle. It cannot withstand our numbers'.

'Well, if you think it will be as easy as you say, take two dozen men and scale the walls of the castle tonight when they are sleeping'.

'By your command'.

As usual the night was cold; an icy wind carried its bite below a cloud covered moon. All around Penste Castle fires of the northern encampment glowed, crackled, and sent tiny sparks upwards to decorate the dark night sky.

A group of twenty young northern soldiers crept slowly forward, and towards the grey walls of Castle Tezz, each carrying a length of rope with a hook attached. The envoy led the way; he felt confident that he would be honoured when he opened the gates for the northern army.

He didn't feel anything else, except a sharp stabbing pain, as an arrow drove through his neck. He fell backwards and sat down on the ground, his lifeblood contrasting with the white carpet of snow. A question that would not be answered was written on his tortured expression; his eyes closed for the last time.

The other northern soldiers looked to the battlement just as a flight of arrows were loosed in their direction. Not one of the twenty northern soldiers returned to their tents that night, instead they laid cold and stiff where they had fallen.

The next morning was the same as before, no armed men could be seen on the battlements, and every soldier was out of sight. As an act of chivalry on the part of the Lord of Penste, a flag was raised to inform the northern commanders that they could, without fear of attack, collect the bodies of their fallen comrades.

'No! No! No! This Lord of Penste Castle is no fool. He keeps his soldiers in hiding during the day so that we cannot count his strength. Well so be it, we will starve them out', said a northern general to his staff.

Unbeknown to the northern commanders, Penste Castle was well equipped and well stocked, and could easily last for two or three months without having the need for supplies. The snow had helped by giving them the means by which fresh drinking water could be collected and stored. Still the northern army waited.

By the River Zarh, the southern troops commanded by General Xante were in an expectant mood when a rider carrying dispatches arrived at the encampment. He was escorted to the tent of the general, and there he handed him the message from Lord Brin. At last it was the authority that would allow him to order the advance. With a smile of satisfaction, the general approached his chiefs of staff.

'My friends', he began. 'May the gods be with us this day and guide us. We march for Penste Castle'.

News of the order quickly spread throughout the encampment. Soldiers hurried to their designated areas. Those who could write composed letters to their loved ones, and senior officers gave talks on caution and defence to those who would listen. Within one hour of the order being received, lines and lines of southern troops were ready to march.

General Xante sat astride his war horse and felt pride in his soldiers, a pride borne out of achievement, dedication and respect. 'For the south!' he shouted. He turned his horse and began a slow walk towards the bridges.

The reply was a deafening cheer as the southern soldiers began to march after him. To see them off the war drums, accompanied by musicians, began to play a marching tune as the bridges were crossed and virgin snow flattened underfoot.

After crossing the bridges, the army separated into two divisions. One travelled to the north of Penste Castle and one to the south.

The weather was bitterly cold, but not one complaint was uttered, even when no fires could be lit did anyone complain. Soldiers huddled together for warmth during the brief periods of rest. It was explained to them that General Xante empathised with the men under his command, but dare not light a fire. If they were negligent and the northerners learned that a relief army was on its way to Castle Penste, the attack upon the castle would be immediate. This would also result in the northern army gaining a secure foothold in the south, and the loss of many southern lives.

It was on the third night that both divisions reached their respective destinations, and fires were lit to warm the soldiers and to dry clothes.

In front of the southern army, and at a distance, they could see the glow of the northern campfires. They looked impressive against the black velvet of the night sky. In the southern camp the fires grew in size bringing warmth to the soldiers who, for the last three days, had suffered the cold for the sake of their countrymen and their land.

It was only a short while before they were noticed by the northerners, and pandemonium quickly followed. Questions were asked of the spies, the lookouts. No-one knew how the southern army had managed to reach their present location. They were supposed to be at least three days march away by the River Zarh.

Northern commanders gathered in a bid to find a solution to the obvious pincer movement by a very clever general, and learning who that general was, sent shivers down each spine. It was agreed that action had to be taken, and taken quickly. Should they turn tail, and under the cover of darkness run for the coast?

Should they try to take the castle in the hope of securing a defence there, or should they stand and fight in the hope of a victory. It was a cruel choice, but one that had to be made, and soon.

Meanwhile at Castle Tezz, and because of the unavoidable conflict which was about to take place, preparations were being made for the elderly nobles and the infirm to be escorted to the coastal village of Caspe. Then, if all was lost, they would travel by boat across Lands Pass to a new country. Once there, they would seek protection from the northern armies. The ageing Lord and Lady Tezz would lead the group, and would in turn be escorted by twelve of Lord Brin's personal guard.

Planned for late in the evening, wagons were loaded with supplies for the journey, and when night came, dark and cold, the small party set forth. All were wrapped in dark woollen blankets, and not only to protect them against the ice cold winds. It was hoped that northern spies would find them difficult to see if they wore dark clothes and lit no fires.

The covered wagons containing the ageing nobility and their travelling companions, and guarded by twelve of the finest soldiers, made their way along the side of the River Powle towards the Forest of Frezfir. Some snow still fell in slow motion: shapes of sky flakes that drifted down to join the deepening mass.

The travellers were finding it ever increasingly difficult as the wagons ploughed through the deep drifts.

On more than one occasion during the night, the soldiers had to urge the horses forwards lest they stand and freeze in the ice cold weather.

Neither a murmur, nor word of complaint was heard from the occupants of the wagons. Huddled together for warmth, they told each other stories of times long past. Lord Tezz sang to them of happier times. He sang to them of the Lord of Ice and Fire. Sometimes he sat in silence remembering his own private stories.

On the morning after the third night of travelling, the village of Hib was sighted in the distance. All were overcome with joy as the prospect of a warm room and hot bathing water filled their thoughts.

A wide natural bridge across the River Powle formed the main road into the stone built village, and Lord and Lady Tezz, for the sake of the other travellers who also longed for somewhere warm to rest, requested that they travel the rest of the way during the daylight hours. The escort, although disagreeing with the idea, saw the sense of it and proceeded with caution.

It was about midday when the tired group arrived and they climbed down from the wagons to stretch their legs. Soldiers who had been posted there by Lord Brin were quick to secure accommodation, and Lord and Lady Tezz were escorted under protective guard to a small inn. There they found the rooms reasonably comfortable after three nights in a wagon and were soon asleep.

While the nobles rested, guards were posted at all entrances and exits to keep away inquisitive locals and as a protective measure in case of an attack by northern skirmishers. The other members of the party were equally looked after and were quite enjoying their celebrity status.

For two days the party rested in the village of Hib and once refreshed, they continued their journey to the village of Caspe by the coast. Travelling once again by night was not welcomed, but Lord Tezz saw the sense of it. The air was still cold and the sky clear of clouds. A thousand stars twinkled against a velvet-black background, and a full moon reflected its light on the carpet of white that stretched before them.

Occasionally, a small nocturnal animal would scurry away out of the path of the wagons large wheels, and the heavy tread of the horses that pulled them. They were not, however, the only creatures of the night that stood and watched the lonely procession as it slowly ploughed its way through the untouched whiteness. A pair of hooded eyes viewed the scene from a distance. The rider stroked his braided locks, and then with the information firmly locked in his mind, he rode away with as much speed as possible.

The morning dawned bright and warm: unusual for that time of year, and a possible signal that winter was almost over. The three wagons halted and began to set up a camp for the day.

One of the soldier escorts informed Lord Tezz that they would soon be entering the Forest of Frezfir. From then on they would be warmer, and sheltered from any severe weather conditions that might arise. This was indeed good news, and it gave encouragement to the travellers. After resting throughout the day, and as the light began to fade, the party readied themselves for another nights travel.

Suddenly there was a commotion amongst the soldiers and Lord Tezz went to enquire what the problem was.

'My Lord', said one of the soldiers. 'One of the soldiers on sentry duty has disappeared. We can find no trace of him'.

The Lord of Tezz, a veteran of many battle plans, feared the worst. 'Soldier', he said.

'My Lord?'

'As quietly but as quickly as you can, head for the forest. It may give us some protection'.

'Against whaaa'. The soldier's words remaining unsaid fell sideways with a battle axe wedged into his back.

'To the forest', shouted Lord Tezz. 'We are discovered'.

The wagons began to move towards the forest as the soldiers scanned the area for any signs of the enemy. None could be seen.

'The Lord of Tezz turned to his wife and smiled. 'Pass me my sword woman'.

'It's been a long time husband', she replied as she opened a bundle to produce a fine bladed sword.

'Indeed it has, but I haven't forgotten how to use it'. He gazed at the shining metal remembering how he learned its uses, and when he had to use it. A hundred and one thoughts crept across the mirrors of his mind.

An arrow took another of the soldiers, and again the enemy was unseen. The Forest of Frezfir stood before them and they quickly entered, regrouped, then scanned for any signs of the enemy.

'There are demons at work here', said one of the elderly travellers.

'Nonsense', said Lord Tezz. 'It's an old method of fighting. It comes from the forest people of some snow covered land or other to frighten their enemies'.

As Lord Tezz described the fighting method, it came to life as figures in pure white furs emerged from the snow dunes at the edge of the forest.

Spending what few bolts they had for their crossbows, the soldiers drew their swords and engaged the enemy in close quarter combat. These were brave men, and although outnumbered three to one, the soldiers gave a good account of the skills they had learned.

The light dusting of snow in the forest turned red as soldier and mercenary fell fatally wounded to be united in death. Eventually after a ferocious fight, the last soldier was overcome by sheer numbers, and fell beneath a hail of sword thrusts.

Lord Tezz with head held high marched towards the advancing mercenaries. His pleas for the safety of the womenfolk were ignored, as were the pleas for the infirm.

His anger rose with the unnecessary and barbaric attitude and he could no longer contain his feelings. In his mind he relived a hundred battles of his youth as, sword held high, he charged. He cut down the first mercenary and severely wounded a second, and then a third. For just a moment the mercenaries were stunned by this unexpected action from an old man. Recovering quickly though, and in front of the Lady of Tezz and her companions, the mercenaries took a terrible revenge upon the Lord of Tezz. Not one inch of his body was left unmarked.

The Lady of Tezz was in a state of shock, and she was oblivious to the sadistic deaths being met by the rest of her party. When her turn came she felt nothing but a longing to be with her husband: it was soon over. The mercenaries looted the wagons for supplies, gathered the horses, then left.

There had been little resistance from the elderly, and now they lay in death's estate with only the trees to remember their final hour. The body of the Lady of Tezz lay in a final embrace with her husband; her unseeing eyes gazing into his.

It was several hours later when, disturbed because of a strange and terrible dream, a woodcutter camping within the forest and on his way through to the village of Hib, continued his journey early.

As he shuffled through the forest with his heavy load, a feeling that he was being watched haunted his every step. The trees seemed to whisper in the semi light: voices in the wind and trees guided him, and caused him to follow a certain path.

Many times he stopped to listen or to cast glances either side of the path he was following.

At one time he thought he saw a black shadow moving cat like close to the ground. He dismissed it as a figment of his imagination. Another time when his heart began to beat faster, he was sure that he had seen a pair of green luminous eyes watching, following.

He had travelled this forest week after week, month after month for many years, never had he felt this way. He quickened his step to almost a run. As he neared the edge of the forest, he came across a scene of terrible destruction; he came upon the content of his dream.

He hurried away towards the village of Hib, convinced that the forest itself had guided him. When he arrived he informed the guard of the terrible slaughter, and after confirmation was obtained, he continued towards Castle Tezz.

Castle Tezz was by now, and because of the forthcoming war, a hive of activity. Designated the main planning location by Lord Brin, messages came in and messengers were sent out frequently.

Update reports on enemy movements, food, clothing and weapons shortages were dealt with, with military proficiency. Battle plans were discussed and discussed again until perfection was reached.

Satisfied that all that could be done was done, Lord Brin summoned Karl, Torran and Edmund to his war room. He told them that he was ready to go to join the southern forces encampment near the village of Yani. The wizards who had arrived at Castle Tezz shortly after the departure of Lord and lady Tezz, began to make the necessary arrangements and preparations.

On the evening before setting out to join the southern forces, Lord Brin was restless. Never before had he been in such a pensive mood. He felt that something was not quite right but could not evaluate the feeling. He was pacing the floor of his study, deep in thought, when Lord Torran entered.

'Would you like to share your thoughts?' Asked a concerned Lord Torran.

'No, my friend, it is nothing but old age'.

'Look who's talking', said Torran with a smile.

'Ha! A friend you are indeed who cheers me in this hour'. Lord Brin made light of his mood, although a deep concern continued to eat away at his very being. Something he felt was just not quite as it should be.

He slept little that night, giving up his attempts in the early hours to pace the corridors of Castle Tezz. A call from the gate snapped him out of his deepest thoughts.

As he walked down into the courtyard, he noticed a bedraggled figure being escorted towards the reception area; he followed. Quiet whispers were heard, but when he entered the room, all went deathly silent.

'Well?' Said Lord Brin. 'Am I a stranger in my own house that no person speaks when I enter?'

The guards and the stranger lowered their eyes. They could not hold the gaze of their lord. For what seemed to be an age no-one spoke, then one of the guards looked sorrowfully towards Lord Brin. 'My Lord', he began, but was interrupted by the stranger who told the guards to leave which, to Lord Brin's astonishment, they did.

'Who are you, fellow, that my own guards obey your commands? Lord Brin was puzzled.

'My Lord Brin of Castle Tezz, I am but a humble woodcutter. I tend with dedication, the Forest of Frezfir in his name'.

'Truly a worthy occupation', said Lord Brin.

'My Lord', continued the woodcutter, 'your guards left this room at my request, for the message I bear is grave indeed. It would not be seemly for a soldier to see his lord in distress'.

It was then that Lord Brin began to understand. The woodcutter was from the Forest of Frezfir, and Lord and Lady Tezz were to travel in that direction. 'Has something happened to Lord and Lady Tezz?' He asked with concern. He began to shiver as the woodcutter continued his story.

'My lord', said the woodcutter. 'It appears that an escorted party of noble men and women were ambushed by mercenaries at the edge of the Forest of Frezfir. My Lord, their deaths were painful and none survived. It grieves me to be the bearer of this ill news but I am stronger than most. I am, my Lord, your servant'.

'You have indeed served me well, woodcutter. What of the bodies of the fallen?'

'Might I ease your pain, my Lord, by saying that although his ring was missing, I recognised the Lord of Tezz. By what I saw it was without doubt that he gave a good account of himself before he fell. My Lord, I travelled here safe in the knowledge that the people of the village of Hib, loyal subjects, my Lord, will tend to the fallen before they are brought back to Castle Tezz'.

'Please convey to the people of Hib, my gratitude', said Lord Brin.

'By your leave, my Lord'. The woodcutter bowed, turned and departed.

When Lord Brin walked back out into the courtyard, he was finding it difficult to keep his self-control. He noticed that the flags of the castle had been lowered out of respect. Two guards stood in salute by the banner of Tezz with swords held in reverse. All felt saddened by the loss. Lord Brin now knew why he had felt strange of late. He had felt the last moments of his father and mother, the Lord and lady of Tezz. The time for mourning, however, was not at this moment. A strong willed man held back his emotions for another time.

As daybreak came and light crept over the castle walls, Lord Brin ordered the guard to turn out.

A bell rang in slow time and people came out of the buildings to gather in the courtyard, for the sound of the bell indicated a death amongst high-ranking dignitaries. Karl, Torran and Edmund joined Lord Brin in front of the crowds.

'My friends' began Lord Brin. 'It is my hope first of all that the Lords Karl, Torran and Edmund will not be angered by what I have to say in public, for it concerns them especially. It also is the concern of all who dwell within the walls of Castle Tezz, and for this reason I have asked you all to attend. 'Early this morning I received a message, a message that has broken my heart, but I am strong. It is my hope that you too will be strong for there are sad times ahead. Some days past, mercenaries attacked and killed without mercy, all who left for the village of Caspe.'

There was a cry of disbelief. Lord Brin had no need to mention names, everyone knew. The crowd dispersed slowly, some weeping openly, not able to come to terms with the senseless murders of the first Lord of Tezz, his wife and their companions. Lord Brin invited the wizards into his private study to confer with them about the incident. Lord Torran was in a raging temper, and swore by all, even unto his own death, to avenge the killing of his friend, the first Lord of Tezz.

Lord Karl held back his emotions as he embraced his father in a bid to comfort him.

'We march north' said Lord Brin after a while. 'From there I give Lord Torran leave to seek justice: to return only when justice has been served'.

'I accept your charge willingly', said Torran.

It was about midday when the lords, along with a small troop of soldiers from Lord Brin's personal guard, readied to leave to join the southern forces in the north. Four banners were held proudly as the procession left Castle Tezz. On the battlements, the flag of the first Lord of Tezz was raised once more in salute to the departing soldiers. It would stay flying in the wind until the soldiers returned to their homes.

CHAPTER ELEVEN

OR THREE DAYS THE lords travelled before reaching the Border
House. There they rested, and then inspected in his absence, the
plans that Captain Dac'ra had made for defence. As was expected,
they were precise in every detail. Tamur, Lord Edmund's squire, would
not stay away from the battle lines this time, and he insisted that he
accompany his lord. He stated that it was traditional for a squire to do
so in times of war.

The lords had no argument, and welcomed him as they began the
last stage of their journey. For a further two days they travelled, and
on the evening of the second day, they saw the fires of the southern
encampment.

'Let's try to sneak in past the guards', said Torran who was in a
mischievous mood. The attempt failed. They were challenged more
than three hundred yards from the southern encampment.

'Who advances?' Shouted an unseen guard.

'Lord Brin of Castle Tezz', replied Lord Brin.

'Advance Lord Brin and be welcome'. The guard remained in his
hiding place.

On entering the camp, cheering erupted throughout the ranks.
Captain Dac'ra hurried over to meet them.

The formalities over with, and after commending the duty guards
for their professionalism and alertness, the lords retired for the evening.
Lord Edmund's squire, Tamur, slept at the foot of Edmunds tent by the
opening, again a custom that could not be argued with.

As the morning dawned and a cool wind blew away the sleep,
Torran was already pacing the ground outside of Lord Brin's tent. Lord

Brin emerged after what seemed to be an eternity for Torran, and he reminded Lord Brin of his promise.

'Alright, my friend. Go with my blessing, but be swift on your return for we have need of you'.

After a shrill whistle a big white stallion came to his masters bidding. Lord Torran climbed onto its back and was soon galloping away. After a while even the horse seemed to sense its master's mood. It gathered that this was not a pleasure trip and made a mental note to hide whenever possible. Challenged on several occasions by allied forces, Lord Torran kept close to the River Powle as he journeyed southwards.

He rode without rest, without sleep, and for two days and one night he kept up a steady pace. He crossed and doubled back on tracks to make sure that no enemy had passed him, and at length he arrived at the Border House to rest before continuing his journey. His anger had still not subsided, quite the reverse in fact. Each time he thought of his friend, Lord Tezz, his rage became almost a separate entity but within the one person, controlling, dominating.

Just as Edmund's rage had overflowed, so Lord Torran's temper was merely simmering. He tried to tell himself that an angry fighter makes mistakes but it was to no avail.

For another four days he travelled southwards, resting briefly at intervals where a clear piece of land would allow. It was then that he sighted the village of Hib resting innocently by the river, a cloudy sky obliterating the marvels that were the stars and the lemon slice of a moon. He began to cross the bridge that would lead him into the village, and a sentry at the far end challenged him.

'Who approaches the village of Hib', called the sentry.

'Who asks?' Replied Torran carefully.

'A soldier from the south'.

'Then we are friends!'

'Advance and be welcomed, friend'.

Torran moved forward to where a nervous soldier recognised him and saluted; he acknowledged the salute before proceeding to the small inn. A group of soldiers who were sat in a far corner immediately stood up as he entered.

'Please, gentlemen, there will be no formalities on my account . . . this visit', Torran tried to smile which didn't quite work, his mind was elsewhere.

'As my Lord pleases', replied a rather robust soldier before returning to his seat.

Because of his mood, Torran decided to sit alone and stare at a small stain on the wall in an attempt to focus on his mission. For the most part of the evening he was still, unmoving, lost within a deep meditative state.

It was quite late when some younger locals entered the inn. They were noisy and undisciplined, and not having the benefit of knowing who Lord Torran was, thought that the stranger wearing red and white robes was a rather comical sight. Torran slowly turned to look at the youthful ignorance and the colour drained from their faces.

After a rather large soldier had had a few quiet words with the youths they were full of remorse and apologised for their behaviour. The soldier was pleased that he had diffused the situation because, like most veterans, soldiers have a way of knowing when another is contemplating the destruction of others. They can smell death even before it happens, and Lord Torran oozed death in its cruellest sense. It reflected in his eyes even though they were still fixed on a single spot on the wall. It was written in capital letters across the lines of his features.

After a while, the large soldier walked over and joined him. 'Begging your leave, my Lord', said the soldier. 'Would I be wrong in assuming that you are on a mission to avenge the death of the Lord Tezz?'

'Does it show that much?' Said Torran.

'A soldier has a way of knowing these things, my Lord. I had expected someone sooner'. He sat on a stool opposite Lord Torran.

'Had it been my choice, I would have been here sooner', said Torran looking directly into the soldiers eyes.

'Let me and my comrades join you', said the soldier enthusiastically. 'We are good fighters and we know the area well'.

'Well-spoken soldier, but alas, I must decline your brave offer. Strange things will probably happen when I meet the mercenaries responsible for the atrocity. It would be best if I spared you and your comrades the sight and the memory of my intended actions'.

'As my Lord pleases. But please keep us in mind should you require the services of loyal soldiers'.

'That I will do'.

'Thank you, my Lord', said the soldier before returning to his companions.

In the early hours of the morning, all eyes were fixed on the figure of Lord Torran. Expressions of disbelief, of horror, and even amazement etched themselves on the faces of the onlookers. Lord Torran was glowing. Still in meditation, he was surrounded by a bright red nimbus. Tiny red and white lights appeared from out of the walls, the ceiling, and the floor; all headed towards him. It was as though he was magnetised, attracting the forces of the universe, and gathering them within.

Torran had started to teach this form of meditation to Lord Karl and Lord Edmund at Penste Castle, and had continued until shortly before he left them. He called it collective meditation.

The small crowd at the inn watched as though spellbound by the display until, as though nothing had taken place, Torran awoke from his meditation and the lights disappeared. The crowd, realising that they were staring at him, averted their gazes and busied themselves with other things.

It was, as the full light of the morning cast away the evening shadows, the time that Torran decided to depart. The large white stallion was called to carry its master. No words were spoken as Torran climbed upon the stallions back; no waves of farewell as he left the village and continued towards the Forest of Frezfir.

The snows had all but stopped falling. Soon the white carpet would disappear to reveal fresh colours, new life. It was still hard travelling through the mounds of crispy snow, and it was not until the sun was high on the following day, that he reached the scene of the ambush of Lord and lady Tezz. The area had been cleaned and tidied by the village folk, but oddments still lay beneath the trees. He lingered for a while watching the silent witnesses, as they gently swayed in the wind, fresh green buds signalling a new cycle of life.

'If you could only speak to me', he said to them.

Continuing along a trodden pathway in the snow which took him northward, he refused to rest. For three days he travelled without sleeping, without eating, and with one purpose firmly fixed in his mind.

The hills of the Dete Beacons rose before him like so many sleeping turtles. A cruel smile crossed his lips as he saw a thin trail of smoke rising in the distance. It wasn't just a cruel smile; it was the evil sadistic smile of one who intends great harm upon another.

He began to glow as he gathered his will, and dismounting, he walked forward to investigate. The white stallion made a hasty retreat to a safe distance, then turned and looked on with a certain interest in the proceedings: that being the safety of Torran.

The mercenary's camp was in a hollow sheltered from the cool wind. At least twenty men sat around small fires sharpening weapons.

Lord Torran crept slowly towards the camp, and then stood to reveal himself: he was in plain view of the mercenary camp.

There was a pause in time as the mercenaries saw, and yet did not see him. One looked directly into Lord Torran's eyes and scratched the stubble on his chin. Lord Torran saw the ring of Tezz on the mercenaries' finger, and his anger rose to unprecedented heights.

'I have come for you mercenary', said Lord Torran. His voice echoed, hovered in the air. 'I, Lord Torran, Wizard of Ice and Fire, have come to avenge the death of the first Lord of Tezz and his Lady. Be prepared, slime of the earth, to meet your makers in the black depths, for I will show no mercy'.

The mercenaries thought this spectacle rather amusing. 'A travelling player and teller of stories. How wonderful!' said one of the mercenaries.

'What a performance', said another.

Then, almost as an afterthought, the smiles faded and they charged forwards drawing their swords.

Lord Torran made no move until they were almost within striking distance. A red glow surrounded him. 'Ice', he commanded.

White octane brilliance flashed from his outstretched hands, and the side of the hill on which the mercenaries were running became like oiled glass. The ground had frozen solid; a sheet of ice covered it. The mercenaries, with no grip to hold on to, slipped to the bottom of the hill and landed in a heap. As sure footed as a mountain goat, Lord Torran walked down the iced slope towards his victims; for victims they would soon be.

The mercenaries were not used to being afraid, they did not know how to be, but they soon learned when Lord Torran shouted his next word.

'Fire', he commanded.

This time red octane light flashed from his fingers and webbed the surrounding hills. The snow and ice melted immediately, sending gallons of water into the hollow in an instant. Most of the mercenaries managed to climb away before Lord Torran issued his next command. 'Ice', he shouted. The water in the hollow froze immediately, and four men were frozen stiff from the waist down. Their deaths were agonisingly slow.

'Fight like a man, coward', shouted one of the remaining mercenaries.

Lord Torran thought that to be a contradiction, but released his will. his black bladed sword slipped into his right hand, a dagger into his left.

'Cut him to pieces!' one of them shouted as the mercenaries charged once more.

With unmatched speed, Lord Torran's weapons were replaced. He held his hands forward and shouted. 'Fire' White hot flame burned four heads to a crisp. The sword and dagger returned to his hands in an instant.

The mercenaries were still in confusion when Lord Torran, shouting the name of the first Lord of Tezz, and with blood lust in his veins, charged.

The black bladed sword severed two heads with one stroke as the dagger was buried into a northern chest. This was no ordinary combat for Lord Torran. His sadistic smile revealed his enjoyment as he blocked and parried, cut and stabbed: his anger knew no bounds.

Machine like, there was no stopping him until the last northern mercenary, pleading for mercy and giving up the ring of Tezz, was consumed in the white-hot flames of Lord Torran's promise of vengeance. A white stallion cautiously walked towards him.

Some distance away and almost at the same time, an incident, not dissimilar to Lord Torran's vengeance, was taking place in the northern part of the land. A group of southern skirmishers had set out from the village of Yani to engage the enemy and to count its forces. For five days they created havoc across the northern lines. No one seemed to be able to corner these masters of the quick strike. Sometimes in northern uniform, sometimes dressed as farmers, they penetrated deep behind the northern lines to bring disruption and confusion, rumour and death.

The northern soldiers began to lose heart amid stories of demons and strange magical happenings. Eventually, Lord Zelfen, tired of the southern bravado, searched for their minds. It wasn't an easy task even for Lord Zelfen. Thousands of minds were in the same area, but eventually he found them. The small party of skirmishers, a dozen in all, were located to the east of the village of Spard, and Lord Zelfen transported himself to where they were camped.

It was sheer effrontery on the part of the southerners; they were mingling with the northern troops in preparation for another strike. Lord Zelfen appeared in the centre of the camp, and amid the homage being paid to him, he pointed out the infiltrators. Quickly the southerners were surrounded.

They dropped their weapons, and offered no resistance, as to try to fight their way out would have been futile.

Lord Zelfen strode towards them triumphantly. 'Are these your demons?' He shouted to the attentive northerners. 'I will show you how to deal with demons'. He came close to the southern skirmishers. 'Why don't you try to make me disappear?' He turned towards a captive audience, and raised his hands for maximum effect, and then his mood changed.

He turned again and looked a southerner directly into his eyes. 'Yes, my defeated friend, I will show you what rewards you will receive for soiling this ground with your southern presence'.

He placed his hands on the southerners head. His eyes probed deep into the man's mind. At first he felt resistance, then the southerner began to tremble, and then the man began to shake as though caught in a fit.

In what was only a matter of moments, the man could not control himself at all. He began to scream, his face became shallow, his bones protruded, his eyes began to bulge and then pop out of their sockets to lie dangling by his nose. He was dead long before Lord Zelfen released him to fall by his comrade's feet.

'Come, embrace me', said Zelfen to the other southerners but they backed away. 'Well, if you do not want to play games with me, perhaps these gallant northern soldiers might let you play a little game with them'. Zelfen turned to face the northern soldiers and gave an order. 'Kill them'.

Axe, sword and mace rained down blows upon the southern skirmishers until they were mutilated beyond recognition.

'Now send them back to their own kind as a warning that I will find anyone who dares try these tactics again', said Lord Zelfen.

It was shortly after the bodies of the southerners had been tied to their horses and driven away, that Lord Zelfen met Lord Barek.

'Do you see, my Lord Barek, delays have caused this to happen. I will not tolerate any further delays, is this understood'.

'There will be no more delays, we are ready'.

'So be it. We will march on the south at first light', said Lord Zelfen with a smile.

The morning came quickly, too quickly for some who would rather have stayed at home than fight for a land that they did not want. The drums began to beat and the musicians began to play a marching tune as hundreds of soldiers readied themselves into battle formation.

There was nervousness amongst some of the soldiers, boasts amongst others as they checked their weapons and supplies.

Just before midday, the big war drums began a slow beat. Orders were shouted and repeated down the lines as the slow march began. Flags were flying, the Black Eagle banner held high, and faces were set in grim determination.

Behind the army, machines of war were being attached to teams of horses. Catapults, crossbows and larger siege engines, all having a variety of uses, all began to move with the northern tide. As they marched away, slowly the encampment emptied of all soldiers except for a token force of caretakers.

These were the lucky ones: the ones that were able to keep warm, the ones who had reasonable sleeping accommodation, and the ones who ate well and thanked their gods for the privilege of safety.

A few dogs barked at the departing soldiers, then cowered, their tails between their legs as a dark shadow passed between them. It did not speak, nor did it take any notice of the trembling animals. It followed the outgoing army with one single purpose. Once the fearsome shadow had passed, the dogs resumed their barking as though daring the intruder to return and fight. A backward glance, a pair of green, almost luminous eyes, and the dogs ran whimpering to the relative safety of a covered wagon.

The snow on the ground began to disappear rapidly as the sun played its warmth upon the land. Spring flowers with their whites, reds and yellows opened their beauty for all to see. General Xante of the southern relief forces viewed the scene before him. His plan had worked and the northern army at Penste castle had been trapped in his pincer movement. He waited now to see what their next move would be.

The northern commanders were still debating, still arguing, and still asking questions. They were waiting for answers that would explain the presence of a southern force so close. No one had the answers.

It was a strange scene: two opposing armies, each waiting for the other one to make the first move. The air was electric as soldiers from both north and south watched each other from raised platforms.

Scribes were recording the event in large volumes, and tacticians were discussing various methods of attack. As custom allowed, a messenger from the southern forces was sent to the northern lines to ask the northern commander to discuss his army's predicament. The messenger came back in pieces.

The times for discussion finally passed as the northern army commanders ordered an assault on Penste Castle. It was their misguided hope that, if the castle could be taken quickly, it would give protective cover for the northern forces, and a base from which to launch a counter stack.

The northern trumpeters sounded the battle call, and Penste Castle raised their flags to indicate that it would shortly be coming under attack. General Xante with no other options open to him ordered the southern forces to advance from both sides.

War drums sounded, minstrels played, and line after line of dedicated southern troops began a fast march forward. The banner of Lord Brin flew from a long pole held by General Xante, as he spurred his horse to lead his men.

A second surprise awaited the northern forces as they neared the walls of Penste Castle: a hundred southern bowmen lay in waiting.

When the order was given, they stood and loosed their arrows upon the unsuspecting invaders. Missiles were launched from catapults within the castle grounds, rocks, firestones and hot oil fell upon the now retreating northerners.

It was at that time that General Xante and his forces were within striking distance, and they too loosed arrows upon the invaders.

The northern forces were fast becoming disorganised and disillusioned. The unexpected had stamped on their hopes for a quick victory. It had taken the arrogance and replaced it with fear, and had taken the fear and replaced that with blind terror.

The northern army commanders could salvage nothing of their plans. They had but one alternative, to retreat, which they did, fast. The scene was complete chaos as hundreds of northern soldiers ran back the way that they had come. Weapons and machines of war were abandoned on the battlefield as fear gripped the escaping masses.

General Xante chose not to order the pursuit, because that in itself may have been a northern trap, instead he brought forward his encampment from the River Zarh to be resituated by Penste Castle. There they would wait until further orders were received. A messenger was sent with dispatches for Lord Brin, saying that only one life had been lost so far, and that a new line of defence had been established.

The northern army had suffered greatly, not only in terms of human life, as over two hundred had fallen in as many seconds, but the humiliation was almost too much to bear. The only consolation was that they were not pursued. It was actually an advantage, for unbeknown to the southern forces, and during the attack on Penste Castle, more northern forces had arrived by ship and were being landed at Penste harbour.

The southern presumption was that if more ships landed, it would be to take away the northern troops, not to land more. When the spies reported that more troops were landing, General Xante was furious with himself for underestimating the enemy as they had underestimated him.

It was fourteen days before a reply was received from Lord Brin, the message read:

> Well done, my friend.
> Do not engage the enemy unless provoked.
> Allow departure from southern soil.
>
> Brin
>
> Clearly, even Lord Brin had not expected a second northern army to land at Penste. General Xante now had to determine what actions he should take. There was not enough time to wait for another reply and so he sent the following message to Lord Brin by the fastest messenger.

Lord Brin

First Lord of Tezz and Defender of the South

Sire

Further northern forces have landed at Penste Harbour.

I have no option but to engage the enemy.

May the gods be merciful.

Xante

General Xante presumed that the northern commanders would expect the accepted form of attack: that being raids by the skirmishers in the first instance, and then the main assault. He decided against this idea simply because it was expected.

Secondly, it would almost certainly allow more time for the northern commanders to prepare, and alter their methods of formation accordingly. Southern spies soon brought information to General Xante, to the effect that the northern forces were massing for a direct assault. This gave the general an idea based upon his well proven pincer movement.

The collective opinion shared by all of the commanders was, that if a direct assault was attempted, they would be driven back by sheer weight of numbers. The general outlined his ideas after examining several methods of advance and attack. He settled on arranging his forces into four main groups. Between each of these groups he would place crossbows and catapults and use some of their own weapons against them. Last minute orders were given to the commanders and chiefs of staff.

'Gentlemen', said General Xante. 'The reason that I have directed the southern forces to be split into four main groups is as follows. Instead of sending our skirmishers out, which is what the northern commanders expect, we will launch a major offensive which is what they least expect.

To confuse the northern commanders even further, the four divisions will act like skirmishers independently whilst remaining part of the whole. Based upon the pincer movement, they will not only attack head on, but we will attack the flanks as well. This I believe will affect maximum disruption with minimum loss of life. It will also give an indication as to their weakest points, and there we will concentrate our main drive.

Before the northerners realise that it is indeed the main assault, we will hopefully be in firm control of the situation.

The crossbows and catapults will be deployed to demolish their central mass. Then, as we advance, we will cut their forces in two. We will have a similar situation to that which we have recently enjoyed.

The centre will be the foundation on which we will achieve success. If the northern forces alter, and adopt a spearhead attack, we will simply move to the sides and let the catapults and crossbows do their work.

In the meantime, two divisions will move to the rear to prevent them from retreating. If they attempt to push forward, southern forces from Penste Castle will block their way. There are a great many fighting men at the castle, and the northerners are unaware of this fact'.

The ideas were unanimously accepted, and General Xante was congratulated on his well thought out plans. The only hope was that they would work in practice. During the following day, soldiers were instructed on the methods of attack, and that the southern forces would advance during the hours of darkness. This was a favourite ploy of the skirmishers, and one that would be expected.

The huge crossbows and catapults were taken to a forward position in readiness for the advance; an advance that would have to be as quiet as possible so as not to alert the northern commanders of the southern intentions.

As a precautionary measure against being spotted by the northern lookouts, a small party of veteran fighters was sent to silence them. That mission accomplished, all was ready, and as the day slowly came to its close and the darkness of night descended, orders were passed, repeated through the ranks, and the army began to move forwards.

Through the hours of darkness the army advanced: a silent sea of southern supremacy, which only halted when daylight came and the soldiers rested. They were close to the northern encampment, but not that close as to affect a visual sighting. The advance was resumed as the light began to fade and evening's darkness descended once more. A bright moon reflected its light upon the moving war machines, and upon a thousand metal helmets.

The left flank was the first to attack as the northern army came into view. A cry from the northern guards echoed in the still night air. 'Skirmishers on the right!'

The cry was soon silenced as the first arrow in defence of the south was loosed with calm expertise.

Food bowls and tankards were thrown to one side as the northern army responded to a skirmisher attack on their right flank. Soldiers hurried across the encampment, swords in hand, as arrows rained down upon them. Another cry came from the northern guards, as the far right of the southern army began to fire their arrows.

'Skirmishers on the left!'

'What's happening?' Shouted a northern officer, as he staggered, half-drunk from his tent.

'Skirmishers to the right and left', said a guard.

It was then that the southern commander, General Xante, gave the order for the centre to display and deploy their war machines. A huge bolt was released from a giant crossbow, and scything its way through the northern encampment, it ended the battle for several would-be heroes.

'Skirmishers? That's the whole damn southern army out there!' Shouted the northern officer.

The alarm was sounded within the northern encampment and hundreds of soldiers began running in every direction. Another huge bolt shot from a crossbow, sliced its way through the northern ranks, and another as the two centre divisions of southern soldiers began to march forwards. So far there had been no southern casualties. Hand to hand combat however, was but a short distance away.

Although utterly confused, the northerners managed to load one of their war machines, and several large rocks were catapulted into the air and towards the advancing southerners. Only one soldier was killed immediately, but several others were injured with varying degrees of seriousness.

General Xante, still sitting astride his great war horse, shouted the next order. 'For the south, charge!' He pointed his sword forwards and rode into the frightened northern soldiers. The central divisions followed his lead and ran, swords and pikes waving, banners flying into the northern masses. The general, a man with a fearless reputation, was in the thick of the fighting as the battle raged, his sword first slashing to the left and then to the right. There were some who believed him to be unstoppable, and this put fear into the hearts of the enemy around him. Others were convinced that the general had a death wish.

Another huge bolt from the giant crossbow sliced into the northerners leaving a path of cut, broken and bleeding bodies.

The sounds of metal against metal and the screams of the wounded and dying filled the air. The general let loose his catapults and huge rocks pounded the back divisions of the northern troops urging them forward to trample on their own soldiers. The northern catapults were also loaded and more rocks were returned to the southern lines. Another machine was being readied for action and then more rocks flew towards the southerners.

'Get rid of those damned machines!' roared the general.

Archers altered their aim and an almost continuous stream of arrows flew towards the northern operators. Torched arrows were fired at the wooden structured machinery which, after a while, began to burn.

As the night drew on, both northerners and southerners alike began to tire. Fires were all around, and their flickering lights made the battle seem a little surreal. Blood-soaked bodies lay in every position: northern and southern soldiers joined in the comradeship of death.

The full extent of the damages could not be seen clearly until first light when, after a trumpeters call, the northern army retreated.

There were no shouts of triumph from the southern troops. Most fell to their knees, thankful for the rest, arms and legs ached, and clothing stank of the smell of sweat and blood.

General Xante had taken an arrow in his left arm. Blood smeared; he climbed from his war horse. Physicians quickly came to his aid, but he would have none of them until he had confirmed that the soldiers were in good spirits. He walked amongst them asking after their welfare, patting a shoulder reassuringly.

'Is it over now?' Asked a wounded soldier.

'Not yet soldier. One more drive and we shall have them', replied the general.

'Then let it be now while they are in retreat and not expecting it', said the soldier.

'Well spoken, my man. You could be right, although it is not usually my way', said the general. On second thoughts, the general called his commanders and chiefs of staff for their advice. He asked about the condition of the men, and could they, if required, continue to fight.

The southern soldiers lay all about, some staring at their dead comrades, some openly weeping with relief, and some simply staring. Some, who were the veterans of warfare, sat around systematically sharpening and cleaning their weapons.

General Xante stood atop a broken wagon and called to his men. 'What say you men? That we strike now for the south and for freedom'.

There was a rallying, unequalled in the general's long history of soldiering. 'For the south and for freedom!' Shouted one soldier.

'For the south', echoed another.

'Aye, and for Xante in the name of Brin', called yet another.

The general was overcome with emotion as he stepped down from the wagon to give orders to his commanders.

The southern army sprang into renewed life as they advanced on the northern positions. With sword, dagger, mace and axe, they fought like mad men possessed. An intense feeling of solidarity, togetherness and indestructibility overwhelmed them.

Ferociously they waded into the northerners, who for their part fought equally as well, but their spirit was weakening. With each passing minute, ground was retaken as the northern forces retreated.

For three hours longer, a pitched battle raged with bodies skewered, bones broken and eyes blinded. As the sun began its descent into the western hills, the main northern encampment was reached.

The caretaker soldiers on sighting the southern forces, fled to the beaches. Another crossbow released its missile and sent the northern commander and several of his men to eternal rest: they had lost.

It was a sad moment when the northern soldiers began to lay down their weapons.

It was a moment of relief for General Xante. He called out to the defeated northerners. 'Take to your boats for there will be no more bloodshed this day'.

He drew his sword and saluted the northern soldiers as they began to depart with a grudging admiration on their faces.

Some wanted to stay and asked if they could join with the southern forces. They said that they had been forced to fight on the northern side, but their loyalties lay with the south. General Xante, however, erred on the side of caution and told them that when the war was over, and if they still wanted to return to the south, they would be most welcome to join the southern ranks.

The rain had almost stopped its rhythmic pitter-patter on the roof of the inn. A mist rolled in from the sea, almost concealing the small village of Arvel from the outside world. In a tiny room that overlooked the harbour, Master Elio continued to instruct Birch in the arts of magic. A willing student, he absorbed all that was said, all that was demonstrated. His mind catalogued each word, each sentence and stored them deep in his vast capacity for recall. Simple spells and incantations were tried at intervals so as not to attract too much attention. Magic, even in its simplest form could be heard, if not seen. Birch continually grew in size and in knowledge. His childish manner disappeared and was replaced by adult responsibility which slowly crept in. Birch became a man. Master Elio was a good teacher, he was also a very satisfied one, and after several weeks had passed, he decided to tell Birch of his hopes, and what he had all along intended for him. They sat by a small open fire that illuminated the room with moving shadows.

'Birch' said Master Elio.

'Yes, Master Elio?'

'Birch it has been a very long time that I have been walking this land. It is the younger ones that should now be caring for it'

'I don't understand', said Birch.

'Let me finish. When we first met in the Timber Wood, I sensed a power deep within you. It was the kind of power that could only conceal itself within a Master, and not be detected even by its host. Well, not until the host was ready for the responsibility of it. From that moment I was sure who my successor would be. The gods have sanctioned my choice, for it was they who gave you that power at the beginning of your life. As for me, my duties almost ended, I will soon be free to join them once more. It is to you now that we must look for our salvation and protection.

If you accept this challenge and allow me my peace, you will probably have to defeat Lord Zelfen in combat. Once beaten, you will then take him to a building by the south coast called The Watch. Once inside that building he will lose his powers, and this land will be safe from the evil threat that he re[presents: it is his prison.

'Master Elio, you have said that you will be free to join the gods. Does this mean that I will no longer have a companion and teacher?'

'Dear Birch, you are almost the teacher now, and I will always be with you in Spirit. When you have completed the chant of calling, power beyond all will be at your command. You will be stronger that even I could ever wish to be. You will become the Master of all Masters'.

'And what about Cat?'

'You and Cat will become as one, and yet retain your separate identities. You will have the ability to interchange, one with the other. You will have the power to change into any form. No other master, past or present and no other in the future, had, has or will have the power that you possess. The awesome power of transformation. You and cat will be able to travel as one. There are endless possibilities. Guard well your secrets, for many will try to learn them'.

As winter closed in and throughout its duration, Master Elio, Birch and Cat lived at the inn. Many more secrets were spoken and learned. Cat travelled the land from time to time hunting, and gathering information. A black shadow, sleek and with unimaginable speed, brought news of the war to Birch and Master Elio.

As winter began to gradually disappear, but before the spring had awakened the hibernating animals and dormant seeds, Master Elio called Birch and cat to his side. 'My friends, I have taken a bud and made a flower. I have encouraged a sapling into a sturdy tree. I have taken a kitten, reared it until it has become a cat. These are the greatest magic's of all: I am now finished and I am proud of my work. It is time for me to leave; are you ready to accept the responsibility that I place upon you?'

Birch straightened himself, and Cat, as though she knew, walked over to Birch and sat by his side. 'Master Elio, we are ready', said Birch.

Master Elio smiled and began to chant. It was almost a song as the ancient words flowed forth. Birch also began to chant a different song, but both appeared to complement each other in pitch and in tone.

At first, the chanting was barely a low humming sound, it was almost quiet. Then it became louder, stronger, and then softer again.

Birch began to feel light, as though in a fever, but still he continued to chant his learned words. The room appeared to spin and then he was standing in the clouds as light began to emanate from Master Elio's hooded figure, brighter and brighter as the chanting continued.

For one hour precisely their songs intermingled, and then there was silence, a warm soothing silence. Master Elio's robes suddenly became hundreds upon hundreds of tiny coloured lights that crossed to hover above where Birch and Cat stood. Sparks of lightening flashed from cloud to cloud.

The light surrounding Master Elio darkened slightly and then grew to a phenomenal brightness. Thunder rumbled and shook the air. A series of coloured lights flashed their brilliance across the sky and then, Master Elio was gone.

Birch and Cat were back in their room. The multitude of coloured lights that hovered above Birch and Cat slowly descended and were absorbed by both. Streaks of octane brilliance fizzed and crackled about them.

Birch began to feel stronger, he felt himself absorbing the power. This is what he had been waiting for since his birth. He knew it, sensed every part of it, and revelled in the drunkenness of its power.

His eyes changed colour to a deep luminous green, and then he was Cat, growling and pawing the air, and then he was himself again. He fell to one knee as the power increased. He shouted. 'EEEELIIIOOOO!'

All was silent. The room seemed unchanged as Birch stood up. He looked for Master Elio but he was not there, and yet he was. His spirit had been reborn in Birch and Cat, and as a new day dawned, they left the inn to journey westward.

Lord Torran sat astride his white stallion. He gazed at the scene before him and almost regretted having lost his temper. Dead eyes stared accusingly from the hollow, his vow of vengeance having been carried out. His regret, if any, was for the way in which he had accomplished his task. His enjoyment bridged to the point of ecstasy as he sentenced the offenders. He now felt empty and ashamed. Turning, he spurred his horse into a gallop and headed north-east towards the village of Yani.

He was clear of the hills when he decided to make his first camp. On the low ground the snow had disappeared to reveal fresh grasses; food for his stallion, and the promise of a warm night cheered his mood.

After eating a meal of ground nuts and dried meat, he settled down to sleep, but a feeling of insecurity suddenly took hold. His senses once again became sharp. His eyes darted from side to side seeking the cause of this strange feeling. It was then that he felt the other presence. Not an equal, but something much stronger. Although it didn't seem to be malevolent, it was certainly dangerous. He knew that the presence watched him but he didn't know what it wanted.

'Who approaches?' He called into the night. There was no answer, only a deathly silence. A red nimbus surrounded him as he gathered his will. He felt nervous with a feeling that he had seldom experienced except in the presence of Frezfir.

'Who approaches?' He called again. The surrounding air felt thick with the strange feeling. He felt it move towards him. He felt it move around him, encircling his small encampment. His black bladed sword came into his hand in one fluid movement.

'I am Lord Torran of Ice and Fire. Cease your games lest I tear this land apart in search of you. Still there was silence. Slightly frustrated, Torran sat down again by his small night fire and waited.

Whatever the feeling or the presence was, whoever was causing it, it was not coming any closer. For this reason Torran felt safe but he knew that it was watching, observing, studying. It was something he failed to understand. If this presence, this feeling was born of the gods, then why didn't the gods show themselves? If the presence was hostile, why did it not attack, it was obviously the stronger. If indeed it was friendly, why no introductions, why did it not join him. To add further confusion to the enigma, his white stallion which stood a little way away from the camp, showed no sign of disturbance, no signs of distress, and no nervous twitching. It didn't appear to notice anything out of place. For a short while, the feeling of being examined hovered over him, and then it was gone. It was as though the presence had never been there.

Although he tried, Torran could not sleep after the unsettling experience, and after several attempts he gave up. He packed his things, and calling his white stallion, he set forth again towards the village of Yani.

A fine spring morning greeted the northern soldiers under the command of Lord Barek, and a warm wind blew in from the west. It was a morning anyone could enjoy if the threat of battle wasn't foremost in the soldiers minds.

Lord Zelfen paced the streets of the village of Spard. He felt a peculiar uneasiness, and was concerned that as yet, the advance had not commenced.

Lord Barek strolled over to him. 'Good morning, Lord Zelfen', he said cheerfully.

'It is not a good morning, Barek. Why aren't the soldiers marching into battle?'

'They must have their rest, Lord Zelfen. We will resume the march this afternoon'.

'Rest? Rest? Those who travelled by sea had rest, plenty of it by all accounts, and look what happened to them. They have been driven back to the edge of the sea, and are now fleeing for their miserable lives'. Lord Barek was visibly shaken as Lord Zelfen continued.

'Yes, my Lord Barek. I can see what you cannot, and I can inform you that the southerners have regained their lands at Penste Harbour. Penste Castle, defended by a bunch of farmers, was not taken as was planned, and even now their General Xante makes mockery of your forces with a pathetic salute. They were not soldiers that you sent, they were cowards; cowards that will face my wrath upon their return.

I will show them what it means to run from a lesser breed of people. Nevertheless, I intend to win this battle. We shall overcome the southern swine, and I will ride victorious into Castle Tezz'.

Lord Zelfen continued to speak of victory as the two lords strolled leisurely along the main street. Shortly after a midday meal of dried fish, fruit and wine, the northern soldiers began to assemble.

Lord Zelfen was still in an uneasy mood: was it something that he had forgotten? He felt as though something was watching him. Although he tried to dismiss the peculiar feeling, it persisted for some time, before suddenly, he realised that it had disappeared.

Feeling a lot better than he had been, he joined Lord Barek as the central northern forces began to advance. Black Eagle banners were raised at the head of the marching army, and musicians played a marching tune in time with the dull beat of the war drums. At a signal given by the commanders, the divisions to the right and to the left of the central columns also began to advance.

A full day's continuous ride had brought news of the northern army's advance to the attention of Lord Brin. Quickly he passed on the information to all of his commanders. The southern army readied themselves for their own advance which Lord Brin suggested, to the cheers of his men, should only commence after a good meal, some fine wine, a woman and some peaceful sleep.

'Tomorrow', he said. 'Tomorrow or the next day will be the day of reckoning. Let us be happy for a short while, and share that happiness with each other'.

'Who approaches?' Shouted a guard.

'Lord Torran' was the reply.

'Advance Lord Torran and be welcome', said the guard before returning to his watch on the perimeter.

Lord Torran entered the camp, and seeing Karl and Edmund, hurried to them. Firm handshakes said all that needed to be said at that time. The three lords continued on the Lord Brin's tent, and found him sitting on a pile of cushions. He stood up and looked directly into Torran's eyes.

'I have fulfilled my promise', said Torran as he handed the Ring of Tezz to Lord Brin.

Lord Brin studied the ring for some time before making any comment. 'What kept you? He said, with a semi-serious grin on his face.

'Now just hold on a minute', said Torran.

'Come on, Edmund', said Karl. 'It's time for these two to get acquainted'.

Karl and Edmund left the tent just as the first insult was thrown. They walked clear of the bad language and settled by one of the campfires. Tamur, Edmunds squire, was singing a lullaby to a group of spell-bound soldiers. He had a sweet, high voice that echoed into the night. He sang of two lovers who had parted, but had met again in the spirit world, and when the song was over, the enthusiastic soldiers insisted that he sing some more.

'Go on, Tamur, it's the custom you know', said Edmund.

'Oh! Is it, my Lord?'

'Indeed it is', said Karl.

Just as Tamur began to sing again, Karl felt another presence, a strange presence. He looked at Edmund, who indicated that he too had felt something.

'Where is it?' Whispered Lord Edmund, so as not to interrupt Tamur's singing.

'I don't know. It seems to be moving all around us. It can't be that close otherwise the guards would challenge it', said Karl.

Lord Torran, on sensing the strange feeling for a second time, left Lord Brin mid-insult to join Karl and Edmund.

'What is it? Torran', asked Karl.

'I don't know to be truthful', he replied. I experienced this feeling some time ago when I was on my way here. Whatever it was at that time made no move to attack. In fact, whatever it was didn't identify itself, it came and then disappeared'.

'Could it be this, Master Elio that you have spoken about?' Said Edmund.

'No, this presence was much stronger than Master Elio', said Torran.

'Lord Zelfen?' Suggested Edmund.

'If it is?' Said Torran. 'We would have some severe problems, but I think not. He would have seized upon the opportunity to attack me at the earlier meeting. To be truthful, I have no idea what, or who it is, but I believe it to be friendly. Let us not do anything rash until we know for sure'.

'It gives me the creeps', said Karl.

It was strange in that no-one else in the encampment could sense anything out of the ordinary, and as Tamur continued to sing; the three wizards began a search of the area in order to locate the hidden power. They searched for more than an hour, but were left with no more an idea than they had at the offset. If they travelled in one direction, the feelings of power came from the opposite direction. If they travelled in that direction, the power source would alter to another. Eventually they sat down on a low wagon to appraise the situation.

The night became pitched in darkness except for the light that emanated from the camp fires and the oil lights in the tents. Edmund was the first to notice the eyes that stared at them from within the blackness. He notified the others.

'Who approaches?' Called Lord Torran.

The deep blue luminous eyes kept close to the ground. They appeared to be drawing closer. This was where the strange feelings were coming from. This was the presence that they had all felt. The three wizards stood and watched, amazed as a huge blue-eyed Timber Cat strolled leisurely towards them, dropped something from its mouth and was gone in an instant.

'What was that?' Asked Lord Edmund.

'A Timber Cat', replied Lord Torran.

'I've never seen a Timber Cat that tamely walked in as though it owned the place, especially one with blue eyes', said Lord Karl. 'Bring light; let us see what this Timber Cat has delivered to us'.

Lord Edmund supplied a burning stick from a nearby campfire.

Lord Torran's face suddenly beamed a huge smile as he picked up the object.

'What is it?' Asked Karl.

'It's a feather', replied Torran.

'A feather?' Said Edmund.

'Yes', replied Torran. 'A very special kind of feather. It can only be obtained from the plumage of a Bemal bird'.

'Master Elio', said Karl, rather excitedly.

'No, I'm afraid not'. Said Torran. 'He would have come in person if he were able to do so. I think that this is his way of telling us that he could not come'.

'Then we may have some problems', said Karl.

'Somehow I don't think so'.

'Would someone mind telling me what it is that I ought to know'. Said Edmund.

Torran related to Edmund their first meeting with the Master, the Magician Elio: the way that the Bemal bird had darted across their path and that Master Elio didn't realise that he was still invisible when he first spoke to them. 'So you can see the connection', said Torran.

'So where do we stand now?'

'That remains to be seen', said Torran. 'But if anything else strange happens tonight, ignore it. It's probably for our benefit'.

It had rained during the early hours of the following morning. A light, penetrating rain. The fresh breeze that followed the rain brought all the smells of early spring. Small yellow flowers glistened with morning dew; opened to meet the morning sun as the southern army prepared to advance.

Lord Brin insisted on all the pomp and ceremony of a parade to instil confidence in his soldiers. The musicians took a forward position, behind them, the banners and flags, regimental standards and pennants.

Two white doves on a background of blue, the colours of Lord Brin, were supported by the red sunburst, the white lightning bolt and the brown diagonals.

All were held proudly as the march readied to advance.

Karl turned to Tamur. 'When the fighting starts keep out of harm's way'.

'As my Lord pleases', he replied.

A mounted soldier, who was dressed completely in black, and with face masked, rode to the front of the assembled army. He was holding a lowered banner: the banner of the first Lord of Tezz. When he had reached a central position, he turned to face the southern army. The banner of the First Lord of Tezz, a single white dove on a background of blue, was raised high into the air. 'For the Lord Tezz'. Shouted the soldier.

Lord Brin took up the shout. 'And for the south, advance'.

There was a pride in the way that the southern army marched forwards to the sound of the pipes and drums. It was a unity that would not easily be broken.

'I wish that I could see a rampant lion', said Karl as he viewed the flags and banners.

'Is he going through the change?' Said Lord Brin to Torran.

Time waits for no man, and evening came quickly as the southern forces marched forwards with purpose, and as the light of the daytime began to fade, orders were given to set up a camp for the night. They could see the fires of the northern encampment about half a league in the distance.

All were in good spirits as Lord Brin, his chiefs of staff, his commanders and the wizards toured the site. Occasionally Lord Brin would stare towards the northern encampment and wonder if Lord Barek was doing the same.

Lord Barek was in a conference with his chiefs of staff when a frightened soldier came running into his tent.

'I've seen one, my Lord', said the visibly shaken soldier.

'You've seen one what?' Said and angry Lord Barek.

'A demon, my Lord'.

'Not demons again', interrupted Lord Zelfen.

'It is true, my Lord', said the soldier. 'A black creature crossed my path almost shadow-like. It was huge and had shining blue eyes'.

'A demon with shiny blue eyes', laughed Lord Zelfen.

'Have you been drinking on duty?' Asked an also amused Lord Barek.

An icy cold wind swept through the tent. Lord Zelfen felt the presence of something with awesome power. He shuddered. 'Where did this demon come from: which direction?' Said Lord Zelfen.

'I will show you, my Lord'. Lord Zelfen and Lord Barek followed the soldier towards the edge of the encampment. 'There, my Lords', said the soldier, pointing to a bushy area beyond some trees.

Lord Zelfen could still feel the presence of an unknown power, but it was not in any particular place. It was all around him. A scream from another part of the encampment echoed into the otherwise silent evening. Lord Zelfen raised his hands and began a slow chant. From his fingertips there came a flash of octane brilliance that illuminated the night sky in that area. The blue eyed Timber Cat raced through the encampment at a phenomenal speed.

'There', shouted a soldier. But the Timber Cat was gone in an instant.

'What was it?' Shouted Lord Barek.

'My Lord, it was a Timber Cat. The largest Timber Cat I have ever seen', said a soldier.

'Take some men, track this Timber Cat down and kill it. The last thing I want at this time, is for a man-eating cat to be loose within this encampment', said Lord Zelfen.

'At once, my Lord', said the soldier.

'Demons indeed', said Lord Barek.

'Even so, my Lord Barek', said Lord Zelfen. 'Let the soldiers bring me the head of this creature'. Lord Zelfen had sensed the power. He did not want to take any chances.

A dozen men armed with crossbows and swords left the encampment immediately to look for the Timber Cat. The tracks were easy to follow even in the darkness. It appeared as though they were left by a cat that wanted to be caught. Before long, the soldiers that were in the search party, came upon a rocky outcrop.

'Okay lads, it's in here somewhere. Fan out and look for the blue eyes', whispered a nervous soldier.

Tense minutes passed by before, breaking the silence, a frightened soldier called out. The leader of the group who was several yards away asked what was the matter.

'It's a demon', replied the frightened soldier.

'Oh no, not that again', said the leader.

The other northern soldiers rushed over to where their comrade stood. He was completely still, looking horrifyingly towards the top of a small mound of rocks. Standing there was a dark cloaked and hooded figure. The cloak had strange markings all over it. At the right breast, a silver staff and around that, two silver snakes coiled themselves.

'Who are you?' Asked the leading soldier in the group.

The hooded figure appeared to look directly into the group of soldiers. He removed his hood. Green luminous eyes held them spellbound.

'It's a demon. I told you it was a demon', said a soldier.

'No', said the dark shape. 'I am Birch of the Timber Wood. Go back to your encampment and tell your Lord Zelfen to cease his meaningless hostility. I am slow to anger, and share not the troubles of mortal men. But to your Lord Zelfen I give this message.

Tell him that he must take himself from this place and that he must travel to a place by the coast called The Watch. There he is to stay for all time, or at least until he has repented of his childish ways. I grow weary and will not abide his meddlesome nature in this land any longer'.

With that, and before the frightened eyes of the northern soldiers, Birch changed once more into the Timber Cat and bounded away.

'Have you gone completely mad? A man with green shiny eyes changed into a cat? Even for me that is impossibility', screamed Lord Zelfen. 'You cannot make and then unmake magic'.

'But, my Lord, we all saw it. A hooded figure with green luminous eyes change into a cat', said the leading soldier.

'And why did you not shoot this figure with the green eyes?' Asked Lord Zelfen.

'Well, my Lord . . .'

'Oh! We've got cats with blue eyes and now men with green eyes that shine in the darkness', interrupted Lord Barek. 'I think that maybe all of you have been eating wild berries instead of doing what was asked of you'.

'No, my Lord. The figure said that his name was, Birch'.

'Are you sure that it wasn't a tree?' Laughed Lord Barek. Then in an instant, his laughter ceased to be and was replaced with a scowl. 'Now look at me and listen carefully. I want that scruffy little cat found and dismembered. I want to eat of its meat at breakfast. If you cannot do this simple thing for me, the dogs will eat of your meat instead, and if you see another tree, kill it. Do you understand me?'

'Yes, my Lord'. The soldier wanted to pass on the message that Birch gave him, but he thought better of it. He didn't want to upset Lord Barek any further, because his life would become extremely short if he did.

The now terrified soldiers hurried away to join several other groups of their comrades that now hunted the cat. 'I want the whole of this area searched for anything unusual, and I want that cat found', said the leader as he loaded a crossbow.

The black robed figure of a southern spy watched with mild interest as the searching parties went about their work. For once in his life as a spy, he was unaware of the two northern soldiers, weapons drawn, who were creeping silently to where he lay. The two swords were simultaneously raised for killing strokes, but the northerners, eyes wide with surprise and terror, dropped their swords as a black mass attacked.

Two throats were ripped open in as many seconds and they fell, still with an expression of surprise on their faces. The spy looked on in disbelief as the huge blue-eyed Timber Cat bounded away without so much as a sound.

The spy, thanking the gods for his reprieve, also slipped away. He mounted his horse and headed back to the southern encampment.

For most of the night, northern soldiers searched in vain for the black Timber Cat. It was just before dawn that a soldier saw the black cloaked figure with the green luminous eyes once more.

'Tell you Lord Zelfen that he has been warned', said Birch.

The soldier did no more than to charge, sword raised high, to his untimely death.

'And so have you'. Birch disappeared.

CHAPTER TWELVE

THE SOUTHERN ENCAMPMENT WAS again a hive of activity as the soldiers prepared for what was to come. It was planned that crossbows and catapults would be situated at the head of the army this time. Archers would then be followed by swordsmen and men with pikes. Mounted lancers would strike into the flanks of the northern forces.

The plan of battle was a simple one, as the army moved forwards; the war machines would then continue their attack from the rear. Being much closer than normally would be the case, the war machines would be more effective. It was hoped that, in its simplicity, the plan would give them victory.

In the half-light of the morning, a sentry noticed a movement in the shadows. 'Who approaches?' He called.

It was not a voice in the true sense of the meaning that replied, because it was not spoken, but the sentry heard it. 'A friend of the south', it said.

'Advance friend and be welcome', said the sentry who became fixed to the spot as a large, black Timber Cat strolled leisurely passed him, said thank you and entered the encampment.

The sentry's mouth opened and closed in an attempt to shout a warning, but no sound came out. Soldiers everywhere scattered as the Timber Cat walked over to Lord Torran. He had seen it enter the encampment and found the boldness a little amusing. Karl and Edmund ran over to where Torran and the Timber Cat stood.

Archers were also running forward but Torran held up his hand. 'Hold', he said. 'Let no man raise his weapons against this beast, for it is more than you realise'. With that the archers retired.

'To my tent?' Suggested Lord Brin who had joined the group.

'Seems like a good idea under the circumstances', said Torran.

The lords walked over to Lord Brin's tent, and upon entering, they were followed by the Timber Cat. It was again not a spoken voice that the lords heard, but it was loud and it was clear. 'I am Birch of the Timber Wood. I am the Master of all Masters and heir to the knowledge of Master Elio. I would speak with Torran, Karl and Edmund.

'We have no secrets from my father, Lord Brin of Castle Tezz', said a slightly offended Karl.

'So be it', replied the voice, and then, before the eyes of the four lords, Birch appeared from within a black cloud that emanated from the Timber Cat, and Cat's eyes turned green. Birch removed the hood that covered his head to reveal a young but determined face. Long dark hair fell over his shoulders, and his eyes were deep blue wells of warmth and knowledge. Hidden only, was the look that spelled death to those who would confront him with violence.

'Transformation! The ultimate power', said an amazed Lord Torran.

'It has its uses', smiled Birch. 'Please forgive my disguise, and forgive me for my previous study of you and your companions. You will understand that I had to be sure before revealing my identity to you'.

'What of Master Elio?' Asked Karl.

'Master Elio's time on the land was limited. He has chosen me as his successor and I have learned his secrets. Now he rests. His spirit is in me and with me: I doubt if he will ever take human form again'. The was a hint of sadness in what Birch said at that point. 'My task here is two-fold. First of all I must end the reign of disruption caused by Lord Zelfen. I will not interfere with the arguments of mankind. That is for you to settle. If I remove the germ, the wound will eventually heal itself. Secondly I am here to give you all a choice'.

'A choice?' Said Edmund.

'Yes a choice', said Birch. 'The fourth, the three's decision be'.

'The riddle! Said Karl.

'Yes, the riddle', continued Birch. 'The choice is simple: to live again upon this land, you must relinquish your powers. You then will be As mortal men, and you will live out a mortal existence. You will age as men do and you will die as men die. The choice is yours to make. The next time I ask, it will be for your decisions. You will answer me for or against'.

With that final word, Birch and the Timber Cat disappeared. The four lords then left the tent; the three wizards with much on their minds.

Whilst last minute preparations were being made for the final advance and men began to assemble, Karl talked at length with his father, Lord Brin. The outcome of that talk pleased Lord Brin more than he would, or could possibly imagine.

Karl would give up his power to control wind and water and would live as others lived. He would take a wife and, it was hoped, he would be able to carry on the family line first started by Lord Tezz. Finally he would die as men die, happy in the knowledge that he had fulfilled his dreams.

Just before midday, the southern army advanced. A smiling Lord Brin, flanked by Torran, Karl and Edmund, together with Edmund's squire, Tamur, led the eager and willing southern troops towards the northern aggressors.

The northern army's commanders, led by Lord Zelfen and Lord Barek, rode to the front of the assembled northern troops. Lord Zelfen turned, and standing up in his stirrups, spoke aloud to the assembly. 'Let every man do his duty to me this day and I will bless you with eternal life', he lied.

A half-hearted cheer filled the air, and Lord Barek ordered the advance as the dogs attacked two terrified victims.

Nearer and nearer the armies came to each other. Lord Torran had ridden over to command the right flank, whilst Lord Edward covered the left, and Lord Karl, sitting proudly astride his mount, stayed central along with his father, Lord Brin.

'Take care, my son', said lord Brin

'And you, my father'.

The southern and northern forces halted within sight of each other. Only five hundred yards separated them.

Lord Zelfen sat on his horse, arrogantly facing the south, convinced that his superiority would win the day. He was just about to launch a feint attack, when there appeared a wind, an unexpectedly strong wind and a sound like a thousand cattle in stampede.

A rainbow of multi-coloured lights appeared between the armies. Within the confines of the rainbow, a white light flashed with an unbelievable brightness, and both armies were temporarily blinded.

The wind and the lights increased for a while before, quite unexpectedly, the wind died down and the lights vanished, but during the brief time that the lights were flashing, a conversation took place between Birch and Lord Zelfen.

'I am Birch of the Timber Wood, and Master of all Masters. I demand that you lay down your arms. I further demand that you, Lord Zelfen, come with me to be judged according to your deeds'.

'And if I refuse, Master of all Masters', said Lord Zelfen mockingly, 'what then?'

'Then I shall have to take you against your will. You will leave me no alternative'.

'Then I shall enjoy teaching you a lesson in the arts', said Lord Zelfen. 'Kill them, kill them all', he shouted to the northern troops and the front section of the army charged forwards.

Lord Brin remained calm. He waited until the northern forces had travelled a fair distance before giving his command to the southern front ranks. 'For the south, advance'.

The first crossbow let fly its messenger of death towards the oncoming northern masses and four soldiers joined their ancestors. The bolt had entered the first soldier just above the solar plexus, and joining him to the other three in a final embrace of death, had emerged between the shoulder blades of the fourth. A shower of rocks fell upon the southern army in reply, and several fell under the bombardment.

Edmund had discovered a new weapon. By using his power, he shaped stone into discs with razor sharp edges. Holding a disc in the palm of his hand and using all of his strength, he hurled the missiles towards the oncoming northerners with deadly results.

The two front sections, one northern and one southern, came together with a mighty clash. Steel echoed upon steel, blood was spilled, men screamed and shouted. Some were trampled underfoot as soldiers fought to survive.

Another disc shuddered to a halt in the chest of a wide-eyed northerner. Another crossbow was fired, cutting, slicing, and stabbing its way through the northern ranks. Shouts continued to accompany the clash of steel upon steel.

Shouts of anger, of frustration, cries for help and screams of the dying. Several men from each side were detailed to carry away the wounded. The dead were left, spirit-like witnesses to the slaughter taking place.

Lord Zelfen was not really taking much notice of the first engagement. He was concentrating on a hooded figure that observed the scene from the vantage point of a small hill that overlooked the battle. Sitting by the side of the hooded figure was a large black Timber Cat.

The southern forces began to gain ground as Lord Torran led his lancers directly into the enemy's flank, and Lord Edmund led his men into the left flank. Long spiked poles jabbed and penetrated, and razor sharp discs found many targets.

'We're surrounded!' shouted a terrified northern soldier. Panic quickly set in, and the northerners began to retreat.

Lord Torran saw the flash out of the corner of his eye, somewhere left of centre. A bolt of brilliant white light totally disintegrated two southern horsemen, and their horses fell to the ground screaming in agony. This gave the northerners fresh courage as the battle took on a new dimension.

Lord Edmund was fighting on the left flank like a man possessed. His black bladed sword striking first right, and then left as he pushed further into the enemy's sides.

Lord Zelfen ordered his archers forward, and disregarding his own front fighting men, he ordered the archers to commence their attack. Arrows fell like drops of rain upon both northerners and southerners alike.

It was like in a slow motion dream that Tamur, Lord Edmunds squire, saw the archer aim and release his deadly missile. Lord Edmund was the intended target but Tamur rode hard through the continuing battle.

A mixture of fear and anxiety caused sweat to form beads on his brow as he kicked and pushed his way through the fighting armies. Finally he leapt, disregarding his own safety, to shield the missiles intended victim.

The arrow caught Tamur between the shoulder blades and sank deep. Lord Edmund quickly dragged him from the thick of the battle, and as he helped him sit up, a green nimbus surrounded them both.

'It's the custom, sire', said Tamur, as he slid into the final darkness.

Tamur was carried a little way away from the battle, and after saying his goodbyes, Edmund asked the earth to accept his friend as Tamur sank slowly beneath it.

The green nimbus surrounding Edmund began to grow brighter as the anger surged through him and as he rode back to the battle the green nimbus was brighter than ever.

Particles of green and brown light rose from around him. Power came from the rocks, from the earth to join his will and the ground began to shake.

Lord Torran had also called upon his powers. He sensed that the remainder of the battle would be fought, not with conventional weaponry, but with magic or a combination of the two.

Lord Karl instructed his personal guards to escort Lord Brin safely back to the main army. Protests were useless after Karl threatened to have him carried back if he resisted.

It was then that the familiar rumbling of Lord Edmunds commands filled the air. Green octane light flashed towards Lord Zelfen with the power of a mountain eruption.

Lord Zelfen blocked with a chant of protection, and sent a black light speeding towards Lord Edmund. The earth rose up in his defence and absorbed the impact, then lowered again to its normal position. Another bolt was deflected by Edmund's sword.

The fighting around the wizards had now ceased. Soldiers from sides, north and south, stood without fighting to watch the light display as Lords Edmund and Zelfen exchanged blows.

Lord Torran decided to join the fight and sent a red light of immeasurable heat towards the black robed Lord Zelfen. Again Lord Zelfen was too quick and blocked the strike.

Lord Karl summoned the wind to carry fine grit in the face of Lord Zelfen, in the hope that it might temporarily blind him and give a small advantage to the wizards. Even this was inadequate.

Lord Torran sent iced missiles of frozen water'

Lord Karl sent storm and Lord Edmund, stone. All were ineffective against the mighty power at Lord Zelfen's command and yet they still sent beam after beam of invisible death.

For more than half an hour, Lords Torran, Karl and Edmund battled to weaken Lord Zelfen's power and his defences.

However much they tried, all was to no avail as their plan began to backfire. They themselves were becoming weak as the power drained from them.

Lord Zelfen sensed this and shouted for his troops to attack once more which, seeing that the wizards from the south were more or less without their strengths, they did with renewed hope.

Lord Brin's personal guard, a group of fighting men unequalled in combat, split into three groups. Fighting as they went, they escorted the wizards back to the main lines.

The southern advance divisions did not lose heart. In fact they rallied and fought more ferociously. Axes, swords and maces, together with lance and pike, crossbow and catapult, rained down blow after blow upon the advancing northern army. Never before was such a bloody battle fought.

Birch still continued to watch as the main divisions of both north and south were ordered to advance. He watched as Lord Zelfen sent forth his power to bathe several southerners in a sea of death. He knew that this was the moment to act. He removed his hood to let his dark hair blow freely in the wind. His eyes were not the soft eyes, the wells of warmth that the lords had seen, but the cold, merciless eyes of one about to seek retribution.

A multi-coloured nimbus gave a new meaning to the word, bright. Two powerful beams of red octane brilliance burst forth from his eyes, and the ground before Lord Zelfen bubbled in its attempt to release the steam trapped beneath it. He jumped back, shocked at the awesome power.

He looked up to see that the Master of Masters, Birch, had sent an invitation, an invitation to match powers. He replied blindly and sent a beam of destruction in the direction of where birch was standing. It narrowly missed Cat, to burn a large area of hillside behind them.

In an instant, the Timber Cat and Birch became as one, and Birch's eyes changed to a deep glowing green.

As the battle between Birch and Lord Zelfen increased in pitch, so the air above them became a stage on which an intricate pattern of flashing lights danced their songs of death. Sparks flew from Lord Zelfen and Birch as they increase the volume of their powers. The air screamed as Lord Zelfen sent another black light towards Birch. An invisible wall of protection absorbed the awesome power and then sent it back to its maker as Birch began to chant. This was a slow rhythmic chant, a chant of total and irreversible power. He raised his hands, his eyes turned red, and then he unleashed power that was beyond human comprehension towards Lord Zelfen.

Where Lord Zelfen had stood, the ground erupted and a huge ball of white heat mushroomed skyward. Fortunately for Lord Zelfen, he had transported himself at the last minute, realising that even he could not withstand the powers of Birch for any length of time.

The two armies had been so engrossed, so absorbed with their own fighting, that very few noticed that Lord Zelfen had departed. The raging and violent battle continued, but the tide was turning. The southern army began to regain ground as once again the wizards joined them. Horses eyes bulged with fright as riders met with shields raised high, and lances struck again and again into the flanks of the northern army.

Lord Edmund was fighting in the midst of the battle when Birch appeared before him. Northern soldiers fled and time stood still.

'Lord Edmund of Earth and Stone, I ask you now for your decision', said Birch.

'I would live again upon this land', replied Edmund.

Transportation was a strange sensation for Edmund, as Birch relocated him and his horse to a nearby hill. He asked Edmund to wait there.

Birch then appeared before Lord Karl and asked the same question.

'Must it be now, in the middle of a battle?'

'It must be so', replied Birch.

'Then I will be as men', said Karl, firmly.

Karl joined Edmund while Birch approached Lord Torran, the longest lived amongst them.

'Lord Torran of Ice and Fire. I humble myself before the favourite of the god, Frezfir. I have come for your answer to my question. What is your decision?'

'I have lived upon this land for hundreds of years', said Torran. I must confess that I have wished for this opportunity on more than one occasion. My service to Frezfir has been rewarding but I would now like my ultimate reward. Gladly I will live as men'.

On the side of a hill overlooking the continuing battle, the three wizards sat holding their horse's reins. Birch stood before them. Once again hooded, Birch looked mysterious as he began to chant in a strange tongue; the clashes of steel and the screams of men below almost drowning out his words.

He sang the words slowly at first then speeded up, the words almost inseparable. Loud then soft, fast then slow as the chant continued. Birch looked skyward and held out his arms as though to embrace the clouds. The three wizards began to feel drowsy like in a dream.

The first lights began to flash and appeared out of Edmund. Miniature brown and green lights that lifted to hover above him, then Karl with blue and white lights and finally Torran with red and white lights. The lights hovered for just a moment before they slowly crossed the space that separated the wizards from Birch.

Birch felt the combination of enormous power, the power that was entering his body. Like the feeling of a cramp it built up within him. He fell to his knees and screamed for Master Elio.

The pain was almost too much to bear as hundreds of years of knowledge built up within him. He folded his arms across his chest and rocked back and forth until the pain eased, then he stood up. A multi-coloured nimbus surrounded him, and power flashed from his body to earth itself at his feet.

'My Lords Torran, Karl and Edmund, you have a battle to fight', said Birch before his disappeared in a confusion of multi-coloured lights.

The lords awakened from their drowsiness, and realising that their powers were gone, embraced each other before returning to the battlefield.

With renewed vigour they charged down the side of the hill and towards the thick of the battle. Lord Brin saw them as they returned. They wore no wizard's robes, just plain clothes with each displaying a different badge of allegiance.

Lord Torran displayed the red sunburst, Lord Edmund, brown and green check, and Lord Karl, three white doves above a white lightning strike. They still rode the same stallions, but even they has a certain aspect of their appearance missing, a lack of lustre.

'For the south', shouted a happier Karl as he invited Torran and Edmund to follow suit and soon all three were in the thick of battle.

Lord Brin had finally come face to face with Lord Barek, the man who for many years had been a thorn in the side of the south. 'Your time has come, Barek', shouted Lord Brin as he brought his sword down from an overhead swing.

Lord Barek blocked the move and tried to counter it, but he was weak.

Although equally as drained through the hard fighting, Lord Brim did not show weakness and again and again he struck out towards his enemy. The northern forces were once again beginning to lose heart, and when Lord Barek was eventually struck down in the midst of the battle with Lord Brin, they began to flee.

Lords Torran, Karl and Edmund found fighting slightly different with using conventional swords, the black bladed swords having disappeared, but they were still fine swords. They began to tire but fortune smiled upon them when fresh mounted troops rode onto the battle field. General Xante and his men had ridden hard to join Lord Brin's forces.

The northern army, or what was left of it, threw down their weapons: the battle was over.

Above the land of Modania and riding on the winds unseen by human eye, another kind of game was being played, the game of hide and go seek. Lord Zelfen was running, hiding from the punishment that awaited him. The seeker was Birch of the Timber Wood and Master of all Masters.

Lord Zelfen finally materialised on Millers Hill. He was determined to destroy the house of Torran. There the gods had met for hundreds of years, and knowing that without this house, the gods would be forever banished to their own domain, Lord Zelfen had decided to take, in his view, a terrible revenge. Little did he know that the house would no longer be needed by the gods as Lord Torran had surrendered his powers.

'Who approaches?' Shouted a guard.

Lord Zelfen made no answer other than to send a bolt of black light that shrivelled the unsuspecting soldier in a ball of flame. Running was no defence for the other guards as Lord Zelfen showed no mercy on any.

The old house stood defiantly as Lord Zelfen approached. 'if I can't have this land; then neither can you', shouted Lord Zelfen to the heavens. He raised his hands, and amid a slow chant, he released his awesome power. At first, the stone and brickwork refused to absorb the destructive force of Lord Zelfen's might.

Then, as he increased his power, there was a massive implosion. The house appeared to fall inwards upon itself and was pulled beneath the surface of the hill. When the dust that had filled the air finally dispersed, there was no sign of the house at all, nor where it had been.

At that instant, Birch appeared, and immediately Lord Zelfen launched his powers against him. Black flame scorched the ground as Birch dodged and weaved.

'See young Birch, I have destroyed the house. Your contact with the gods has gone forever. Soon you will join it in the pits of damnation'. Black fire once again shot forth from Lord Zelfen's fingertips.

Birch side stepped and sent a white searing flame that scorched a surprised Lord Zelfen on his left side.

Furiously he returned the insult with a red burning flame.

Birch protected himself with an invisible shield of pure energy that absorbed the deadly power, and then returned it from whence it came.

Lord Zelfen leapt out of its path, rolling badly on the hard ground. In an instant Birch was upon him. Powers forgotten, they fought a close quarter combat of strike for strike, punch for punch. Birch was without a doubt the stronger of the two, but Lord Zelfen didn't give up easily.

As he slowly began to tire, Lord Zelfen made one last and desperate attempt as he pushed Birch to one side. Gathering his powers, he sent forth a thick black beam of pure destructive energy. Birch had little time to dodge the blast and so he quickly gathered his will. He took the full force of Zelfen's power in his chest. Lord Zelfen was ecstatic; he leapt about with utter joy.

Birch then stood up, unyielding to the power that was sent to destroy him. Lord Zelfen was visibly shaken by the invulnerability of his adversary. Standing motionless, Birch began a slow chant.

It was not a song, but groups of solid words spoken in the ancient language that etched themselves into the air around Lord Zelfen. He realised too late that this was a spell of binding. His mind tried to resist. Sweat beads formed on his brow as he tried to force the spell from him.

Birch continued without pause. The deep wells of knowledge that were his eyes focussed on the slowly submitting Lord Zelfen. 'Zelfen', said Birch. 'You will go from this place to a place of concealment, The Watch.

There you will stay until such time as you have truly repented of your misdeeds'. Birch pointed a finger at the cowering Lord Zelfen.

A white beam of light escaped from his fingertips, and Lord Zelfen disappeared.

The flag of the first Lord of Tezz was slowly lowered as returning soldiers, some walking, and some riding, passed under the gate arch of Castle Tezz. Everyone was celebrating the victory over the northern army.

'Did you see the way I fought those two axe wielding men', said Lord Brin.

'How could you fight? You was always surrounded by a regiment of guards', said Torran.

'And I suppose that you won the battle all by yourself, pigs' breath'.

Lord Karl turned to Lord Edmund. 'Time for us to leave'.

Epilogue

Although Birch travelled back to his cottage in the Timber Wood, peace was not to be for he was the Master of Masters. He was the arch enemy of Lord Zelfen, and Lord Zelfen was planning his revenge.

Look out in 2013 for 'Birch—The Shadow of the Cat'